INSIDE
LOOKING OUT

TIM FORD

www.pandamoniumpublishing.com
pandapublishing8@gmail.com

FB: Pandamonium Publishing House
Instagram: laceybakker
Twitter: @laceybakker1
Youtube: Pandamonium Publishing House
Podcast: Podbean Pandamonium Publishing House

OTHER TITLES BY TIM FORD

THE WAY OF THE WARRIOR IS RESOLUTE
ACCEPTANCE OF DEATH

-MUSASHI

1

I have never been locked up for an extended period of time, lots of time in juvie as a teen, but not as an adult, and certainly not sober. There were several times when I was in the Army I would be on leave and get thrown into the drunk tank because I was wasted out of my face. Fuck, come to think of it, I remember spending two days in a drunk tank in Saigon.

I just came off a three-day recon mission and my company commander called me into his office. I could tell by his facial expression and demeanor that things were not good. You know you start to replay everything you have done in the past couple weeks to see where you fucked up.

But this time it was not me that fucked up. He handed me a letter. A letter from Rachel stating that Jake was killed in San Quentin. My older brother Jake was the toughest and baddest mother fucker that walked the face of the planet. How could this be?

Rachel said there was a full-scale prison riot in San Quentin and Jake was stabbed more than one hundred times and then was thrown over the fourth-floor railing to his death. Prison officials assured her those responsible would pay, but to this day no one has ever been charged.

That night, there weren't enough booze for me to drown my anger, frustration, and sorrows. I had what they call an *alcoholic blackout*.

I don't remember shit; it took me two days to sober up. And here I am now sitting in a jail cell waiting to go to prison. Fuck, I did follow my brother's footsteps after all. Natasha was right.

Well, Rachel will not have to bury another brother who gets murdered in prison. I will make sure of that.

Just after dinner was finished in the bull pen cell, two guards approached and said I was moving upstairs to a pod. *Thank fuck.* This tiny cell was getting on my nerves.

As I stood in front of my pod waiting for the guards to open it, every single prisoner stopped what they were doing and eyed me up and down. The Blacks, Asians, Mexican and even the Whites; it all reminded me of basic training, the testosterone flowing through the place trying to intimidate the new meat. Fuck, even the old bastards were eyeing me.

Everyone's thinking they're the toughest and baddest. But rest assured I was also eyeing each one of them up and down, seeing who a true threat was, who was a phony fuck tough guy, and who the bitches were.

Now jail is different than prison as a lot of guys are locked up for summon violations, unpaid parking tickets and other misdemeanors.

But this certain pod was for convicted prisoners waiting to be shipped out to the various prisons in California. All of them are going to be pen-timers.

The head guard for this pod told me he was the king, and everyone inside was a court jester. Any fighting and I would spend my whole time here in the hole eating bean cake and pissing and shitting in a bucket.

I looked at him and said, "Yes, Boss."

Funny, as my respect for him didn't make the bastard smile. Then again, my words are empty, and I am sure he knows it.

As soon as the Walking Boss said, *"Ok, Strongbow, here is your cell. Johnson over there will be your celly until you are shipped out."* Everyone stopped what they were doing once they heard my last name. The Strongbow name strikes fear, or anger into others especially those in the criminal world.

So, you put your shit inside your cell then go back into the common room. There is a TV going but you don't watch it. You are more interested in what everyone else is doing. You're trying to size everyone up. Some guys are playing cards, some guys are pacing back and forth while others are doing pushups or shooting the shit.

I decided to sit in a chair against the wall and observe. My new celly Johnson came over and introduced himself. I could tell by his muscular physique and his shitload of homemade tattoos this guy was a steady pen-timer.

"How exactly are you a Strongbow?"

If I've learned anything from Jake, Jerry, and also fighting in Nam, it was to never show fear and always be ready for a fight.

I looked at Johnson with a death stare and said, "I'm Jerry's first cousin, and Jake was my older brother, is that a problem?"

Johnson smiled and said, "Not a problem at all. I liked your brother Jake. Did some time with him at San Quentin back in '70, he was a good man. God bless his soul."

"Thanks, he was indeed."

Johnson and I hit it off pretty good. He introduced me to the rest of the guys in the pod. Gave me a heads up on who to trust and who was a rat.

Before I knew it, the lights were flashing which

meant lights out in five minutes. So, you go into your cell and wait to be locked down for the night.

Within a couple minutes the guard slams your cell door shut and you are locked in till dawn. Now for me, I knew this would be a rough night, a night of deep, negative thoughts and reflections of past failures.

Unlike in the jail cell at the police station, I could not pace, bang off pushups and dips till physical and mental exhaustion hit, but not here and not now; I have a roommate who appreciates quiet time, and a good night's sleep.

So, I go back to what my Grandfather taught me during the Inipi; controlled breathing, controlled thoughts, only positive thoughts to be exact. I eventually fell asleep and before I knew it, I was rudely awoken by the guards turning on the brutally bright lights.

I had a sore throat from all the cigarette smoke in the jail. *Fucking gross.*

After breakfast, a guard told me I had a visitor downstairs; I'm thinking it is either Uncle Karl or Rachel, but to my surprise sitting there talking to a guard was Joseph O'Reilly; the Leprechaun himself.

As soon as I sat down, Joseph nodded at me and then he ordered the guard to leave us alone.

Without hesitation the guard said, "Yes, Sir! " and did as Joseph directed.

I just shrugged my shoulders and started to laugh. Joseph didn't laugh along with me though. He still had a stern look on his face.

"How are you doing Lad?"

"All things considered I am doing better, Joseph, nice to see you."

"You still shooting that shit in your body?"

"No I'm clean, almost two months now."

"You look healthier than last time I saw you."

"Thanks, man."

"Now, I'm not one for *told you so*, but I warned you that bitch would bring you down.

Look at you now."

"She never forced me to inject heroin or to even get hooked on it in the first place. Fuck, Joseph; I was either shooting or smoking that shit back in Nam."

"I know you loved her, but she was a heat score wherever she went. A troubled soul, Mitchell."

I won't lie to you. My back was up with Joseph talking shit about Lucy even though he was bang on. But I also know how powerful Joseph is in the Bay Area underworld and he also is in possession of a lot of mine and Lucy's cash which now makes it all *my* cash.

"I know you're right. Love is blind. Listen, I need a favor."

Joseph's eyebrows were raised in anticipation of what I wanted.

"I don't think the authorities will let you out of here to put flowers on her grave, Lad."

"I just don't want her buried in a pauper's grave."

Joseph shook his head slightly as he rubbed his forehead.

"She was a heathen; she deserves to be buried in a pauper's grave."

"No, Joseph. She was my woman, a woman I loved. I want you to use some of my cash and give her a proper burial with a proper marker."

"Fair enough, Mitchell. I will make sure she is buried in a Protestant graveyard with a marker. I will not have her buried in a Catholic graveyard, understood?"

"See if you can get her buried in the same graveyard as my Mom and sis, Pam."

Joseph nodded his head.

"How much time do you think you will be serving?"

"Not sure, Uncle Karl says anywhere from one to three years. It is what it is, you know?"

"I know, Lad. Donnie sends his best. With him being an ex-con, he is not allowed to visit you in the city jail. Once you are sentenced to the federal penitentiary he will come and see you. Do you need anything at all, son?"

"Not right now, Joseph, but thanks for the offer. I plan on staying clean by the way."

"Well, that is the best thing I've heard all day. You stay clean and I will have a job waiting for you when you get out."

"Oh yeah, doing what?"

"I can always use a solid doorman and maybe doing some odd jobs with Donnie. I hear you two have worked quite well in the past. Is this something that would interest you, Lad?"

"Like a problem solver?"

Fuck how many guys have the balls to come down and ask you in jail if you would like to be an enforcer and contract killer for them? Only one-Joseph "Leprechaun" O'Reilly. Joseph smiled at me and waited for my response. Not sure why, but I started to snicker which also caused Joseph to snicker. Then we both burst into a full laugh.

"Of course, I will."

"You made this old Irishman happy. I will go down to City Hall and get Lucy buried forthwith in the same graveyard as your Mom and sis. You need anything let me know, Mitchell."

"Thanks, Joseph; much appreciated"

As I went back upstairs, I knew what I was getting myself into with working for Joseph. I'll be doing the same thing I did in Special Forces and SOG. And just like in those groups the crew is small, mighty, and most importantly, trustworthy with your life. I trust and have more respect for Donnie more than my own cousin Jerry. He has kept every single promise he made to me before I went to Nam. And Joseph; No way would he ever allow any of his men to inject any drugs. He keeps a tight ship and his men are always paid well. Joseph always shares the wealth and that for me is also huge.

I know I could never work in a Monday to Friday world with some dickhead university goof ordering me around. No way I could handle being stuck in some dead-end factory job either.

The Government paid a lot of money training me to be a killer. Perhaps they knew what I am best at. I guess they ain't that fucked up after all.

Over the next couple days, everything became routine. Rachel would come daily; I eventually told her to take my car as I didn't want it sitting there rotting. It worked better than her fifteen-year-old junker. I would work out with the guys in my pod; we would get to know each other a little more and when a new guy came into our pod, I would be giving him the same look I had placed upon me on my arrival.

On the third day Uncle Karl came by as my lawyer to tell me I had my sentencing hearing the next day. He went over what questions the judge would more than likely ask and how I was to respond. He said my response could be the difference between one and three years in prison. That caught my attention.

Can't say I slept the greatest that night; it reminded me of when I was kid being sent to the Principal's office knowing I was going to get the strap, just not sure how many whacks I was going to receive. I guess part of that are the values my Mom and Dad placed upon me.

But now I am an orphaned adult. I fucked up and I will pay. I am a man; I can take it, bring it on.

The next morning, I barley ate my breakfast, grabbed a shower, and waited for them to come and get me for my sentencing hearing.

Shortly after ten, they came and got me. I was handcuffed, shackled, and then put into a paddy wagon and driven to court.

You sit downstairs just like at the DMV and wait for them to call you.

I guess I waited around forty-five minutes which felt like an eternity.

You are walked from the back of the holding cells to the courtroom and are on display like some circus show freak. Right off the bat I see Uncle Karl and his assistant sitting at this desk waiting for me.

I look into the gallery and see Rachel and our cousin Jerry, Donnie and Jeanie Terek, Connor and Joseph O'Reilly, and Kerry and Fraser Dalton. Nice to see some familiar and friendly faces. Kerry's face and gut are huge like she is ready to give birth, fuck man good thing I banged her when I did as no way would I ever touch her now.

I give each one a nod and smile. Uncle Karl asks me if I remember my correct answers for when the judge questions me, *yes, I do* is my answer.

It was like my answer to my Uncle was the cue for the court bailiff to tell us to rise as he announces Judge Harris' entrance into the court room. The Judge looks first at the D.A., then us, and asks us all to sit.

He reads over the notes and periodically looks over his glasses and straight at me. For such a frail looking man this guy gives me the creeps with his beaky nose and liver spotted forehead.

Harris then looks up and asks the D.A and Uncle Karl if the plea bargain satisfies both parties. Now I know you are not supposed to disrespect a Judge especially one that is about to sentence you to a prison term, but he sounded like Elmer Fudd.

Both the D.A. and Uncle Karl said *yes*.

He then looked at me and asked if I understood exactly what I was agreeing you.

I said, "Yes, sir."

"Very well," he responded.

He then asked the D.A. if Miss Thom had any family members willing to address the court. The D.A. said Miss Thom had no immediate living relatives.

"That's a shame," was his response.

Judge Harris then asked me to stand. Fuck these handcuffs and shackles feel like they weigh a ton as I try to stand up.

The Judge rolled his pen with his fingertips as if he were rolling a joint. He asked me if I had anything to say before he rendered his sentence.

"I am sorry for the results of my addictions. Lucy was not just a fellow heroin addict; she was my girlfriend and my lover. I had envisioned a life for us together when I first returned home from Vietnam."

Judge Harris smiled after I finished talking and then he nodded to my Uncle.

"Mr. Strongbow I have read your pre-trial report and while I respect you for serving our country and trying to defeat the communist forces in the far east, people like you buying and using heroin is supporting those communists in their fight to rule the world. I hereby sentence you to a term of twenty-two months in a federal penitentiary with the possibility of parole after serving seventeen months. Do you have anything to add District Attorney Smythe?"

The D.A. said, "No, your honor." Same question to my Uncle and same response.

The judge slammed down his gavel and that was

that.

I thanked my Uncle and as soon as I turned around to see everyone two big court officers jumped between me and my family and friends as another officer whisked me right out of the court room and back into a holding cell.

What the fuck was that all about? Did they think my family and friends were going to bust me lose? Fuck, if I wanted freedom, I would have headed for Canada in the first place. Fucking assholes.

As I was sitting in the holding cell waiting to get sent back to County Lockup, you would think I would have a sense of relief, but I didn't.

Another dark storm cloud is headed my way, I know it, my gut is never wrong. I was sentenced on a Thursday, and the next day I would find out where exactly I would be serving my time, and then on the following Monday I would be shipped out.

That Friday before being told where I was being shipped out, I had a very interesting and kind of a mind fuck visit from Kerry Dalton. It was nice seeing her big smiling face. Man, pregnant chicks really put on a lot of weight, I guess twice the amount of perogies have to be digested considering she's Polish.

"Mitch do you know why I'm here?"

"To see me off, wish me luck?"

"Well…that, but also this baby I'm carrying might be yours."

I flash back to that night of the car accident and the two of us had unprotected sex. My gut flipped more hearing this then it did while being sentenced yesterday.

"Does Fraser have any idea about us? About that night?"

"No he doesn't, and I want to keep it that way. It was a huge mistake Mitch; I really love him, and I don't want to end my marriage because you and I had one night of stupid, reckless fun."

Kerry's eyes filled with tears which made me feel

like shit. I had lots of those emotions lately.

"He will never hear any different from me. The last thing I ever want to do is to ruin your marriage hon; we did it just once, how many times have you had sex before and after that? I highly doubt you got pregnant from us doing it just once."

"I think you're right, I am sorry for laying this on you, Mitch, but you just disappeared off the face of the planet and lately the guilt of what we did is consuming me."

I thought of Liz O'Malley right away and what Jake did to her for fooling around on him with me. Made me kind of nervous for Kerry's safety if she did breakdown and tell Fraser what happened, I can't let that happen.

"I think right now it is a hormonal thing with you being pregnant. Never ever tell Fraser anything different. All will work out for the best, I promise. You tell him you will break his heart, since Caleb was killed you are his shining light.

Yeah, you and the baby."

More tears rolled down Kerry's cheeks. I smile back at her even though I'm hoping she leaves; the tears and guilt are fucking brutal.

But that didn't happen. A jail guard said I had my meeting upstairs with the Department of Corrections staff. Rescued? Well, sort of. Kerry was still sitting their crying as I was escorted upstairs. As I was making my way upstairs, the jail guard asked if that was my pregnant wife that was crying. Nope just a buddy's wife was my response.

This caused him to snicker, glad he found in humor in it, *goof*. There were three people already seated, waiting for me.

They said because I was a local boy who they didn't deem a threat to become a career criminal, they would allow me to serve my time locally.

I knew exactly where they meant even before they said the words…San Quentin.

And just like in court I was whisked back to my cell.

Fucking San Quentin, the same prison that Jake was murdered in.

Lunch came shortly afterwards but I really didn't feel like eating. Once again lots of emotions running through my brain and the biggest emotion of them all? Revenge on the bastards who killed Jake. But there is also that part of me that says seventeen months and I will be a free man to start my life all over. Jake was a full patch executive of the Hell Hounds. Should they not have sought revenge by now and if not, why?

Shortly after lunch, which I didn't touch, a jail guard came up and said I had another visitor. I really hoped it wasn't Kerry still crying like a blathering fool.

It was Joseph O'Reilly with a bit of a stoic look on his face.

"So, I hear through the grapevine that you are being shipped off to San Quentin to serve your time."

The guy knows everything that happens in this city, especially of the criminal nature.

"You heard right"

"I know that you are not in that motorcycle gang like your brother was. But there are others inside who may not know this or even care. It is the Strongbow name that they will recognize"

I nodded *yes*.

"Listen, my cousin Michael Callaghan is serving a five-year sentence in there for selling guns. He is a high-ranking member of the IRA which makes him a man to be feared. He will look out for you, lad."

"Thanks, Joseph. I really appreciate it. How come I've never heard of him before?"

"Because you never worked for me before. I always take care of my crew."

"How did you make out with getting Lucy moved to my Mom's and Sis' graveyard?"

"Done. Next Tuesday the body will be exhumed and reburied. I have also asked Father

Duffy of my parish to say a few words for her at the burial. That girl needs all the help she can get to get her into heaven."

"I need another favor."

"What is it?"

"If something were to happen to me in prison, I want all the money owed to me going to my sister, Rachel."

"Fair enough, Mitchell. You have my word on this."

No sooner did Joseph answer me when a jail guard came in and apologized to Joseph for cutting his visit short as Uncle Karl, who is still my lawyer, and sister Rachel also needed to see me. Joseph raised his one hairy eyebrow and literally struck fear into the guard. Fucking power and respect indeed.

As they passed each other Rachel chose to shake Joseph's hand even though he went to hug her. Uncle Karl shook his hand but look confused as to who the hell he was.

As soon as Rachel picked up the phone she said, "Irish mobsters…really, Mitchell?"

Then my Uncle asked who I was just talking to. I tell him a good friend who is Irish.

"Mitchell, I really hope you are not getting into organized crime. You looked into my eyes and said you want a fresh start at life. I took your word on that."

"You still have my word. Let's be honest, with my last name I don't think I'd have a problem joining the Hell Hounds and yet I haven't. Joseph is a good man; he has always looked out for my best interests."

My Uncle didn't believe a fucking word I was telling him. I guess being a criminal lawyer he knows, just like Santa, who is naughty and who is nice.

"Have you been told yet as to where you are to fulfill your sentence time?"

"Yeah, San Quentin."

"Your sister and I have some very serious concerns about your safety, especially because of what happened to Jake in there."

"Once again I am not Jake; I don't wear the Hell Hound patch. I will be fine. As far as I know I don't have any enemies in there. Any prison I go to I could get me into trouble with my last name."

I glanced at Rachel who was not impressed with me either; fuck her too.

"Come to think of it, Rachel, you might be cursed in the legal world with our last name. Maybe you should change your name to Kohler."

Rachel mouthed *fuck you* before punching the two-inch glass between us and then storming out.

I looked at my Uncle and said, "They teach her that in law school?"

"You are a first-class fucking asshole, Mitchell. That girl has cried so many tears over you and this is the way you treat her? Grow up, son."

Then it was my Uncle's turn to leave. Fuck him too! That night I had no problems eating dinner at all. A part of me wonders if I am subconsciously trying to disassociate myself from Rachel. Will I turn into the animal I must become in order to survive prison life?

I know I need an edge, I needed it in Nam to survive and I will use that ruthlessness that I was hoping to have buried in the last helicopter crash along with my fellow Special Ops team members who perished on that last ill-fated mission.

So, I start doing knuckle pushups, more stretching than normal. Shadow boxing and kicking, I feel yourself getting meaner and nastier. I recall taking the enemies life; I recall even taking some of my own countrymen's life. And every recall is based on hand to hand, slicing throats, poking their eyes out, remembering where every single organ and major artery is located. CURRAHEE RANGERS.

For the rest of the weekend I only had two more visitors. Jeanie Terek, who is like an older sister; she told me that her and Donnie love me, and to be safe and if I need anything, they will always be there for me.

And the second visitor was one of the very few members of the Hell Hounds without a criminal record. Scott Kantonescu came with all kinds of messages from my cousin Jerry.

Jerry said to get involved with Scott's older brother, John the "Mad Dog," who is actually only seventy-seven days away from being released from San Quentin. Back in sixty-seven, John took a baseball bat to a bunch of members from the Thunder.

Scott said John was a *"Shock Collar"* inside San Quentin which is like a gang leader. The gang consists of either Hell Hound members or associates and other white supremacists, Nazis, I guess. My safety would be guaranteed. Between Jerry and Joseph, my criminal family will have my ass covered and my friends are key; I'll be untouchable.

Monday morning right after breakfast, the guards came and gathered up six of us, we were headed to San Quentin. I said goodbye and good luck to the guys in the pod I was leaving behind; I'm sure at some point there will be some sort of criminal interaction between us down the road.

Like some crazed animals, we are shackled and handcuffed and put on an older school bus converted for transporting prisoners.

One driver and two shotgun toting guards are also along for the ride. It is a short, but very quiet ride, no one says anything. What the fuck is there to say anyways?

As we pull up to the front gates, it almost has this Disneyland feel to it. And just like Disneyland, you pay a fee to get inside. My fee to get past the front gates was Lucy's overdose and death.

Yeah, I will be paying that fee to the state of California for the next seventeen to twenty-two months. My gut tells me I will end up doing all twenty-two months, if not longer.

My heart also tells me I will be paying for Lucy's death for the rest of my life.

As a prisoner, as soon as you get off the bus, you realize the nickname for San Quentin, which is called The Arena, makes perfect fucking sense. You're automatically put on display for all to see- the cons, the guards, fuck…everyone is checking you out.

I guess Emerson Lake and Palmer said it best, *Welcome back my friends, to the show that never ends.*

And for most cons they are repeat offenders. For me being a newbie, I am fucking nervous as all hell. In some aspects, it reminds me of when I first went into basic training for the army; I was lined up and given a quick medical by an old, crusty male nurse, who was taken aback by all my battlefield wounds. I am now officially State of California prisoner 31727382.

Fingerprinted once again, and a new mug shot taken.

I was then put into their version of a bull pen and waited for a prison official to have an official welcome to San Quentin, *here are the dos and don'ts*, bullshit spiel. I sit and wait to have my talk; the loud noises from the prisoners are really starting to get to me. I hit the floor and start pumping off pushups. I was really starting to feed off the negative and evil energy coming from the prison, and Christ, I wasn't even in the worst part yet.

Eventually a guard came down and got me. He said I must be someone special as the Warden himself asked to speak to me.

I didn't reply, but my brain went into overdrive wondering why. So, I had a seat in the warden's waiting room with the guard eyeing me the whole time.

Just like in the bullpen, I waited, but unlike the bullpen, my ass was told to sit the whole time, no pushups, no pacing to burn off the nervous energy. Fuck it was like I was a kid waiting to see the Principal all over again.

Eventually, the Warden's secretary says he'll see me. The guard tells me to get going. Warden Lopez is sitting at his desk reading a file, that file would in fact be *my* file. He was a short, balding man, a serious bastard…maybe a little too serious. Lopez looks up at me with a stern look and then looks again at my file.

"Mr. Strongbow, I like to run a smooth and very uneventful prison. Since I took over as Warden four years ago the murder rate here at San Quentin has dropped by seventy eight percent.

Now, having said that, I have a little concern about your stay here in my prison; in those four years one of those murdered was your brother, Jake. So, my concern is that you will be seeking retribution for those responsible for his murder. And quite frankly, after reading your Military records, I am even more concerned. I too was in the military and was Deputy Warden at Leavenworth. Reading your file here and seeing at how you were not just Airborne, but also Special Forces, I know that taking another's life is not strange to you and I assume that you have no regret or remorse. Am I correct on that?"

My turn to give him a stern look as I nodded my head *yes*.

"Are you also a member of the Hell Hounds or any other gang, Strongbow?"

"Not at all."

"I believe you. I had a friend at the San Francisco Police do a background check on you. So, now the bigger question, do you have plans on seeking revenge on those who murdered your brother?"

"I plan on walking out of here in seventeen months' time. I have wasted enough of my life in Nam fighting a war that we had no right being in. I am sure your cop friend has never heard of anyone being charged with an accessory to a drug overdose. I made a mistake, it cost me my girlfriend's life and now I am paying for that mistake. If the Hounds want to go after whoever killed my brother, let them. Like I said, it's gang shit and quite frankly they call each other *brother* and yet still no retaliation, fuck them all."

Lopez now looked long and hard at me. He didn't know how to take me; he didn't know if I was feeding him a line of bullshit or telling the truth. In some respects, it was a bit of both.

"Well, Strongbow, I will give you the benefit of a doubt. Don't fuck up and you will be out of here in seventeen months."

Even when I got up, he was still trying to figure me out. I was taken to South Block and that's where any similarities of the army end. In the army everything is discipline and respect. South Block was like walking past monkeys at the zoo and carrying a bag full of bananas-total fucking madness and confusion. Yelling, screaming for no apparent reason at all.

Here, you walk past a cell and people ask what the fuck you're looking at. Calling you pretty boy, asking if you are a tough guy and wanna show how bad you really are. Anger; lots of anger. It was like Tet all over again.

I was taken up to the second floor with my new prison garb, a couple towels, and set of clean sheets. Much to my chagrin I wouldn't be having a cell all to myself, a fucking ginger would be my new celly until I get shipped out of this block.

The kid was young, *really young*, and scrawny. If I was a little freaked out, and I know how to handle myself, he must be beside himself.

Kevin Stillman was his name, and young Kevin was a repeat offender. He fucked up his parole by being drunk and stealing a cop car and eventually losing control of it and taking out a liquor store. And what was Kevin on parole for in the first place? Stealing cars of course. Kevin boasted to me there is not a vehicle he can't steal. Fuck I thought of Blais MacTavish right away.

So, Kevin being a repeat offender gave me the heads up on the dos and don'ts of surviving San Quentin. Rule # 1 Mind your own business. Don't get involved with prison politics. Rule # 2 If someone comes onto to you, you gotta go at 'em. Rule # 3 It don't mean shit if you and some Black on the outside are the best of buds. In here the Blacks stay with the Blacks, Whites with Whites, especially the Arian Brotherhood.

Now, the Mexicans are a little different; they are divided into two groups: Northern Mexicans and Southern Mexicans. Make no mistake about it, both groups hate each other.

There are the Asians that for the most part stick to themselves. Russians and other Baltic groups, who can be very nasty, are not to be trusted.

And then, there are the queers. Right now, I can't see ever crossing that line. Hell, I went in the bush without seeing any poontang, and if worse comes to worse, early lock for a quick, one-hand shake with my cock.

Kevin was from Modesto and with any cellmate, you sort of feel each other out, right off the hop. He knew of the Strongbow name and asked if I was a Hell Hound. I am sure having a celly with a patch on his back is also more protection for him. I let him know I am just a civilian, but a civilian with lots of friends…scary, solid friends.

Within an hour of being in my cell, I thought I saw something out of the corner of my eye, fly by. Kevin saw the same thing and before I knew it, he jumped up and stuck his skinny arms through the bars and started to pull a string inside, all the while looking in both directions for any signs of a guard.

I was shocked and asked what the fuck he was doing as he was now reading a piece of paper smaller than a fortune cookie note.

He turned to me and said the fish line was the underground prison mail system. Kevin had a quick read and then passed the note to me. The writing was too damn small, so I asked Kevin what it said. Once again, Kevin looked for any sign of a guard.

"It says certain people in here are not happy to see you, watch yourself until you get moved."

"No shit, who sent it?"

"The initials are JK. You know who that is?" I knew it was from John Kantonescu, but I also know to trust no one inside here.

"I do." Kevin didn't dig any deeper.

In South Block, we're locked up for twenty-one hours a fucking day. The only time we're out is chow time and, in the yard, which is one hour, max. I figured if someone were coming after me, it would be in the yard where it's wide open with more distractions and activity.

The bigger question is *who* and *why?* Well, I have several in the *why* category, but in here, fuck…I don't know who is who.

When I was younger, and I would go from one school to another, I would have to fight to prove myself. I always would get the talk from my Mom saying to use my brains and not my fists. Dad would roll his eyes while the conversation with Mom was taking place. She would look at my Dad to back up what she just said. Dad would say, *Listen to your Mom, she's right.* Then, he would take me aside and reiterate what he has always instilled into all of us Strongbow's male or female, *show no fear, hit to hurt, and hit to win.* And I would, can't even remember the last time I lost a fist fight. But fuck, this is prison and there are people in here that hit not just to hurt, but to kill.

We would have yard time every afternoon at 14:00 to 15:00, before that was lunch. And like everything in prison, lunch was also about politics and marking your territory. Kevin so far was a great celly and told me to hang with him until I fully understood how things work inside San Quentin.

Now, San Quentin is so old school that each cell must be unlocked manually. So, when lunchtime came around the guard would unlock each cell one by one while you stood outside and then we'd all go to lunch, single file, like little ducks in a row. I felt every single set of eyes in South Block where watching me; first view of the fresh, new meat. In here, you walk proud, you flex your lats, and stick out your chest. And every fuck that eyes you, you fucking eye them right back. I also clenched my jaw. You let the guards know that you're not a push over, not weak, and most importantly, for all to see and know, not a fucking rat.

As we were standing in line, Kevin assured me that in time I would find the food not that bad and it would take a while to get used to it.

"I've eaten rats, snakes, and bugs in the jungle. Trust me, I've eaten worse," I said to Kevin.

"You are one sick fuck, Strongbow."

I noticed one guy serving the food, looked familiar; I knew him from somewhere, just wasn't sure where.

Then he turned sideways, and I recognized his flat, busted-up nose. He could still kiss a wall. Fuck me, it was Billy Davidson, Oakland Hell

Hound member that I haven't seen since I shipped out to Nam.

"Little Mitch Strongbow ain't so little anymore. I heard you were in. Mad Dog is working the dinner shift. You need anything let me know."

It was nice to finally see someone from the outside world. Someone who reassured me that my back would be covered. I guess at dinner time I'd see the one and only John "Mad Dog" Kantonescu.

Fuck, it was going be weird seeing John in kitchen whites rather than black Hell Hound leathers. I noticed as soon as we took our spot at pre-selected table, that Billy was pointing me out to certain members going through his line. All would nod at me and give me the thumbs up. Yeah, that made me feel better. What didn't make me feel better was this pig slop lunch.

Fuck…snake did taste better. Kevin wasn't bullshitting me.

Kevin said to put ketchup on everything, so that's what I did. I noticed that the mess was like everything else in here, you stayed with your own color and group. By the time I was done my meal, at least a dozen hard core white supremacists, or Hell Hound associates, came up and introduced themselves to me.

All of them were under orders from Mad Dog to make sure my back was covered until I get shipped to my permanent block, which John ran. I thanked each and every one of them, but I also know everything comes with a cost; the question is, what's the cost for this protection?

After lunch, we went back to our cells for about an hour until it was yard time. Protected or not, I was still anxious, still too many people out there I know want me dead. Fuck, I am sure this is not the first time, nor will it be the last time in my life.

I could feel the tension building inside of me the closer we got to the yard. As soon as I stepped onto the concrete, I felt a charge of rage flowing through my body. This feeling was the same after getting off a Huey and stepping into a hot LZ. The sunlight was blinding and the warmth I felt from it didn't mask how cold this area truly was.

Kevin told me to follow him as each gang in the yard has their own area. For a white man to walk into a territory of a Black, South or North Mexican would start a war.

I did as instructed. Each group also had their lookouts making sure I didn't show any disrespect and walk into their territory. They reminded me of prairie dogs as they stood at attention looking for any signs of danger coming their way. Fucking losers.

Kevin took me to the Arian's piece of property in the yard. The Shock Collar or the ringleader was Tommy "Unborn" Capello.

Tommy was a big muscular guy, shaved head, blue eyes and was also a member of the Battaglia crime family. A made man. Kevin introduced me to Tommy who eyed me up all the while without smiling.

"So, you're a Strongbow. Sonny and Mike Battaglia speak highly of you, I personally don't know you from shit. So, until I know I can trust you, count yourself on probation. I heard you were Special Forces in Nam so you should have no problem pulling point duty, understood?"

I just nodded my head, *fucking goof.*

Kevin took me to where my standing post was. He told me the dos and don'ts. This is fucked, but this is the cost of protection, I guess. The hour seemed to drag, I wanted to lift weights and hit the heavy bag like the others, but I know this is part of prison politics, I guess no different than being a Cherry in Nam. Latrine duty for thirty days straight.

So, after we went back to our cell, I started to do pushups, burpees, dips anything that was physical enough for me to blow off steam.

At dinner that night I sensed John "Mad Dog" Kantonescu's presence even before I saw him.

"STRONGBOW!" was all I could hear.

John had grown twice the size since the last time I saw him.

John jumped over the counter and gave me a big bear hug. The guards didn't think much of John's long-lost greeting as two of them pumped their shotguns and told John to get back and serve food.

"Why don't you dicks put down your guns and see how tough you really are!"

You could tell there was in fear in the guard's eyes but none in John's, even with the shotguns pointed at him. John eventually went back in line after laughing at them and of course under his own accord and started to serve food.

"Anyone giving you problems, brother?"

As much as I wanted to say Tommy, I kept my mouth shut for now. Jake drilled into my head about being a rat and Dad said all Strongbow's can handle any problem that *cometh thy way*.

I noticed that Tommy stared at John and I the whole time. I don't trust him. Over the next couple days, I took my position as lookout in the yard. But on day five, Tommy asked if I would rather do something else, as he could tell I was getting pissed.

I asked what I had do to get out of it.

"I want you to stick this guy in the yard."

"Fuck man, I am out of here in less than

seventeen months, I don't want to do a life sentence."

"I don't want you to kill him, I want you stab him in the leg with a pencil. Look at him in the eye and say next time it will be a shiv and it won't be just a warning."

I knew better than to ask *why* but I did ask, "In the yard?"

"Yep in the yard, right now, prove yourself to me."

"Sure, who?"

"See that cigar smoking Commie playing chest, the one with the goatee? I don't think he understands English very well, enlighten him, would you?"

So, I nonchalantly strolled over to the cigar smoking Commie with a couple of the other guys. We were watched the whole time, and not just by Tommy, but a couple of the guards patrolling the yard. I decided to sit beside the Commie.

He just looked at me and asked in his best broken English what I wanted, *what for is the problem?*

I smiled at him and said, "His knight will have your queen in two moves."

His eyes left me and looked towards the board; that is when I drove the pencil into his thigh. He grimaced in pain but never called for help. I got up nice and slow and said what Tommy asked me to say and then I walked back towards Tommy and the rest of the boys.

"Nicely played, Strongbow. There is hope for you after all."

I said nothing but inside I don't remember asking for his help, yeah, not at all.

Over the next couple days, I watched Tommy bully a lot of other people. His famous line that he always used was, *Don't you know who I am?*

Fuck, I am sure everyone in our block knew exactly who he was. I was becoming someone who I hated, a fucking bully. I like people showing fear and respect toward me, but to pick on the weak for cash or favors, can't say I liked it much.

I have never heard Mike or his Dad Sonny Battaglia talk to people the way Tommy talks to people. Made person or not, if he comes onto me for cash, favors, or blowjobs, I will slice his fucking throat.

Right now, his crew is the strongest on this block, and with being a first time con, I am still learning the ropes so I have to play the game. Now that I was off lookout duty in the yard, I would super set weights for forty minutes and then spend the final twenty minutes pounding the shit out of the heavy bag.

I knew everyone was watching me and one day I even broke the chain holding up the bag. The whole yard stopped and stared at me in disbelief. I stood over the fallen bag and growled.

2

DAY 17: I was finally being shipped out and to my new block that would be my home until I was paroled out of here. Kevin was surprised how quick I was moved out considering he had been there more than a month before me and still waiting.

Tommy made sure to let me know I owe him, seeing at how he took me under his wing and protected me. *Thanks*, was my only response. He did fuck all for me; if anything, he brought heat onto me as the guards will now see me as part of his crew, I ain't part of his crew, fucking dick.

My new block was the same block as Kantonescu and Billy Davidson. I was on the fourth floor, cell number twenty to be exact.

Just like before, I'd have another cellmate. The new one was an older guy who was finally getting out of San Quentin in just over two months after serving the past forty-two years of his life behind bars.

Now, for a sixty-five-year-old, George Daniels was in great shape, broad shoulders, chiseled muscles much like his jaw line and fists that were huge. George was an amateur boxer, three-time golden glove before coming to prison. He should have fought in the 1932 Olympics, but he was apprehended and convicted of robbing over twelve banks back in 1931.

Even in prison, George continued to box and was the reigning Super Heavy Weight Masters champion. George's was also famous for being part of John Dillinger's gang. Just like Dillinger, George was betrayed by a broad. The courts told George if he gave up information on Dillinger, he would get a reduced sentence.

George's response, "Fuck you I ain't a ratfink."

That solidness cost George the next forty-two years of his life. He should have been out in just over twelve years, but George never shied away from trouble in prison and kept getting charged with everything from assaults, and not just on fellow cons, but also guards. Possession of contraband including drugs, hooch, and porno mags.

Not all his time was spent here, just the past ten years after they closed Alcatraz. George has done stints in Joliet, which was his first prison, and the first prison he broke out of, which added another five years to his sentence.

"What's your name, kid?" were George's first words to me after he eyed me up and down.

As I went to respond, George was flexed his back and neck muscles and clenched his jaw.

"Mitch Strongbow."

"You don't look like a full blood."

"My Father was Sioux; my Mom was German."

"What do you mean was?"

"My Dad died in Nam back in '63, my Mom was killed by a drunken cop in '67."

"You're too young to be an orphan. I remember a Strongbow in here, he was shived a while back. Any relation?"

"Yeah he was my older brother, Jake."

"They don't live long in your family, do they?"

"No, they don't."

"How much you got left? Pen time, not lifetime."

"Just over sixteen months."

"Well kid, I'm out in eighty-two days and I want to keep it that way. Do you plan on seeking those responsible for taking your older brother's life?"

I smiled at George and wasn't sure how to

respond.

"Look kid, I'm not a rat. I've spent the past four plus decades in prison by *not* being a rat, I just want to know whether others will be coming to our house looking for you."

"I'm not sure, George. I'm not going to look for trouble, I just want to get out of here and restart my life. Like you, I have wasted a fair amount of my life doing time, not in prison but in the army, then I found the needle and that took not only time off my life, but ended my old lady. That's what I am in here for, her accidental overdose."

George then stuck out his hand in friendship and officially welcomed me. He said he would have my back and that he expects the same in return.

That would not be a problem. I was then assigned the top bunk and George let me know what was sacred to him and the dos and don'ts of our house.

We were given yard time twice a day, and that's when I got to meet the rest of John's crew. A couple full patch Hell Hounds, a couple club hang-arounds, and a couple guys striking for the club even while being in prison. There were also all kinds of pure, Arian skinheads.

I was accepted into this crew because of my last name and the SS tattoo I have on my chest. John said if I were smart, I would ask to work in the kitchen with him and the rest of the boys.

I asked why I don't need the thirty-five cents a day they pay.

"Working in the kitchen you get clean clothes daily, you eat like a king and are given longer yard time which is little incentive the prison does for us brother, so we don't poison the other inmates."

Sold was my answer. After the first yard break I asked the walking boss if I could work in the kitchen.

The walking boss smiled and said, "Good choice Strongbow, idle hands are evil hands."

Unlike with Tommy's crew I didn't have to prove myself to John with him being a shock collar and all. Guys striking for the club would do the lookouts.

On day four, one of the lookouts told us a couple guys from the Thunder were making their way over with a bunch of Southern Mexicans.

Everyone stood up as the tension grew with each step, they came closer. John and Billy met Jorge Cruz who was the Thunders national enforcer. He was serving a triple life sentence. I heard he's the one who took Jake's life.

Jorge was stocky much like John, which meant he too must be juicing. He had dead eyes and a real nasty scar running from his ear to the point in his chin. He was evil, pure fucking evil. Jorge looked at me and said he heard I'm coming after him.

"Someone has been telling you lies; I don't even know who the fuck you are."

"Well, Tommy Capello tells me otherwise, you calling him a liar?"

"If that is what Tommy told you, I would be asking Tommy what he has to gain by this."

I could tell that Jorge thought about my response. One of the other Thunder members who they call Mutt answered though without thinking.

"He is fucking stupid just like his dead brother; you wanna join your brother?"

John told Jorge he better put Mutt on a leash before he ends up in the pound and put down. The whole yard including the walking boss noticed this gathering and fired a couple shots in the air as he and several guards approached us.

Everyone hit the ground but me and Jorge. We just stared at each other.

The riot siren went off and the yard was full of gun toting guards. That was the end of yard time as we were all taken back to our cells. On the walk back I was approached by a little guy who introduced himself with a strong Irish accent as Michael Callahan.

"You do know lad you will have to kill them before they kill you."

At first, I just nodded my head. I just wanted to do my seventeen months and get out and start my new life.

"That includes Tommy Capello. I hear from good sources he is a rat for the FBI."

That stopped me in my tracks. Is Michael wanting me to kill Tommy for whatever reason? Fuck, prison is nothing but a mind fuck of games.

"Normally, I would ask who your source is, but I know better than that."

"Joseph says you are a smart lad. Listen, I will get you weapons if you wish, I highly recommend you having weapons as today was only the start of things to come. I hear you are pretty fearless and a tough bastard who has killed many in Vietnam. Do you remember what it was like to kill, Mitchell?"

"You never forget it long enough no matter how hard you try."

"Don't quell those demons in here, let them out, Mitchell."

I took a deep breath and knew Michael was right.

"Yeah, I will take a weapon, what do you recommend?"

"Something with a sharp end you can put between your knuckles and when you punch aim right for the juggler. I have such the thing made from an old bed spring."

"Thanks, Michael. How much?"

"This one is courtesy of your Uncle Joseph O'Reilly."

"When can I get it from you?"

"The walking boss will want all cells checked for weapons, he will know there is tension in this block and a lot of that tension is aimed at you. So, in a week once they get frustrated not finding anything. Until then, watch your back, I will also be watching your back."

I thanked Michael and gave him my weekly supply of tobacco for being a standup guy.

Once we got back to my cell George was pacing and cursing out loud to himself. His eyes bulging out, his fists were clinched and then he started to spout all the while spraying spit all over the walls.

"Those fucking Thunder think they are tough; they are fuck all. Let's go and kill each and every last one of them, Strongbow. How dare they threaten my celly? I have sliced and diced bigger men then them, I swear I will put a grin under Jorge's chin. Unlike your brother I will finish that cocksucker off."

"Jake gave Jorge that scar?"

"Yeah, he certainly did. Jorge started off crying, as the blood was flowing out of him like a river, he began screaming, that big phony fuck. If the guards wouldn't have shot your brother, he would have bled Jorge to death like a pig."

George was so wound up I had to try and calm him down so I could hear the whole story. Fuck, this is the first I ever heard about Jake being shot in prison.

Eventually George settled down and told me how Jake was murdered.

"Tensions were running high in the prison as there was a battle for the lucrative drug trade between the Hell Hounds and the Thunder. After a few dustups in the yard, a couple Thunder killed a full patch Hell Hound named Garret Moore, he was a Los Angeles Hell Hound. But he wore the club colors and he was killed because he was a

Hell Hound. Yeah, three members of the Thunder jumped Garret on his way back to his cell. It was too well orchestrated to the point the Cops knew a guard had to be involved. Just couldn't prove which guard. Your brother was the Shock Collar and had no choice to go after Jorge with him being the highest-ranking member of the Thunder. So, in the yard a mini riot started, Jake grabbed a shiv and headed right for Jorge. Both men were armed and ready, your brother eventually sliced Jorge and the only reason he didn't finish him off was that a screw in the watch tower fired a shot that hit your brother in the shoulder that knocked him down. Your brother was charged with attempted murder. Your brother ended up in the local hospital for about two weeks and then he spent about another week in the infirmary here. The prison was hotter than a cat on a tin roof, yeah, I remember we were on lockdown for about two weeks or so afterwards. Then, one day while in yard, there was another riot between the South Mexican's and a group of Muslims. I believe it was orchestrated by the Thunder. While the riot was going on, available screws were sent to the yard. The one screw that was watching the infirmary was killed. By the way guess who else was also in the infirmary with Jake recovering from his wounds. Yeah, Jorge. Then whoever killed the screw then went after your brother. I guess a chase started until eventually they caught Jake, then the bastards threw him over the fourth-floor railing to his death. Because there were no witnesses no one was ever charged. You know prison code; you talk you die. Jorge swears it wasn't him as he was too weak. He blamed the Muslims as your brother had run ins with them also over the drug trade."

I went deep in thought after George told me the story. I thought of Jake fleeing for his life, and now my thoughts of revenge.

Later that afternoon, us guys working in the kitchen were now going to be serving dinner once again as the lockdown was lifted. The walking boss had a long talk with me and said I was going to be watched a little closer and if I started anything, I would lose any chance of early parole. Fucking cocksuckers, they should have kept a closer eye on Jake, he would still be alive if they had.

While serving dinner that night I saw Mutt in line who smiled at me. Kantonescu picked up on this and said in time we'd get even. I was starting to seethe the closer Mutt was getting to being served.

On the dinner menu that night was a beef goulash dish. I grabbed the scooper and put a spoonful on Mutts tray while shooting daggers through my eyes.

Mutt looked down at it said, "This slop looks like your brother after he fell four stories and splattered all over the concrete."

Yeah, the whole vicious killing mode never leaves you. I didn't think of losing my five months off for good time served and getting out early.

I thought of my murdered brother, Jake and rammed the handle end of the scooper right into Mutt's Adam's apple. He grabbed his throat and was now gasping for air. I then slammed his head onto the counter. Then I pulled him up by his hair and drove my thumb into his right eye socket. Mutt then went flying backwards and hit the ground and tried to scream out in pain.

The riot alarm was going off, but I wasn't done

with Mutt. I scaled the counter to finish him off but was met with the butt end of a guard's shot gun. It was now my turn to hit the ground. My nose was busted and both eyes watered. I had no control of my legs even when I tried to get up. Then I was gang tackled by a bunch of other guards until I was properly restrained and then handcuffed.

I was not taken the infirmary I was taken right to the hole. After about thirty minutes or so the cell door opened up and three of the biggest guards I've ever seen told me to lay on the ground face down with my legs wide apart. I was then re-cuffed and taken to the infirmary for a nurse to look at me. The bleeding had stopped by then.

The nurse was cute and seeing at how this was the first time I have seen a female in over three weeks I got hard as soon as she felt around my nose. She confirmed what I already knew, my nose was busted.

She asked if anything else hurt. No was my answer. She told me to sit still while she went and got me a couple pain killers. Where the fuck was she expecting me to go? The three guards didn't leave my side, talk about a cock block. As I waited for the nurse to come back, I looked around for Mutt and he was nowhere to be found. *Good,* I thought, *I hope he is fucking dead.*

When the nurse came back, she handed me a couple pills and a paper cup full of water. It was impossible to put the pills in my mouth while being handcuffed and holding a cup full of water. She saw this, and as she went to take the pills out of my hands, a guard beat her to it, grabbed them, and told me to open up.

As I opened up my mouth, he shot the pills into the back of my throat, this made me gag until the nurse gave me a sip from the cup and said, "Are you all right, Mitch?"

I nodded yes while still coughing. I never gave her my name. How did she know it? Fuck, she does look kind of familiar. No sooner had I stopped coughing when the guards said *let's go.*

I stared at the nurse which seemed to piss off the one guard as he gave me a shot in the kidneys and told me to look straight ahead. I was then taken to the deputy warden's office. Yep, just like going to the principal's office after a scrap.

The deputy warden was on the phone as the one guard told me to sit down and keep my mouth shut. I did as instructed, but that didn't stop my ears from listening in on his conversation.

Right off the bat I heard him say, "So, is it too early to tell if he will lose sight in eye?"

This put a smile on my face as I know they were talking about Mutt.

"No, I have the perp right in front of me. Ok, sheriff let me know if he does lose his eye then we can up the charges."

At first, I foolishly wondered how I could be charged with anything, as I am already in prison. As soon as he hung up the phone, he looked at me while tapping a pencil on his desk.

"And what provoked this attack?"

"He said the slop I was serving looked like my brother, Jake, after he was pushed to his death."

This stopped his tapping of the pencil as he

clenched his teeth and pointed right at me as his face turned beat red.

"There will be no vigilante justice in my prison, do you understand me, Strongbow? Sixty days in the hole and sixty days added to your sentence. Guard take him away."

I said nothing as I was being walked to the hole, part of it was because the pain killers were kicking in, the second part is now I am more determined to get even with the Thunder members who took my brother's life.

Stoned or not, my resolution for the next sixty days was to get into Ranger shape. Practice strikes against the wall, get that fighting coordination back and I just don't mean hit to hurt, I mean hit to kill. Get my knuckles tough enough to break a cinder block.

3

DAY 82: I'm ripped and ready for whatever comes my way for the rest of time spent here. I am ready to kill Jorge and any other Thunder member who crosses my path.

Time in the hole also had me thinking smart, Special Ops smart. Too many witnesses in here to get away with a rage murder. Everything must be plotted and planned, I will need allies.

George was in our cell folding his clothes when I came back. I noticed my bunk was covered with mail; fucking bastards take away your mail privileges when you are in the hole.

George gave me a hug and said I was looking

good. He then looked at my knuckles that were now a nice shade of brown, the skin that first would peel off when doing knuckle pushups had now calloused over.

"So, what's the word on the street, George?"

"Thunder wants to get even with you for what you did to Mutt. By the way, nice job on that, I was quite impressed."

"Fuck them, fuck all of them. Kantonescu working the afternoon shift?"

"John is back on the street, man. Just over two weeks now. And that Fenian Callahan was deported back to Ireland but he did give me something for you. A shank, but it's hiding in the yard right now. And Mitch I am out of here in a couple weeks myself."

This is not good; these two were big parts of my allies. George picked up on this right away.

"But there is a new guy on the range who was asking about you, a real tough fucking guy."

"Not Tommy Capello?"

"No Albert "Boom Boom" Maganini. I am hearing Tommy is in protective custody and he is now a rat offering up shit on the Battaglia's to the FBI. Billy Davidson is also the new shock collar. He took over for John. A few people voiced their concerns and he took care of matters the old-fashioned way."

This made me smile as I asked what the old-fashioned way was.

"Moose Johnson is one who thought he should take over seeing at how he is supposedly the biggest and baddest Mother Fucker on this block. They found his body stuffed in a cooling vent; he was stabbed over one hundred times. Gonzo Griffin from the Hitler youth thought the same. Billy broke his jaw right in front of a screw. Fucking screw just turned his back and walked away. If you and Billy are tight, he will be the one to keep you alive. I know you have friends in that cycle club. But add a made man like Albert, as he does, or will hold a lot of power."

"And where is Albert right now?"

"He is about eight houses away, also on the

fourth floor. Should we go down and see him?"

I nodded yes and said, "After you, George."

Outside of Albert's cell was some other guy I've never seen before.

He was a pretty solid guy, about six three maybe two hundred and fifty pounds who eyed us up and down and asked us what the fuck we wanted.

"I hear Albert is looking for me."

"And who the fuck are you?"

Before I could answer I heard a voice from inside the cell say, "Mitch the bitch Strongbow. Frankie let our guests in."

Albert came over and gave me a big hug.

"Albert, what the fuck did you get pinched for?"

"I got a deuce for possession of stolen property. Fucking rats. Speaking of rats, I want to have a talk with you about something. Frankie why don't you and George go outside and make sure no one is listening to Mitch and I talk."

Both men did as instructed.

"Have you met Frankie "Knuckles" Bisiganni before?"

"Can't say I have."

"He is a good guy, solid guy from Vegas. He is a bone breaker. Now let me tell you who is not solid, Tommy Capello is not solid, in fact he is a rat. Mitch certain people who we both know, want me to make sure Tommy doesn't get a chance to squeal on certain people. I understand you just got out of the hole for poking out some guy from the Thunder's eye."

"He said the wrong thing to me; he was slamming my dead brother."

"Well Mitch, the Thunder want you dead for your actions. Jorge approached me himself and said he was going to kill you. I told him that ain't going to happen. And do you know why that ain't going to happen?"

"Because I made sure we all got out of Yosemite alive?"

"That is one reason, but Jorge doesn't give

two shits about that. I told him you are protected by the Battaglia family."

I know I am not protected by the Battaglia family, not totally anyways even if I saved Mike's life back in Nam. So, what is the catch?

Albert got up and looked outside his cell to make sure George and Frankie were doing their jobs and no one else was listening to what Albert was going to say next.

"Mike Battaglia knows you killed Gifford and General outside Electric Ladyland. He says you did him a favor as it turns out General was working for the FBI and Gifford was a rat. Now Mike wants one more favor and he will make sure no one harms a hair on your head in here and you will be taken care of once you get out."

"You have my interest, Albert."

"He wants you to kill Tommy Capello."

Suddenly he went from being a Shock Collar in general population to asking to be put in protective custody. Rats and pedophiles are the only people in P.C. Either way him going in there signed his death warrant.

"Why me and not you or Frankie?"

"Because you work in the kitchen and you just went from serving food to delivering meals to protective custody."

"I don't think the screws will just let me waltz in there and kill Tommy."

"All the screws except for one will be called to the yard as a riot will be starting there. This will coincide with Tommy making his way back from the infirmary for his daily shot of insulin."

"Fuck, you have really thought this out quite well. When does this go down?"

"Tomorrow at lunch time. You can do it, Mitch. And as a bonus, I have this one screw that will make sure that Jorge's cell is left open. Put the murder weapon in Jorge's cell and let him go down for the murder."

I was thinking about it, thinking really hard about it.

"Jorge got away with murdering your

brother, everyone knows it Mitch. Let's call this Karma."

"And what about the screw that is walking Tommy back to P.C.?"

"Blindside him, knock him out cold, do it quick enough so Tommy can't get away on you."

"Fuck man, I barely know the layout of this prison."

"Mike would tell me stories about you in Special Forces. He would tell us how you wouldn't need a compass or map, you had these instincts, natural, God-given instincts. Fuck Mitch, you got us all rescued out of Yosemite with no map or compass."

"Yeah there are some dark places in here I could hide. And where am I getting the weapon from? You know they will be shaking me down with just getting out of the hole knowing I have enemies in here."

"The weapon will be on the trolley with the food. It will be under one of the dishes. I'll have gloves hidden on the trolley too."

I know I can use the protection of the Battaglia family, it would be nice to see Jorge go down for Capello's murder, never liked that bastard to begin with.

"I will do it."

Albert smiled, shook my hand, and thanked me.

"Make sure he's dead Mitch."

"I will."

I left Albert's cell and headed back to mine. *Why do I think I just made a deal with the devil?*

George could sense something was up and asked if I was all right. I said I was fine, that I just wanted to read my mail.

For the first time since I could remember, I knew that there was a letter from Natasha, it was like the paper and ink were calling me. One by one I went through all the return address until, sure as fuck, I saw one from N Hotz, Queens NY.

I didn't even have to open it as all the mail was already opened. *Fucking screws.* As I opened it, a small picture fell out. It was Katrina. Her grade one school photo. As much as I wanted to read the letter, I couldn't put away the photo. It consumed me. I looked at every inch of her smiling face, her eyes, smile, dimples, and features. She had hair in tight pigtails or at least that is what I think they're called. She is so cute, so innocent, a cross between Rachel and Tash. I finally put the photo down and read the letter Tash wrote me:

Mitch, I am sorry to hear of Lucy's passing and that you're being held responsible for her death. You always told me you would never be like Jake and yet you are in prison just like him. I hope now you realize why I left San Francisco to have our baby, Katrina. I loved you, I truly – loved you, but I could see that unfortunately, Jake had more control over you then me and our child that I was carrying. I sent you this photo of Katrina hoping that she will help you stay off the drugs and help you leave a life of crime once you are released from prison. Rachel didn't tell me of your incarceration, Glen read about it in the news and he let me know. Please don't write me back as I will not open the letters. But I'll regularly send you photos of Katrina for inspiration. And I don't want to make you feel bad as society and the law of the land has already punished you, but your Mom never envisioned this life for you even if I did. Be smart Mitch, I know you can. Stay out of trouble in prison. Get a good job once you're out and one day, I will introduce you to Katrina, this time as her Dad, not just a friend of Mommy's and Aunt Rachel's brother. -Natasha

Just like the picture of Katrina I had to reread the letter several times and each time I would get something different out of it. Eventually, I came to the conclusion to get mad, mad at the world. Mad for everything that had gone wrong in my life. And this rage would be taken out tomorrow on Tommy Capello.

*

Can't say I slept the greatest that night. Between Tash's letter of *I told you so* and plotting and planning the death of Tommy, I tossed and turned. I think once I did finally close my eyes enough to shut down my over worked brain the lights in the cell came on.

Time to go to work; time to go and kill that fucking rat, bully Tommy Capello. As soon as I

got into the kitchen the manager took me aside
and said I am now going to be delivering meals as
part of my extended duties and did I have a
problem with that. Like a good soldier I said that
was fine, good excuse for me to stretch my legs.
So, we made the oatmeal for all the cons, then
came making lunch. You try and act normal as to
not let the screws know something was up.

George on the other hand could sense something
and asked what was wrong. I said the letter from
Tash brought me down and fucked up my head.
George's response, *fuck that cunt*, made me smile.

At 11:30 the one screw said it is time for me to
deliver the food to P.C. He said if I am not back in
twenty minutes this would be my first and last
trip. I smile and say *yes boss*, and off I go with my
cart of death.

P.C. is in the far side of the prison; fuck I am
going to have to haul ass on this one. Didn't know
I had a time constraint. As I am walking, I watch
all the different screws and sections of the prison
looking for the perfect spot to take Tommy's life.

Clusterfuck number two, what time does Tommy

go down to the infirmary at? At the first opportunity I root through the cart until I find the shiv but no gloves. Not the greatest start.

I am about two minutes from P.C. when I notice two people headed my way. Fuck, it's Tommy and a screw; I look around and no place to hide in the shadows. I also don't hear the riot alarm going off. This is reminding me more and more of typical army intelligence failure.

As we pass each other Tommy just snarls at me, *fucking goof, if only you knew what I have in store for you.*

I then pull up to P.C. and help the screws and cons unload the food, time is precious. On the way back I haul ass and find a dark corner and get ready. I have the shiv all set; I just need Tommy's throat.

The shiv is short, I would say maybe four inches in total. This is going to be almost hand to hand death. Another scenario I didn't think out. Sure as fuck I am now going to get blood all over me, how the fuck do I explain that?

Think, Mitch, think. As I am plotting and

planning, I hear the riot alarm go off. My heart pounds, I am starting to think fuck this mission, I will get Tommy tomorrow or the next day.

Just as I am about to head back to the kitchen, I hear a screw saying, "Tommy pick up your pace".

I feel like I did during Tet, a virgin killer all over again. Anything but confident. But just like Tet, that dark demon we keep locked up broke free of its chains and morality. The screw is walking ahead of Tommy. I hit him in the jaw as hard as I could. I heard his jaw pop as he fell limp to the ground.

Tommy is stunned and vulnerable. His eyes now light up as he recognizes me, so I square him right in the nuts as I throw an overhand to Tommy's head with the shiv and land it right into Tommy's temple. His knees start to buckle as his eyes roll back in his head. We both hit the ground together in a bloody mess. I once again strike Tommy in the temple, but he is now flipping and flopping like a fish out of water. The shiv is now stuck in his skull.

I go to pull it out several times and then the cheap version of a knife breaks off. So, like I was taught in Special Ops, improvise. I start to choke him to death. You notice I said *start*, not finish? Tommy is so close I can hear the death gurgle start up when I hear a screw telling me to cease my actions.

I don't stop until I hear a shot gun being discharged. Once again improvise.

"For fuck sakes I am trying to help him, quick, get a Doctor!"

The screw now comes closer all the while having his shot gun pointed at me. I move my hands from his throat to his temple.

"If continuous pressure is not put on his temple he will bleed out!"

The screw doesn't know what to do now, he is totally confused.

Eventually he has a couple more screws join him, and they tell me to lie on the ground spread eagle as they put a call in for the Doctor to tend to Tommy and the knocked-out screw. I am covered in blood. My only hope is that the knocked-out screw didn't see me strike him at all.

Eventually I am handcuffed and taken to an interrogation room. I am still covered in Tommy's blood. I still don't know if he is alive or dead. Fuck, even if he lives, he will have as much brain substance as a head of lettuce. My only concern was if the guard saw me.

San Quentin has its own cops working inside the prison walls. Detective Frank Trower, California Department of Corrections was the first to interview me as to what my side of the story was.

I tell him I am coming back from delivering the food to P.C, I hear the riot alarm go off and I do as instructed and lay on the ground. I hear some commotion going on ahead of me and I see a huge black man stabbing Tommy. I yell, what the fuck are you doing? when he takes off. I get up and see Tommy down and hurt bad. I know from my days as Special Ops how to treat life threatening wounds.

Next thing you know I have a shot gun going off. I know with no witnesses, a riot taking place in the yard I just might get away with it. And the one factor I have going for me is no past bad history with Tommy. And of course, I must act really concerned as to whether or not Tommy lived.

Pretty sure Trower could tell I was pulling a regular Pinocchio tale to him, but I had in my favor no witnesses, and thank fuck my nose doesn't grow when I am telling a lie, and this lie is so epic, my nose could break through all the cinder blocks in here and help me escape.

I was then allowed to go back to my cell and get cleaned up. I knew there were rats on our block, and I know I would be watched so I didn't stop off and give Albert a full report.

I headed right from my cell and grabbed a bar of soap and headed straight for the showers. By the time I am done showering and head back to my cell, the walking boss and two other screws are waiting for me.

They tell me to get dressed and come with them. I do as instructed and head right back to the same interrogation room that I was questioned in earlier.

This time there are two guys in suits and these two guys I recognize, Agents Stone and Calder of the FBI.

"I see being locked up hasn't stopped your murdering ways, Strongbow."

I guess I now know Tommy "Unborn" Capello is dead.

"I ain't saying shit unless my attorney is present."

"You won't talk to us, but you will talk to prison cops?"

"They're not total dicks, sorry I don't trust feds, and yes, that is being personal. I want my lawyer present."

"Innocent people don't need lawyers"

"Miranda rights say differently," was my smart-ass response.

They tried to bait me to get me to talk, but all they did was to piss me off even more. Fucking cocksuckers.

"No lawyer, no talk, bottom line"

I kept reiterating this every time they would ask me something or baited me. For some supposedly composed people they were getting pretty pissed off, and I just don't mean good cop bad cop shit. They were totally frustrated with me.

Eventually agent Stone called Trower over and said he wants me thrown into the hole until I learn to talk.

He smirked, looked at me and I just shrugged my shoulders.

"And what is he going to the hole for?" he asked Stone

Agent Stone face was beet red, "For not communicating with a federal agent regarding the killing of an organized crime witness."

I have to give Trower credit as he just shook his head no and said, "First off this is my prison with my fucking rules. Secondly, I am not going to lose my job because you have denied him his Miranda rights. Allow him to get his lawyer in the room, then question him."

Agent Stone then handed Trower his card and said

once my lawyer showed up to call him. Both agents then got up and left the room but not before giving me the evil eye. Boy am I fucking scared. Trower then asked who my lawyer was. I almost said my Uncle, but he would be the last person I would call for assistance.

"Actually, I let my last lawyer go, if he was any good, I wouldn't be here."

This made him snicker as he answered true enough. Time to find out how much Joseph cares about his men.

"Can I call a friend who will get me setup with a Lawyer?"

"Sure Strongbow, come with me."

I called the Drunken Leprechaun and was lucky enough to talk to Joseph himself. You have Trower and two other screws present so you can't say too much.

"Joseph it's Mitch, listen, I need a lawyer can you send someone to the prison for me?"

"That I can do lad, I will send the finest lawyer in the Bay area. Everything ok?"

"This fucking rat got murdered in here, and the FBI wants to ask me about it."

"And who would that be?"

"Tommy Unborn Capello."

As soon as I said his name, Trower hung the phone up on me.

"Don't socialize on my dime. You can tell your friends all about it during visitations."

I know not to bust Trower's balls as he went to bat for me against the FBI. I also know he might be playing a mind fuck game with me, being nice. So, I just answered *you're right*. I was then taken back to my cell.

Within twenty minutes of being back in my cell, Albert and Frankie paid me a visit. Albert asked how it went; I looked at Frankie and told him to keep guard. I trusted Albert, but as I have learned in the past, trust very few with your life.

"San Quentin now has one less prisoner and one going out in a pine box. You were right about him being a rat."

"How do you know that?"

"Prison cops questioned me about the murder, then the FBI came in and talked to me about the murder of a star witness against organized crime."

"Fucking rat, dead fucking rat, good job. What did you tell the FBI?"

"I refused to answer any questions without my lawyer present. They got pissed and left. I contacted the Leprechaun who is sending a lawyer for me."

"And what story are you going to tell them once your lawyer is present?"

"Same story I told the prison cops, returning from dropping off the meals and found him on the ground severely wounded. Tried to stop the bleeding."

"Did you manage to get the shiv up to Jorge's cell?"

"No, it broke off in Tommy's skull. There were no gloves in the cart also. I really don't mind taking care of business for certain people. But I don't want to be setup to fail, you know?"

Albert look confused about the gloves, "I know. Sorry, Mitch. I was told there would be both. I will take care of the fuck up."

That night when we went down for dinner, I noticed the one guy Moore who was serving us had two black eyes, he didn't have them at lunch time. I guess he was the fuck up.

By the time we were finishing up dinner, a screw came up to me and said my lawyer, and the two FBI agents were waiting for me. For the most part I have always been a calm and cool killer, but this felt different, I think deep down I know I can do my convicted time, but fuck, having to do another 30 plus years, I'm not too sure about that.

As I went inside the interrogation room, I only saw one person, a short kind of dumpy guy in a suit wearing a Kippah.

"You must be Mitchell Strongbow. Mr. O'Reilly says you need a lawyer. My name is David Levy, and I would like to represent you if you wish."

"You are Joseph's lawyer, correct?"

"Yes, that is correct."

"Then yes, I need a lawyer and would like to hire you."

"Very good, I don't come cheap, but I will be totally devoted to your case. Before we talk, I need more privacy, that is a two-way glass where the people on the other side can hear our conversation, most notable the FBI."

David then walked towards the glass and tapped on it and said he wanted a private room to talk to me first. Within thirty seconds the door to the interrogation room was opened, and a screw said to follow him. And where was our private room to talk? The prison chaplain's office. The one screw said he would have to stand outside the door but assured he wouldn't listen in. Levy reminded him if he did, that would be a violation of my constitutional rights, and he would have him charged, and fired.

I told David my side of the events, the side where I stumbled upon Tommy already stabbed and fighting for his life. David was smart, he knew when someone was bullshitting him.

"So, there were no witnesses at all, none? And you have had no previous altercations with him all?"

I shook my head no.

David then said he will answer all questions first; I will not answer any questions unless David instructs me to.

The two of us were taken back to the interrogation room and within a minute in came the two FBI agents. The agents asked me to tell my side of the story which I did. Then the volley of questions and theories started to try and nail my ass for this murder.

"Mitch, you are quite the teller of tales, fables at best. We have your prints on the murder weapon."

I automatically want to answer and as soon as I opened my mouth, before I could get the first syllable out, David taps my hand and answers for me.

"Mitch admitted trying to get the weapon

out so he could put pressure on the wound, next."

"We find it strange that someone with ties to the Battaglia family, finds someone brave enough to testify about them in court. And Mitchell just happens to find him dying."

David turns to me and asks how exactly how I have ties to the Battaglia's.

"Mike was one of the helicopter pilots in the unit I served with in Vietnam."

"So, had you met Mike before going to Vietnam?"

"No sir."

"And are you an associate of the Battaglia family, Mitchell?"

"I have visited his strip club in San Fran, but so have a lot of horny males who appreciate the dancers there."

David then asks the FBI agents a question, "I would like to know, for the record, as to whether or not my clients name has ever been associated with any criminal activity involving the

Battaglia's."

At first both agents just look at each other until David pushes them for an answer, "A simple yes or no. If it is an ongoing case just say so and we will respect the sensitivity of an ongoing investigation."

Eventually they both say that there is no history of me working for the Battaglia's.

David then asked the prison afternoon shift supervisor if there were ever any problems between me and Tommy. None that they were aware of was his answer. David then smiled and looked at the agents and asked if there were any witnesses to this heinous act.

"None that we are aware of, but your client has a history of violence and has taken many lives in Vietnam."

This made David laugh.

"If I am not mistaken, this prison probably houses over four hundred convicted killers. You do realize that Mitchell turned himself in for his girlfriend's tragic overdose. He could have run with the skills he learned in Vietnam serving his country. But no, Mitchell was a man of integrity and did the right thing, he is a righteous man that is trying to turn his life around. Now, either charge my client or let him continue on his journey of forgiveness."

As if rehearsed, Agent Stone said this will still be considered an active and open case until further details present themselves.

Both agents left the room. Trower stayed in the room. I thanked David and said I liked his Moxy.

"Thanks, Mitch. That is why people like Joseph have me as their council. They come back and want to talk, you have me called."

David handed me his business card.

As soon as David left the room, Trower looked at me and said, "I have no doubt in my mind you killed Capello; you might have even got away with it. But be forewarned my staff will be watching you a little more closely, Strongbow."

I knew better than to answer him back like a smart ass. I nodded my head yes.

*

It was already lockdown by the time I got back to my cell. George asked how I made out. Good, really good was my answer.

"Time to go fishing, Albert wants you to let him know. Lack of communication in this place is a bad thing. People get quiet, people get nervous."

"The prison detective said they are going to be watching me a little more closely now."

"Use code Mitchell, you don't write a book for the whole word to see, a few simple words to reassure him that all is good."

Fair enough. So, I wrote as small as I could. GLZ which in military terms meant Green Landing Zone, all is safe. I was still pretty wound up, so I opened up the rest of my letters.

One put a smile on my face and it too contained a picture of a baby girl. Fraser and Kerry's baby girl, Lisa. On the back Kerry wrote *eyes just like her proud Daddy, Fraser*. Another coded note that said all was fine.

The next morning, I opened my eyes and it took

me a couple seconds to try and figure out if it was just a bad dream that I stabbed Tommy Capello to death or not, I was drenched in sweat and felt a bit queasy.

As soon as I entered the kitchen the manager told me I would no longer be portering the meals, and I would be stuck washing the pots and pans for the next bit. I guess that is one way the prison would be able to keep an eye on me.

At yard time I told Albert everything that went down with the FBI. Fuck them and fuck their rats was his response. Then he said let's lift some weights. And we did.

Albert also had access to the same steroids that John would get. So, living with a bunch of caged fucking animals where only the strong survive, I made sure that not only did I do set for set and rep for rep with Albert, but I also did the same amount of steroids.

Working in the kitchen, I ate healthier than most cons. I also told Billy Davidson about Ralph General working for the FBI and at how Gifford was also a rat.

When Billy asked how good my source was, I said, "Gospel."

*

The next day sure as fuck I had a pair of visitors, my cousin Jerry and Donnie Terek.

You go into this big common room with screws walking around, no privacy so anything you say personal you almost have to whisper.

They both said they had tried to visit me in the past but being in the hole meant I lost all my visitation privileges. Both asked how I was doing inside. I said well, they asked if I had any trouble with the Thunder members.

"The reason I was in the hole was because I gouged out Mutt from the Thunders' eye."

This made them both smile, Jerry asked if there had been any retribution.

"I am running with Billy Davidson and Albert's crew. So far so good."

"A little birdie told me a story about General and Gifford. Is it true?" asked a very inquisitive

Jerry.

"I wondered why the FBI questioned me so hard about their deaths. They wanted any info. Someone in here told me a story about General working for the FBI and Gifford being a rat. I told you several times they were no good and not to be trusted. I also told you I knew all natives in the 101st, I didn't know him."

Jerry was very humbled by this and said sorry and asked how he could make it up to me.

"Just trust me next time. I know I am not a patch, nor do I want to be a patch, that doesn't mean I don't have great street smarts."

"You're right little cousin, I should have killed General."

"I killed General and Gifford even after Lucy and I were treated as outcasts in Texas. If it weren't for a rat named Fagan, Jake would still be alive. I fucking hate rats and that is why I killed him. Not for the Hell Hounds, for you Jerry, and for you Donnie."

Things then got really quiet, uncomfortable quiet.

"Fuck, Mitch. I am not even sure what to say other than sorry and thanks. Listen, I hate to put this on you, but the club took a lot of heat from the Feds after their murders. Now I know why. Would you be willing to say to Von Kruder that I asked you to take out General?"

Donnie also reiterated what Jerry said. Yeah it was weird seeing these two guys so humbled and almost sheepish.

"If worse comes to worse. You know what I would really like?"

"Ask away, Mitch."

"Things didn't end well that last time I talked to Rachel. See if you can get her to drop by and see me. See if you can talk to her without my Aunt and Uncle knowing."

"First thing in the morning I will head over to Sacramento. I will convince her."

"Thanks Jerry, much appreciated."

"Anything else, Mitch?"

"Yeah, second thing; Donnie has access to

cash of mine in case if something happens to me in here. Jerry if you also make sure Rachel doesn't have anyone cause her grief throughout her life."

"That goes without saying Mitch, she is a Strongbow. Secondly?"

"I have to get laid, starting to get a bit edgy you know? This one cross dressing Asian looked too much like Lucy. Kind of getting me hard, you know?"

They both broke out in laughter.

"I can have one of the Splashers come down and give you a weekly hand-job here as long as you are not shy."

"I shit outside in the yard where everyone can see me, no roofs or walls; fucking pigeons are always shitting on you as you are shitting. I shower with a bunch of guys. Shyness left me when I was as a school boy."

Before they left, they told me to be safe and if anyone gives me grief to let them know. I told Donnie to say hi to Jeanie.

I felt I had to get that off my chest and let them know that I was not pleased at the way I was treated in Texas; I bargained multi-million-dollar drugs deals and then was kicked to the curb. I am pretty sure that will never happen again with Jerry as club President.

A couple days later when I was in the yard working out, a screw came and told me I had a visitor. My first reaction was the Splasher better not pass out from my sweaty balls. Fuck her. I am sure she's smelled worse and I bet after a hard night she has smelled pretty ripe.

I should have told Jerry I wanted one with big tits, fuck I miss playing with big tits. As I entered the visitation common room, I looked all around to see what gift Jerry had sent and then I smiled and realized he has sent the perfect gift. It was Rachel.

Fuck, I was happy to see her, the happiest I have been since I was first locked up in here. As soon as Rachel saw me, she smiled as tears rolled down her cheeks. She came over and hugged me and said she loves me and misses me.

"I love you too, Rachel. Thank you so much

for coming to see me. You look more and more grown up each time I see you. How are you doing? How is school?"

"School is great actually, and you are looking more and more muscular each time I see you, holy smokes, Mitchell."

"Lifting weights helps keep me out of trouble, it also keeps me off the drugs and helps control the anger I had brewing inside of me."

Time to bare my tortured soul.

"I am so sorry for losing it on you last time. I hated my life; I still have guilt inside of me for Mom and Pam's death. I spent those four years in Nam trying to bury those tormented thoughts, and I couldn't. I really tried to live a normal life, but Rachel, if you saw the shit I did in Nam, it fucked me up even more. And I fed off all the insanity. And then I had this crazy idea when I came home Tash would forgive me for what I did back in '67 and Katrina would be that one salvation to set me straight. Once again, another kick in the nuts. And unfortunately, I have taken a lot of my frustration out on you, and Uncle Karl. I know he is a good man, and he has done a wonderful job raising you. Part of my frustration was I am the big brother; I should have been looking after you."

Rachel was totally shocked by my apology and honest sincerity. To a certain degree so was I.

Rachel cried, this caused me to tear up.

"Not going to lie, Mitchell, back in '67 I hated you so much. I blamed you for Mom and Pam's death. I blamed you for my best friend Natasha moving to New York City to have my niece. But I was an immature sixteen-year-old who still hadn't fully got over Dad's death. I just want you to get out of here alive. Did you know it was me who had to identify Jake's body seeing at how I was next of kin? You come home from Nam all shot up, could barely walk and you get into the same criminal lifestyle as Jake."

"You do know that I am not a Hell Hound, right?"

"So I have been told"

"Jake died in here because of a gang fight between the Hell Hounds and Thunder. I don't get involved with gang stuff."

Rachel forced a smile; I don't know if she believes me or not. Part of it is the truth; I am not a club member.

"So, what are your plans when you get out of here, Mitchell?"

"I am not sure, what do you recommend?"

"Well I know you can get your grade twelve diploma while in here. Have you thought of that?"

I started to snicker; a confused Rachel asked what was so funny.

"Back in high school I would pay people to do my homework either through weed or have girls seduce guys."

"Are you kidding me, did Mom ever find out?"

"No, she didn't. I think Mom would be happy if I had finished my grade twelve. You know what? I will do that, for Mom and you."

Rachel was smiling ear to ear.

"I received a letter from Tash."

Rachel's whole face change and swore she kept her promise to me that she wouldn't tell her where I am for the next couple years.

"Her brother, Glen, let her know. She sent me a photo of Katrina. She said if I promise not to write back, she will send me updated photos."

"Are you happy about that even if she is sort of blackmailing you?"

"I accept it for what it is. I don't love Tash anymore; I also don't hate her either. I will always love Katrina. I will find another to love, and one day, Tash will have to let me see Katrina, and I know I will have to prove to her and Stan that I have changed for the better."

"Holy fuck, Mitch, you have changed. Prison actually works?"

"Fuck no; prison is the ultimate mind fuck. Grandpa cleansed me of these bad thoughts towards Natasha and Stan. He said I was putting so much negative energy into what I can't change, and it was consuming me."

"I love Grandpa; he is so wise and just. You know, speaking of being blackmailed, Jerry dropped by Stanford with about six guys from the club. He said if I didn't go down and visit you, he would have the six guys he came with, ride through the campus naked, yelling at the top of their lungs how they all loved me. I dreaded coming here, now I am so happy I came. This is the big brother I love, nice to have you back."

"Nice to be back, sis. I love you too, Rachel. I think Mom and Dad would have liked hearing that."

Rachel promised before she left that she would come up once a week and see me. I said I would really like that. To a certain degree I meant what I said. Tash and Stan were too much negative energy. Grandpa showed me that. But I also know in prison only the strong survive.

No sooner after Rachel had gone, me and Billy Davidson broke all the fingers on the right hand of a guy who owed money for cigarettes. Not roll your own smokes, but tailor-made cigarettes, or as we call them in here, TMs.

George may have been sixty-five but every morning him and I would do a boxing workout. Caleb Dalton taught me a lot about boxing, what he left out, George finished off.George taught me how to throw 'em off my front leg for power not just my back leg. He also fine-tuned my left hook.

This one big, and I mean *big,* mother fucking Muslim said I was interrupting his prayers in the yard by singing Black Sabbath as I was jumping rope.

Just made me sing louder. He got up off his mat and said my lyrics were evil. I believed he was wrong as my left hook and right overhand were pure evil. Knocked him out cold. My actions almost started a riot right there in the yard. Billy being our Shock Collar, met with the Muslim Shock Collar to try and calm the waters.

No one wants a full-scale riot. For us, it's bad for business as you know the screws will stop our drug, cigarette, and booze enterprise. For the Muslims they know they would have to contend with us and the North Mexicans who the Battaglia family does drug business with outside prison walls.

So, it was agreed that the Muslims would have their prayer time in one section of the yard and not near the exercise area and we would not exercise in their prayer area.

Now, for me, I am not a pure Nazi as I have some black friends on the outside. One of them is Black Paul, fuck, he helped me get out of San Fran when I was on the run.

And when the day came that I spotted Black Paul who was just sentenced to eighteen months for having four stolen VW Bugs on his property, I couldn't go up and give him a big, welcome to San Quentin hug. It bugged me a bit at first with these rules. But it helped to keep me alive and to also show trust and respect to the others in the prison gang I belonged to.

4

DAY 99: Prisoners come and go all the time in San Quentin. And when the day finally came, the forty-two-year prison career of George Daniels came to end. He seemed almost as scared leaving as one of the new cherries coming into this place.

"George you should be happy man, fucking freedom!"

"You know for the past forty-two years I was told when to get up, eat and go to bed. I missed two world wars, Korea, and Vietnam. I think eight different Presidents, I have lost count. I am not sure I am going to know how to survive outside these walls. I just know how to survive behind these walls."

It was sad seeing George this nervous. I have never seen fear in the old fighter's eyes before, now I see it.

"You are going to be living with your sister in Florida; you have family who will take care of you, man. There is so much to see and do out there. Strip joints who legally serve booze, not just speak easy joints. You can now go and see a prize fight live; you can call Ali a bum and traitor in person instead of yelling at the television, George."

"I guess you're right, kid. Getting out of this place is the hardest thing to do, getting back in is pretty easy. You watch your back in here and get out in one piece and show that ex-cunt of yours she made a big mistake."

"You always had a way with words, George."

And like that, he was gone. Never thought I would say this but having a whole cell to myself felt pretty empty.

The only advantage was that I could jerk off in peace. Who was my mental focal point? Barbara Eden. Fuck, her master was such a moron. I would be tapping that ass daily and my wishes would involve two or three other chicks, weed, and an endless supply of beer and steak.

5

DAY 102: First thing this morning, two new inmates added to our block would change the course of my life in prison.

First off, I would be getting my new celly; his name is Herschel Adler.

For the common person, that name meant nothing, but if you watched porno and actually read the credits at the end of the movies it would say Writer, Producer and Director, Herschel Adler.

Now, Herschel was not imprisoned for having sex with anyone or anything or any other sick shit that took place in his movies; the IRS said he owed over thirty thousand in back taxes. This cost Herschel fifteen months of his life in San Quentin.

Herschel was in his mid-forties, he was stout and wore a really bad toupee and a goatee, but he was also wearing a pair of black eyes. He was a very nervous guy and within ten seconds of putting his stuff in our cell, he raced to the toilet and sprayed the bowl.

"I am so sorry, please don't kill me. Hey, you're not a killer, are you?"

He was sweating and I honestly thought he was going to have a heart attack right there on the shitter.

"I haven't actually killed anybody in over a year."

"Oy vey, a killer, they put me in with a killer, no offense."

"Relax man, I am just fucking with you."

"Not funny, not funny."

Then I saw Herschel turn whiter than a ghost when I took my shirt off to get washed up.

At first, I thought maybe it was the scars all over my upper body from Nam, or the fact I was really starting to not only get big muscular wise, but also quite ripped.

Then I realized he was staring at my 1st SS tattoo on my chest.

"Herschel, you are either not a fan of tattoos, or you are a Jew."

"I have money, whores, whatever you want. Just don't hurt me."

"I am not going to hurt you man; my ex is a Jew and that makes my daughter Katrina half Jewish."

I then walked over and asked Herschel who gave him the two black eyes.

"He told me if I said anything to anybody, he would kill me, I believe him!

"My house is now your house also. No one brings grief to this house."

"I will be honest with you, Mitch; you actually seem like a nice guy. I am also a businessman. In the outside world I pay people to make sure no grief or harm comes my way. I am willing to pay you for protection in here."

Prison has turned me into something or someone I never wanted to be. The Army turned me into a ruthless and fearless killer until I was broken down in the line of duty. Fuck yeah, I will take care of Herschel. I will of course talk to Billy and make sure he gets a kicked up some cash as well seeing he is the Shock Collar.

"And how much is your ass worth saving?"

"I was thinking maybe twenty-five dollars a week, what do you think of that, Mitch?"

"I don't have to think. I know your white, Jewish ass will be sold to the Muslims. Not only will they take turns fucking you, they will also take turns stabbing you to death. I am willing to bet they are already in discussion about what your butt hole is worth. And let's not count out the hardcore Nazi's who I will have to keep from killing you. In here, the Shock Collar decides who gets protected and who we go to war over. Billy Davidson is the Shock Collar and one of my closest friends. Have you heard of him?"

"He is a Hell Hound, correct?"

"Good. I'm glad you know who he is, and the power he possesses."

I felt Herschel's nose, it was clearly broken.

"I will talk to Billy and tell him you are willing to pay each of us seventy-five dollars a week for protection."

"That's a lot of money, Mitch."

"You don't think your life is worth that much Herschel? Or if you think others will offer cheaper protection let me know, I am more than willing to let Billy know you turned us down. And he will say fuck you, then after you get out of the prison infirmary and approach us again, Billy will double or even triple our first offer. Or he will say fuck you, not good enough then, not good enough now. And I will have a new celly because you will be leaving here in a pine box."

Vey iz mir was his response.

"Herschel, remember one thing; like I said, my ex is a Jew and her Mom and stepdad hated me. I learned some Yiddish. I promise this is not just a shake down. You will be protected. Who did this to your face?"

"His name is Chris Downs, and he is nothing but a schoolyard bully. You know him?"

"I have heard of him and what I have heard is nothing but shit. I think he is a member of the Jokers Wild Motorcycle Club, which is just a puppet club for the Thunder. Yeah, schoolyard bully sounds about right."

I felt sorry for Herschel, he was soft and not able to fend for himself and all in all, he was a decent guy. Great sense of humor, lots of insane stories about the girls who star in his pornos and you really believed all his stories were true.

Albert also liked Herschel, as Albert the businessman knew there was also money to be made off Herschel and his whores once we were all released from prison.

The Muslims and true, hard-core Arians on the other hand hated Herschel so we earned our pay, not just another scam.

Jerry, as promised, had a Splasher from the club drop by for a quick tug during a visit. You try and be discreet as possible, but not touching a woman or one touching me in over five months, I swear it took four strokes before I shot all over her legs.

I think the screw finally clued in as to what was happening as my eyes were rolling back in my head as I moaned out, "Holy fuck."

6

DAY 113: A screw came and got me from my cell and said I had a visitor. The one thing you never want to do in prison is to make a screw look stupid or weak. You can get away with a lot of shit in here, but this is their so-called *line in the sand*.

I knew this time there would be no moaning when shooting my load. On the walk down I was fully hard anticipating another successful hand-job manipulation.

Last chick was blonde, was kind of hoping today would be a red head, yeah, I will mention that to Jerry, every week should be a different hair color. After all, variety is the spice of life.

We passed the visitation room and kept heading east, my hard-on went away, and I had this really bad feeling come over me. Fuck, did a rat finally come forward and say he saw me kill Tommy Capello?

Sure as fuck we stopped right in front of the interrogation room. There were two other screws in there and they told me to spread eagle against the wall. The patted me down as I was plotting and planning what to say to my lawyer.

I was handcuffed and leg shackled which was weird as the FBI only had me handcuffed last time. As soon as I was walked in the room, I was surprised to see two cops in uniform and not two guys in suits.

The one cop I didn't recognize, the second cop had his back to me and as soon as he turned around, I said, "Holy fuck!"

But this time there was no moaning and no pleasure and I knew only pain was about to cometh my way. It was Kurt Wilson, who is now a San Francisco cop. Kurt asked the screws to leave and told me to have a seat.

"Fuck you, asshole!" was my response.

His responded with a shot to my midsection. It took the wind right out me and doubled me over. Kurt then came and grabbed me by the hair and forcibly sat me down.

"You killed my fiancée you cocksucker. You broke my great-grandparents kitchen table, and you fucked my sister's head right up!"

Fuck him, the self-righteous cocksucker.

"Guess what? I loved Lucy as well, she didn't fucking love you, Kurt. I never forced her to do anything she didn't want to do and that included putting a syringe in her arm. You fucking smothered her you bastard. She was going to break off your engagement as soon as you got back stateside."

Kurt grabbed my hair again, but this time smashed my head on the table. That one had my eyes water up as I now felt dazed. He must have concussed me as I saw the door to the interview room open, and Frank Trower came in all fired up at Wilson. He gave Wilson a scathing lecture about using his position of power.

I am still trying to shake the last attack off when I

heard Trower tell Kurt to keep his hands to himself, that he is responsible for my wellbeing in San Quentin. Any more assaults on me by Wilson, he will be asked to leave, or even charged by the prison itself.

The older cop also agreed with Trower. He reminded Wilson that he is still on probation and a convict can still press charges against the police.

"I would never charge anyone for assault and not even a cop; only a pussy would do that. Wilson why don't you show me how tough you really are and take off these cuffs and shackles and we can settle things right here and now."

All eyes in the room now focused on Wilson. He was always a chicken shit. His face was now turning beet red in anger as he stood up and said,

"Once you leave this place your ass will be mine. I will watch your every move, Strongbow. You will fuck up and I will have the pleasure of sending you right back."

I stood up and said smugly, "Funny, your sister always liked it on her back."

Hook-Line-Sinker. Wilson now charged at me and with not being able to use my hands or feet, how exactly did I break Officer Wilson's nose? He tried to throw an overhand and missed. He was now inches away, so I gave him an old-fashioned Glasgow Kiss.

Wilson hit the ground; his face was covered in his own blood. He tried to get up but had a case of Bambi legs. His mouth was still running, telling his partner to charge me for assaulting an officer.

"Kurt, the guy is in cuffs and shackles, you assaulted him twice. This kind of shit will sink a guy's career. Let's go, rookie."

His partner pointed at me the whole time while they were leaving. I can only imagine what he was thinking, well you know what, fuck him too.

To tell the truth, I did feel a bit concussed, but that nurse has been on my mind and in my pants ever since I first met her. I was puzzled that she knew my name. So, I told Trower, I should really get looked at. Trower turned to me and asked what I was going to say about what happened.

"I slipped on a wet floor and hit my head."

He took a deep breath and knew that I know how to play the game. Fine was his answer. As luck would have it, she was on duty.

She smiled at me and asked what happened.

I kept my promise to Trower, seeing as how he stood up for me. She felt around my neck which once again got me hard and looked into my eyes with a small flashlight.

She then turned to the Walking Boss and said I have a slight concussion and she would like to keep me over night. Walking Boss said fine and then he left.

I was assigned a bed in the infirmary and was told I must stay in it. I flirtatiously asked if she was going to join me. She pointed to her wedding ring and shook her head no. One of the two screws assigned to the infirmary asked if there was a problem.

She said no, all is fine. I stared at her, still trying to recall how the hell I know her. I looked at her name tag and it said *Hartman,* that drew a blank, so I asked if she served in the Armed Forces.

"That's a negative, soldier. Katrina has your eyes by the way."

My gut now flipped as my head spun and it wasn't from the concussion.

"Nurse Hartman, I am at a disadvantage being concussed and all. You seem to know a hell of a lot about me, you look familiar, but I can't place it. What's your first name?"

Before she answered she made sure the two screws weren't listening in.

"My first name is Amy and last time I saw you, well you were pretty stoned."

"I have spent a good deal of my life stoned. Before or after Vietnam?"

"Before. I know you're in prison, but I also know there is a good guy inside of you. You saved me at Monterey from that animal."

"No shit! Little Amy, you have grown up quite nicely, Abby was your twin sister, right? Muriel was your Mom?"

"Yes, Muriel is my Mom, my Mom who you

shot sperm all over. Heck me and Abby still laugh at that!"

"I remember Tash was so uptight about me making a good impression, and I don't think that was the perfect first impression."

"Not really, but we also knew why Tash loved you. You made up for it introducing my Mom to Janis Joplin, she still tells her friends about that. I read why you are in here, sorry to hear about your girlfriend. That animal at Monterey is the kind of creep I thought for sure I would run across in here."

"I am pretty sure if you want to run across him it would be in a graveyard." Amy's eyes widened. "I had nothing to do with his death!"

"I am glad to hear that. I want to thank you once again, Mitch for making sure he didn't do anything to me and for also helping me when I was throwing up. I do remember that and haven't forgotten what a good guy you were."

"I am still a good guy; I am just in a bad place and I have to do what I have to do to get out of here in one piece. Be honest with me, has Tash asked how I am doing in here?"

Sheepishly, Amy said *yes*.

"If you really want to thank me for taking care of that creep Salvatore, then please tell Tash I am a model prisoner. Katrina gave me the strength to keep me alive in Nam. I should have died on my last mission."

I told Amy the whole story, showed her the surgery scars, showed her the bullet wounds. Amy promised me she would do as I requested.

We talked right up till the end of her shift which ended at 23:00. Amy also said she is a newlywed whose husband is at the Naval Academy and once he graduates, he will be going to flight school to be a pilot. I was saddened when she left. I hate Natasha for all the shit she has put me through, but deep down I look at Amy and see Tash, maybe hate is too strong a word.

For the rest of the night the nightshift nurse woke me up every two hours to make sure I didn't slip into a coma. The next morning, I was cut loose just in time so I wouldn't miss my shift in the kitchen. My nose was a bit swollen and I had a pretty good bruise on my forehead, well worth breaking Wilson's nose.

It doesn't take long for news to travel fast throughout the prison. Either good news or bad news. Billy Davidson said he heard I knocked out the cop that was interrogating me.

"He wasn't interrogating me; he was there to fracture my skull and let me know he is coming after me once I am a free man. That is when I broke his nose and fucked him up."

This statement made everyone's morning, everyone but Albert and Frankie. Albert took me aside and said a screw told him that Carmen D'Angelo was just convicted of trafficking a hundred kilos of coke and that he is going to be sentenced to spend the next dozen years or so here at San Quentin. He asked if I knew who he was. I said I didn't have a clue.

"Carmen D'Angelo is the underboss to his brother Sal. They are the head Mob family out of Sacramento. They run everything from Sacramento to Carson City. Ruthless bunch of old school mobsters to say the least. About two years ago they tried to dip their toe into the Bay Area water. This didn't sit well with the Battaglia's and what started off first with just guys breaking each other's skulls turned to a couple bodies missing from each side. New York eventually got involved as the heat was no good for business. A truce was called, and they went back to Sacramento."

"They know exactly who you are?"

"Yeah, they know I am a Capo, there is no love lost between us. They blamed me for being directly involved with one of their missing guys. They actually asked New York permission to kill me."

"Was this guy some high-ranking member who went missing?"

"He was a brother-in-law. Because I was a Capo and of course I denied anything to do with his disappearance their request was denied. Yeah, I was the last item on the table for the truce."

I knew better than to ask Albert if he killed him or not, but his smile gave it away.

"And guess who they use for muscle?"

Let's see if I can go two for two in the guessing game, "Thunder?"

"Ding, ding, ding Mr. Strongbow you win the cupid doll."

"You think they will break the truce and come after you in here?"

"I have no doubts in my mind they will. Carm will make sure it doesn't come back to him. He will reward who ever does it quite well. Yeah something I forgot to tell you, after his brother-in-law went missing, I said I guess his sister will now wear black for the rest of her life and will never have sex again. He asked what I meant by that. I said no one else is going to be that desperate to fuck a filthy, whore, pig like his sister. We had quite the fist fight over that one."

"I am sure old Bill Shakespeare himself couldn't have said it better, you crazy bastard."

Albert laughed but I could tell he was, I don't know, worried or plotting and planning on what is the next best course of action.

That night as I lay in my cot, I know that I too, will be a target with D'Angelo coming here. I can see him backing the Thunder also coming after me. Albert and I could be the old proverb killing two birds with one stone.

The next afternoon I noticed Albert did not show up for lunch. Later in the yard, he told me that Mike Battaglia had come to visit him. He sends his thanks for me taking care of Capello and I will be rewarded once I get out.

He also told Albert to do what he must do to stay alive, if at all possible. And if it comes down to killing Carm, make sure it doesn't come back to him. Albert, being a loyal soldier, said he will try his very best.

That night we talked to Billy Davidson to hopefully join us and to give him the heads up as to what might be going down. Of course, you don't say you are going to kill a Mob underboss, you tell Billy that the Thunder in here is going to get an important ally.

Billy said that right now throughout the whole prison there are three full patches, five strikers, and about a dozen loyal associates.

I laughed inside as Fagan was supposedly loyal to the Hell Hounds and he turned out to be a rat. Yeah, watching him take his last breath before he drowned still puts a smile on my face.

7

DAY 122: It's about thirty minutes before lights out. I am alone doing pushups when I noticed a figure standing in my doorway has totally blocked the outside rays of the moon. The fucker is huge. The sweat rolling into my eyes burns as I strain to look up and see who it is. I am also a little nervous as my arms and shoulders are totally exhausted. If someone has come to fight me my feet better not fail me.

I jump up and am ready for the fight, head rush and all, when I hear, "Please don't stop on my account, Mitchell."

That familiar Rhodesian accent is uncanny.

"Big John Derksen, how are you brother?"

"Well I am doing a double life sentence, how are you, Mitchell?"

"Great to see you, John. And sorry to hear that, man. What the fuck happened?"

"These two stupid fucks tried to rip me off, make that two dead pricks. I shot them both dead. Problem is that the cops saw the whole thing go down. They were being watched by the cops in the first place, bad luck for sure."

I asked if he saw Billy Davidson yet, he said yes, and that Billy told him where my cell was. I asked if he heard what is coming down with the Thunder. John just smiled and said he wants to kill Jorge himself.

"I will never see the light of day again, what's another murder charge?"

I took John down to meet Albert and Frankie. I could tell that Albert and John have met before; I could also tell there was a hell of a lot of tension between the two. John said he wanted to get caught up with Billy and left Albert's cell.

I looked at Albert and said, "Is there something I should know about?"

"I was in a high-end poker game with him

years ago. The pot got big. He put up his Harley, I put up a Camaro Z28, I won the hand, and he was pissed. I offered to sell it back to him. He said I was overpricing his bike. I told him to fuck off and it went to fisticuffs. You cousin Jerry and Donnie Terek paid me a visit the next day and Jerry and I agreed on a price."

"You know we need John's help dealing with the Thunder and D' Angelo's?"

"I know we do; I will try and smooth things over. But I do have my limitations also, I ain't sucking no man's cock or kissing any one's ass in here. I am a Captain for the Battaglia family and that means something in here, not just with the cons, but also the screws."

I went back to my cell, pissed. When I was in battle in Nam, I didn't give a rat's ass who was beside me in a firefight or if it was a Marine Corp slick coming to haul my ass out of a hot LZ. Herschel picked up on me being pissed and I told him what was going down.

Herschel was one of those wise Jews, you know the kind that can tell a story and it has a life meaning behind it.

"In the middle east, Israel is a small country surrounded by large Muslim countries that out man and out gun us ten to one; these countries, with their main goal, to destroy us. In Israel we have several different sects of Jews who don't always see eye to eye with each other. But the one thing we all have in common is to protect every single Jew from the Muslims who are bent in destroy us and wiping Israel off the map."

"You're right, Herschel; we have to come together as a formidable force, or we will be destroyed."

I lay on my cot that night thinking I am the one who is pissed, and I am a civilian. I am not a Hell Hound or a member of the Battaglia crime family. Fucking egos, this is what the whole problem is all about.

Sitting back and not getting involved will just come back to bite me in the ass because, sooner than later, the Thunder will also come after me.

*

Next day, while serving breakfast, I noticed a couple of Thunder associates had more attitude and seemed to be sticking their chest out and yapping off a little, no make that a lot, more than normal.

Something was up and I knew what. Once my shift ended and it was yard time, I asked Albert and John to join me in a walk and talk.

I laid everything on the line, I didn't care that Albert was a made man. I didn't care if John was a full patch who I grew up thinking he was the biggest and baddest Mother Fucker I ever met. I explained to them what I learned about brotherhood in Nam and also what Herschel told me about Israel.

Albert put out his hand first to John as a sign or peace and brotherhood. John was a bit hesitant at first and then growled and said fine as his hand met Albert's.

Later that night, Albert, Frankie, Billy, John and I discussed what our game plan should be. Each one of us had our own ideas. I was the only civilian, but I had more combat experience then all of them put together. I strongly suggested we kill D'Angelo within twenty-four hours of him coming in here.

My thought process is that we don't want him gathering up favors and support in here. The longer he is in here the more power he will gain.

If we kill him before any known hostilities go down, the less chance it would come back to us. If we could somehow have it come back that the Thunder did this, it would be the perfect scenario. Just not sure how. We all went to sleep that night united and ready for the kill.

The next morning, I had a visitor. It was Joseph O'Reilly.

I trust Joseph with my life, but I am not sure where he stands with the D'Angelo family so I ain't going to tell him what we have planned for dear old Carm. Joseph asked if I had any more problems with members of the Thunder or anyone else. Not really was my answer.

"Well then, Mitchell. I hear trouble is coming to this prison in the name of Carm D'Angelo. And that trouble is not meant for you.

Don't get involved with the bullshit lad, you hear me?"

"And what makes you think I would get involved in the first place?"

"I had Sal D'Angelo pay me a visit yesterday and he asked if you worked for me."

"And what did say?"

"I said yes you are one of my men, what seems to be the problem? He said there won't be a problem as long as you stay out of his brother's way and make wise decisions as to whom I run with or run against."

"You do know the D' Angelo's use the Thunder for muscle."

"I know that, and it concerns me."

Joseph went deep into thought. More so than ever I know we have to kill Carm.

"I have some pretty solid and loyal friends in here who have my back and vice versa. I will be fine and thanks for your concern."

"Sal is an underboss; he wields a lot of

power and respect, Mitchell. People wanting to make a name for themselves will do whatever he asks of them. And yes, that includes murder in the name of a fucking dummy."

"I have no grief with him; do you think he would come after me because of my friendship with Albert and Mike Battaglia?"

"He knows you are not in their crew, but he knows you have some sort of bond with them. He did come to me first. And if it were me, yeah, I would come after you. Anyone that bares a threat for his power and safety I would go after."

I just nodded my head yes in agreement and clenched my jaw.

"Mitchell, whatever you do, have it come back to anyone but us. If this comes down on your head not even I or Battaglia could protect you. Killing a made high ranking full-fledged made mobster is suicidal, be smart, lad."

After Joseph left, the walls seem to get a little tighter on me, yeah, they were really starting to close in.

I headed right to Albert who was doing handstand pushups at the time. I told him the whole scenario. Albert now knows that Carm wants to run all criminal activities inside San Quentin and anyone who opposes him, or who he views as a threat, will be taken out. That means Albert, Frankie Knuckles, every single Hell Hound and, of course, yours truly.

Albert's face at first went beet red as he started to curse and swear, then he stopped and smiled, a devilish smile if I've ever seen one.

He turned to me and said, "I think you are wrong with whacking Carm within twenty-four hours of coming in here. You said you worry about him getting more and more powerful. I say we knock out his biggest allies before he comes. I know exactly what guys in my world will support whatever he says or does. We know he will have the Thunder in his pocket. I say we kill all of them before he even steps foot inside. Let's neuter this bastard before he gets a hard-on."

*

It was now almost 16:00 on Friday. Carm is

coming next week so this weekend will be the perfect kill time. Billy, Albert, Frankie, John, and I ate dinner at the same table that night. Call it a war council at its nastiest. Billy said he has a guy working in the yard grounds and he will make sure we all have weapons ready for us tomorrow during yard time. Billy said each one of us will be assigned a certain area for the weapon.

Tomorrow he will know exactly where each weapon will be hidden. Billy thanked me for the weapons. I was shocked and asked him what he meant.

"That crazy, IRA terrorist, Callahan left a leprechauns pot of weapons for you."

Never go into battle empty handed. So, all of us played out every single scenario and exactly the precise time the attacks would begin.

13:00 was time. All of us were confident and ready for battle. I slept not bad that night, considering. Confidence knowing we have really thought through this whole mass killing, put me at ease. I guess the only unknown variable for me was this; I know Albert has killed before, being a

Nam Marine vet, Derksen is in here for a double murder and lord knows how many he has killed while in Rhodesia.

Davidson and the other Hell Hounds I am not sure they have the kill monster inside them. Anyone can throw punches and act tough behind their club's patch. And Frankie Knuckles is a made mobster. Rumor is to be made you would have killed to be part of their exclusive club.

That morning, I told Herschel he really didn't look so good and that after breakfast he should go and see the nurse. He was dumbfounded by this.

"Herschel you pay me to protect you, I might not be able to that today in the yard, don't ask, just go and see the nurse."

I know he got it when he said, "Awe."

No one can say that half word half moan *awe* like a Jew. That morning during breakfast, something just didn't feel right. Both my head and gut knew. I have killed too many people in my life for this to be nerves.

The Thunder members sitting at their table

seemed happy, relaxed, and almost jovial. Jorge also kept making a point of looking over at us like the cat that swallowed the canary. Derksen said that Jorge is his; he is going to personally rip out his intestines and force Jorge to eat them.

"Fuck John, you been dropping LSD with Charlie Manson?"

That made us all laugh, but it did nothing to ease the tension that was burning in my gut. By the time we were done eating, the kitchen manager came out and told me that Little Earl just left for the infirmary and my afternoon shift is starting right now. I was dumbfounded and shocked, Albert told him to find someone else.

"Strongbow, you have two seconds to get your ass in the kitchen or you can spend the next thirty days in the hole."

By now, two of the other screws overheard the heated conversation and asked if I wanted to be walked down to the hole right now. Albert told me to go to work and we will have the push-up contest tomorrow. I knew exactly what he meant, so I said that works and headed to the kitchen.

No sooner did I get dressed into my kitchen whites and headed to help take the hams out of the ovens, I heard the prison riot alarm go off. You automatically hit the ground. My mind was racing.

I know Albert said we would wait till tomorrow, and fuck, it is just after nine, so nothing is coinciding with our plans. Must be some other shit going on.

The manager, under the watchful eye of a shotgun toting screw, locked us in our area where we eat, and then they headed off to wherever the riot was taking place. Within twenty minutes we were unlocked and told to go back to work.

I noticed the one screw made a little too long eye contact with me, really red flagged to tell the truth. The whole time all of us in the kitchen are trying to get answers, but all we heard was silence. Then you are told the entire prison will be locked down for the rest of the weekend.

Whatever went down was big. A screw must have been attacked or even killed and they are punishing the rest of the population. So, instead of serving inmates you pack up meals that are to be delivered to every single cell.

Several cons helped to deliver the meals and as soon as they would come back you asked for info.

The first thing confirmed is that it was a murder and not a screw but a con.

The older cons tell me to have the whole prison locked down it must have been someone high ranking in the con world.

Fuck maybe D'Angelo came early, and Albert already whacked him. By the end of my shift we still hadn't heard shit. All of us were shackled and walked back to our cells. Once inside I could tell by Herschel's face that all was not well.

"Herschel, who was murdered today?"

"John Derksen"

I had to sit on my bunk and collect my thoughts.

"Did they catch who did it?"

"You have a couple fish lines from Albert, too small for me to read."

My heart was now racing as anger filled my body.

Mitch, I am hearing John was stabbed more than one hundred times. A screw came and told him he had a visitor. John on his way was to see that visitor when he was blindsided. The whole prison is to be locked down till at least Monday. By then our guest from Sac will be wearing prison garb. This was an organized kill. I see Jorge and the rest of the Thunder involved. C.D. knows he needs the upper hand in here and right now the H.H stop that.

Things didn't get better as the weekend went on. The whole prison was ripped apart looking for not only the murder weapon but also any weapons that would be used in those seeking revenge for John's murder. And yes, that included the weapons we had stashed in the yard.

One by one anyone that was a friend or foe of John was interviewed by the prison staff including, yours truly. I was not a suspect, but they asked me if I knew who would want him murdered.

Now, these guys are actually better the cops for

questioning you and here are my reasons why I say this; they already know who you are, who you eat with, hang with, and work out with. You are always under surveillance in San Quentin, twenty-four hours a day whether you like it or not. And these bastards don't need a search warrant or probable cause.

So, you don't insult their intelligence when you are not a suspect. You don't talk like a rat, you just be yourself, and for me that means being solid.

Before I left the interrogation room, Trower sternly reminded that anyone with gang connections was going to be watched even closer. He also reminded me I am a short timer, *don't fuck it up*. I know what he was saying is true, but in here you must become part of a crew to survive. In Nam, and all over South East Asia, I liked being the Lone Wolf. There, I could disappear in the jungle. Here, there is no place to run and gun. No quick kills. Fuck, the more I think about it, I did get away with murdering Capello.

*

Monday morning, you could feel a change in the flow. It just seemed different. There was an electric charge in the air. The lockdown was lifted, which I am not sure was the right thing to do, but then again, this place is called The Arena. I was working the breakfast shift, one of the first guys I served was Mutt, the fuck was wearing an eye patch. I smiled at him while putting oatmeal in his bowl.

"You think this is funny, Strongbow? Your time is coming very soon."

"I think what is going to be even funnier is when you are using a white cane. Next time I will ripped out your other eye from your socket, and then put my cock in there and skull fuck you."

The kitchen manager sensed the tension and told him to move along and for me to stick to serving breakfast. I wanted to serve up a heaping helping of death, not oatmeal. I know I am targeted just like Albert. Fuck, Army Intelligence told me the Viet Cong had a bounty of ten thousand dollars on my head. Nice to be so loved isn't it?

After my shift, I went out to the yard and headed

right for Albert, Frankie. and Billy. Right off the bat you make sure that you are still solid with whatever comes down.

Albert said he had been watching Jorge and his crew bothering with a bunch of Southern Mexicans.

And so, it begins. Just like in any war, each country is looking for allies. Well, time for us to start making allies. If we stand back, we will all be dead by Halloween.

Now, I knew several of the Muslims and Africans from San Fran and Nam. Billy said he would rather die than ask the Blacks for help.

So, that leaves the Northern Mexicans who are always one step away from fighting the Southern Mexicans, the Asians who keep pretty much keep to themselves, and the Russians who are ruthless, but just can't be trusted.

I know that the Hell Hounds and the Battaglia family get a lot of dope from Mexico, fuck, I helped set up the deals in the first place. I don't know how much Billy knows about this as he is not an executive in the Club. I know that Albert knows.

I believe we now must get help outside the prison walls. And that help is from my cousin Jerry who will be pissed about having one of his club members murdered. You know Thunder is behind it. Yeah, if we can get Jerry to talk to Hernandez and see if he has any control over either the south or north Mexican gangs in here.

Now these of course are logical thoughts, since being in prison your logical thoughts often slip through the bars to never return. Within a day, Donnie and Jeannie Terek paid me a visit.

I gave Donnie a quick lowdown as to the going ons in here. He said the Club is going to hold those responsible and seek revenge. I told him if we don't get some help he may as well get ready to bury a couple more of us. I said our friends in Mexico would be a great help right now.

Donnie agreed and said he would talk to Jerry as soon as they get into Oakland.

*

The next day during yard, a bunch of the senior

Mexican gang members called the La Neustria Familia came over to our designated area.

I knew they were not there to fight us as their Shock Collar was with them. No way would they start a rumble with him this close. Like most Generals, they sit back and order the troops to fight.

Marco Garcia was their Shock Collar. He had more tattoos covering his body than exposed skin. His eyes were pure evil. Just like the rules the screws impose on us, there are also rules for prisoners involving other prisoners.

Marco being a Shock Collar would only talk to Albert and Billy, one Shock Collar and one Capo.

"I understand you are in need of some help."

"I might be. Depends on how much it costs," said Albert with a tentative smile.

"You are right, everything comes with a price. My price to start off is this; my cousin, Juanita, owns a restaurant in San Francisco. It seems the city won't issue her a permit to sell liquor. Fix that for her."

Albert said he would see what he could do and asked what else he wanted.

"If a war is started in here, I want a life for a life. For every life we take in here for you we expect five hundred dollars and if you want D'Angelo himself taken out, that will cost you five thousand dollars. I assure you that it won't come back to you or the Battaglia family."

Albert agreed to all aspects of Garcia's deal. Billy wasn't too happy with the demands but knew to keep his mouth shut until Garcia went back to his side of the prison yard.

"I will kill all the Thunder members in here myself, Albert. They are mine."

Albert said he will respect Billy's personal need for the revenge kills. And what did I think of all of this? I know in Nam and Laos the Army always had deals with local tribes to hunt the Vietcong. But I also learned that it is just as easy to be betrayed as it is to seek help and make a deal.

I trusted Albert as we have been to hell and back together and Billy will seek revenge for the murder of his club brother. Garcia? Fuck, I know shit about him other than he controls a gang of over three hundred members and associates. That in itself is scary I guess that's why Albert did the deal.

A couple days later, Garcia and two of his men approached us in the yard and said his cousin now has her liquor license.

He also said one of his men who are a spy in the South Mexican gang confirmed that D'Angelo has reached out to them for muscle for hire.

Looks like we are going to war.

8

DAY 135: The morning started off with business as usual. I had the early shift in the kitchen. I also talked Herschel into working in the kitchen as Black Paul told me on the sly there is going to be an attempt on Herschel's life very soon.

The Muslim population despised Herschel for being a Jew. They have found out he makes porno movies, fuck they are all taking numbers to slice his throat after they rape him of course, fucking hypocrites.

I noticed when we were serving breakfast several members of the Muslim Brotherhood seemed to be like sharks tasting blood. They were all giving Herschel the death stare.

Sure as fuck at yard time a couple members of the Muslim Brotherhood approached Herschel as he was playing chess.

Billy and his crew weren't exactly fond of us protecting or even having a friendship with a Jew. But Billy did admit that Herschel was not your stereotypical Jew, so he didn't mind standing beside me when I asked, Sayed what he was doing away from the Monkey Bars

"You don't think the Jew exploited your people, Strongbow? His people helped to have your people enslaved onto reservations."

"I am actually only half Sioux, the other half is full blown Nazi SS. So, from that aspect, no."

Sayed's eyes got really big as he went to shiv Herschel. I was able to push Sayed out of the way causing him to balance and fall to the ground.

This caused a huge free for all between our crew and several members of the Muslim Brotherhood. Within throwing several punches and kicks the riot alarm was going off and guards were firing shots into the air telling all to get on the ground.

In Nam I knew when the sights of the rifle were pointed at me. I had a quick glance at the guard tower and saw a screw with his rifle aimed right at me. Reluctantly I did what every con is supposed to do when the alarm goes off. I hit the ground face down.

I felt someone kick me in the ribs and then I heard a rifle go off. I heard a sound that I have heard one too many times in my life, a bullet coming closer and then whizzing just over me. The next sound I heard was someone close grimace in pain and then the thud of someone hitting the ground hard. I felt the vibration when they hit the dirt.

You stay in the spread-eagle position, but you look around to see who is shot, you hope it's no one from your crew. Within an arm length I see some black dude on the ground with his guts sprayed all over the place. I also notice Sayed hasn't moved from the same location I bowled him over onto the ground.

Not even thirty seconds later, you are surrounded by shotgun toting guards screaming at the top of their lungs that if anyone moves, they will be shot dead. So, you do as ordered and one by one you are told to get off the ground, patted down for weapons, handcuffed and then taken to the hole.

Eventually, you are taken to an interrogation room and questioned by prison authorities.

I was told right off the bat that Sayed is dead. They pulled a shiv out of his chest. It seems the blade went right through his heart. Seeing at how several witnesses saw that I was the last person to make physical contact with him, they now want to hear my side of the story.

There is an unofficial code of conducts for solid cons and being a rat is at the top of the list of what not to do. But me doing a life sentence for the accidental death of Sayed is not one of those solid con rules. I told them exactly what happened even if they tried to say they have witnesses that saw me shiv Sayed.

So, you tell what went down and leave nothing out. They ask you questions to try and trip you up. Not much to be tripped up on as Sayed came to us; we didn't go looking for trouble.

They take all kinds of notes and say that they know where to find me if they have more questions. You are taken back to the hole and you are a little scared. Not because he is dead, but because you truly had nothing to do with his death, well directly anyways. Is this Karma for me getting away with Capello's murder?

Next time they want to ask for more details, or arrest me, I am clamming up until my lawyer is present.

Just after midnight I heard my prison door open. I got butterflies as the two screws came closer. They took me back to the interrogation room where Trower interviewed me earlier. He seems to be more tired than I am though.

"Well, we have some good news and some bad news for you, Strongbow."

"What's that?" Fuck, I almost feel like throwing up.

"The good news is that your side of the story has been confirmed by not only by several prisoners, but also prison staff. The bad news is that you are going to be doing the next week in the hole for fighting. Count yourself lucky on this one."

All and all not a bad deal, one week in the hole for

a dead Muslim.

I also realize that someone in the Muslim Brotherhood will seek revenge for his death. They might as well get in line behind Mutt and the rest of the Thunder members.

9

DAY 142: Another week spent in the hole and after one of two very vivid dreams I will be in no hurry to come back.

After my first dream or nightmare I was surprised I could even fall back asleep.

I dreamt that Jake and I were back in the diner in South Dakota in the fall of 1963. The same diner were those rednecks accused me of stealing their leather coat I was wearing.

This time though, all three of them were laying a beating on Jake. He was screaming at me to help him, but I was frozen and fear and couldn't move to help him.

Jake was a bloody mess. A voice from inside the kitchen told me to help out my brother. Fuck even my voice was mute.

That voice kept getting louder and louder until I was able to finally regain my own voice. I said I can't.

"I never raised you that way, boy."

I turned around and saw a figure come out from the shadows of the kitchen. The voice was that of my Dad who was wearing a white cook's outfit.

I said sorry, sir. My Dad pointed at Jake on the ground. I watched a horrified Jake stare at me with pain and fear in his eyes as I did fuck all and watched him take his last breath.

My Dad then walked over to Jake. Kneeled over him with a tear running down his face and said something in Lakota that I didn't understand. Once my Dad stood up, he was now dressed in his 101st Airborne dress parade uniform.

He slapped me in the face and said I am not worthy to be a Strongbow or a member of the 101st Airborne.

He said he will personally court martial me and have me kicked out of the 101st and will have my last name changed to Custer.

I woke up from this nightmare covered in sweat. Even my fingertips were pruned. I felt like puking. The nightmare was so real; I felt Jake's pain in his eyes. I felt the wrath of my Dad for not coming to help Jake when he needed me the most.

My second dream was not violent at all, but I felt just as sad once I finally woke up.

Once again, another flashback in time. 1967 Monterey Pop Festival to be exact. Tash and I are scrapping about me getting high with her twin cousins Amy and Abby. Nothing is going on and yet, Tash loses it on me and says she never wants to see me again; we are done forever are her exact words.

She storms off and Amy and Abby are right behind her. Fuck her I think to myself as I finish off the joint, we were sharing. By the time I get to the roach I burn my upper lip with the heater of the joint.

I hear a voice saying she will kiss it better. Out of the blue smoky haze appears Amy. Like a seductress she makes her way back into my tent. Amy asks to see the fresh burn. She smiles and says she has the perfect lipstick ointment and slowly and softly begins to kiss me.

I am pissed at Tash, so I don't resist her advances. My lips are eager to meet her lips. We kiss until Amy forces my singed lip on her bare breasts.

Her nipples are erect, they are pink and perfect. As I am kissing her, I feel her hands undoing my jeans as she then starts to stroke my cock. I am rock fucking hard.

After a couple minutes Amy lays me down and straddles me. She rides me like a gymnast on a balance beam. *Fuck me, Mitch! Fuck me hard!* She screams. I am now biting on her nipples and sticking a finger up her ass, asking if this is what she wants. She moans *yes*, and before I know it, I am starting to blow my load. I am shooting everywhere. All over Amy and the tent, this time it is Tash's head, not her Aunt Muriel, who opens up the tent flap and gets shot with sperm. But she is not blinded, she sees exactly what is going and she starts to scream and cry. Amy now jumps off me and looks down at me and also starts to cry and says *I am so sorry, so sorry*. Both sets of tears from the girls now drip onto my singed lip and burn as if vinegar was poured onto an open wound.

The pain is so strong it wakes me from my dream. This time I am not only drenched in sweat, but my legs are covered in cum.

Even though I have no love for Tash, even seeing her upset at me in a dream still bothers me, I hate making her cry.

And Amy, fuck, I think I am going to find a reason to go to the infirmary today. I figure married or not, she owes me at least a hand-job for saving her from Salvador at Monterey. I don't need to fuck her I just want her to beat me off.

I am getting sick of seeing my hand around my dick all the time. This dream about her had to mean something. Jake's death dream and my Dad belittling me, still not sure. I was just in time to catch the tail end of breakfast. It was good seeing everyone again. Herschel made sure to give me extra scrambled eggs and to say thank you.

I grabbed a seat with Albert and Frankie. Both stared intensely at a table on the other side of the room. I looked over; three Thunder members were sitting there with some greasy looking prick.

I asked Albert if that was D'Angelo. He said yes. He also said Marco Garcia told him that D'Angelo has put a bounty on all of us sitting at this current table including, yours truly.

I asked if he believed and trusted Garcia. Albert said her heard the same from other criminal groups in here.

Seeing at how Albert is the main, or should I say, prized target I ask now what.

"I told Garcia that we need some weapons."

"And what was his response?"

"He said the weapons would be free, and as you know, Mitch, nothing in life is free and, in this case, certainly not death. He said if we want weapons, we must get all our dope from him or quit dealing ourselves."

"The only time those Mexicans get busy working is if it is illegal shit. So, what was your response?"

"I told him if his cost to us is decent we

have a deal. He said he will charge us ten percent above his cost. It was a decent price, so I said fine. Billy said fuck him, so you better have a talk with Billy and tell him to think bigger picture. We are not dealing from a position of power here."

I promised Albert that I would have a talk with Billy. We needed strength in numbers.

When I asked Albert where Billy was, he said he had a gut ache and the shits and was resting in his cell.

As promised, I gave up heading to the yard after breakfast to talk to Billy. What I didn't tell Albert was that I still had a shiv that George gave me before he left, hidden in my cell. I think each time we go to yard, which is the most dangerous place to be attacked, I will bring it with me.

I had walked up to the second-floor landing when I heard a loud commotion coming from the yard. It was a full-scale brawl. I took one step to go down to make sure none of my guys were being attacked when I heard someone screaming in pain and yelling for help.

The screams were desperate, the screams were

that of Billy Davidson. Someone was giving it to him in his cell. I start to fly up the next two flights of stairs as fast as humanly possible. Billy's cell is three away from mine. Time to see how well the shiv George left me works.

By the time I hit the third-floor stairs, the riot alarm was going off. I heard weapons being discharged in the yard.

I am taking two steps at a time as Billy's screams are getting weaker and weaker. I finally hit the fourth and haul ass to Billy's cell. At this time, I hear nothing but very faint moans.

You know I should stop off at my own cell and get my shiv, but I think I am now at the point where Billy is seconds away from dying.

So, I run right past my cell, I am so focused in saving his life I don't even think about my own safety. In the cell before Billy's I see a shadow out of the corner of my eye. Then I feel a searing pain in my gut, and I fall forward onto the ground. My momentum is so fast I just slip and slide past Billy's cell.

Everything goes into slow motion. I am sliding on

my back. I look down to where I am feeling intense pain and see the blade of a shiv sticking out of my blood-soaked shirt. I can't catch a full breath and I certainly can't get to my feet once I stop sliding thanks to the guardrail.

I know this feeling all too well being stabbed in Hue while on leave in 1970.

Two men start walking towards me. It is Mutt and Jorge. Both have an ear to ear smile. They now swagger as they start to laugh at me on the ground.

"Mutt looks like we have a two for one kill tonight. You should be one of the musketeers with how well you stabbed him!"

"Thanks Jorge, I told you I would have my revenge on you, Strongbow. You're as fucking stupid as your dead brother."

Jorge then told Mutt to pick me up off the ground. Mutt grabbed me by hair until he had me up enough to grab me by my throat. My eyes were watering, and I didn't have the strength to break his death grip. I couldn't fully straighten up as I was getting weaker from blood loss.

Jorge curled his lip up just like Elvis Presley and said, "I am not sure which one of you two fucking Indian brothers I will have enjoyed killing more. You or that piece of shit brother of yours. I guess the only way to know for sure is to have you both die the same way. Jorge, throw this useless fuck over the railing. Kind of ironic for a member of the Airborne to die that way wouldn't you say, Strongbow?"

In the four years I spent fighting in South East Asia I have been in hundreds of fire fights. Been shot and stabbed several times.

At least a couple dozen suicide missions. Been in two bad helicopter crashes including that last one where I was the only survivor. Plane crash back home that took Caleb Dalton's life. One drug overdose and yet I have been able every single time to see the next morning's sunrise.

This time I think lady luck has run out on me. I have had a really good run, all things considered. Having said this, I will be dammed if these two cocksuckers see the sunrise tomorrow. Damn straight, Airborne.

Mutt smiled at me and then grabbed me by my underarms to lift me up and throw me over the railing.

I smiled back at him and with every ounce of courage, I channeled all the pain from my body to another dimension.

I pulled out the shiv that was still sticking out of me and drove it right from the start of Mutt's nuts and ran it right to the top of his sternum.

The smile left his face fast. He had a horrified look on his face that was paler than Arctic snow. His lifeless body fell to ground. A shocked and enraged Jorge screamed, grabbed hold of me, and spun me around to throw me over the railing to my death.

This time I would not be as lucky as I dropped the shiv that I used to kill Mutt. I knew to use my body weight and fell to the ground. Jorge was strong, really strong, so he picked me up by the seat of my pants with one hand and the back of my shirt with the other hand.

As he attempted to throw me over, I used my legs to straddle the railing. Jorge punched me in the back of the head. I figured two or three more punches and I am either going to lose leverage or I am going to pass out.

I yelled *Currahee* and as Jorge threw another punch, I grabbed his arm and used the momentum of falling over the railing to bring him over.

If I am going to hell, I am taking him with me. I made sure not to let go of Jorge. I wanted to make eye contact with him the entire time. I also kept saying *Strongbow* all the way down. I wanted him to always remember who took his life when the both of us are shoveling coal in hell.

As we passed the third floor, I had a death vision. I saw my Dad in his full military dress uniform. Beside him was Jake dressed in his Hell Hound colors. Dad was saluting and Jake was smiling with one thumb up.

The exact same scene on the second floor. Just before we hit the ground, I roll Jorge on his back with my forearm on top of his windpipe to ensure he dies. I believe seeing Dad and Jake means they will now be waiting for me and will walk with me to the happy hunting grounds.

I have been welcomed for avenging Jake's murder. You hit the ground so fast and so hard that you black right out. Maybe that is the best way to die, fast and with a cause, even if it is double murder revenge, rather than slow and painful like Nicky Evampolous.

Once again, I find myself fighting between life and death. For a fleeting second, just as in my dream, I see Amy over top of me crying. The pain coming from my gut tells me I have to be alive, but I also can't fully awaken which takes me back to a death state.

A state where being related to Red Cloud is sometimes a blessing, and sometimes a curse with these visions. On my ill-fated last mission in Laos, I was surrounded by death. Out of a crew of six, I was the sole survivor. As I lay between life and death, I had a vision where I had the choice to join my departed Mom, Dad, Jake and Pam, or suffer in pain as I saw Katrina and Natasha asking for my help.

I chose to live knowing that I would be suffering in pain. Never realized part of that pain was more mental than physical as Katrina doesn't even have a clue who the fuck I am. Natasha decided to marry someone as I was running through the jungles of South East Asia.

Once again, death has decided to pay me another visit and yes, another vision to fuck my brain up.

I am paddling my canoe through a river of fire. It takes every ounce of courage and strength for me to make it to the island, an island I have seen and visited before. A young, muscular Sioux brave warrior waits for me along a shoreline and helps me pull my canoe onto land. He tells me to hurry and come with him; the elders have become impatient in waiting for my arrival.

The young brave has a perfect rhythm of running; I swear, every time his foot hits the ground, I hear a drumbeat. Mine is just an out of sync thud. I find myself falling behind, my legs feel sluggish, almost bogged down in thick blood red mud. I find myself sucking wind big time, my lungs and legs are now burning. Sweat is rolling from my forehead and stinging my eyes so I can barely see the young brave as he is now distancing himself from me.

I shouted for him to slow down, but my voice was mute. Within seconds he was gone, like a phantom nowhere to be found. His saying to me, that the elders have become impatient with me seem to smack me upside the face. So, I continued in my journey, a desolate journey at that.

At one point, I stopped and looked around for any sign to where he had gone. I felt alone and not sure what to do next.

Think, Mitch. I looked up at the darkened skies. The North Star jumped right out at me. It was dynamic and putting a show on just for me.

A single ray cascaded from it and shot the beam to the ground two feet in front of me. The brilliant light shone upon a set of footprints. I knew what to do next. Just like my Dad and Uncle Jack had taught me, I followed the set of tracks. Suddenly, my legs were no longer heavy. My lungs were no longer burning, and my breathing was back to normal.

Not sure how long I was following the tracks as time was not a dimensional factor. Before I knew it, I heard the sound of beating drums, I heard a gourd rattling and could smell a fire burning. I was feeling stronger and stronger. I came to a clearing and in that clearing was a burning fire and tent. I recognized both from my Inipi cleansing. As I came closer, some of the fruit my Grandfather and I left for the elders, was gone.

I looked around and saw no one at all. My senses told me someone was inside. Someone was waiting for me.

It had to be the elders that the brave told me about. I started to snicker to myself, do I knock and wait for them to answer the tent flap? Nah, if they are growing impatient, I better get my ass in there.

As soon as I touched the fabric of the tent, I had a chill run down my spine. A bad vibe came over me. My heart was pounding right out of my chest. I had a vision that on the other side of this flap was my Grandfather and Great Grandfather, Red Cloud. They were both ready to take me to the other side. That death has finally, after so many chances, managed to catch me. My eyes were now starting to tear up and I don't know why.

I said I would always accept death. I guess I feel I am letting down Rachel as she will no longer have any living members of her immediate family. And Katrina, I never did get a chance to tell her that I am her Dad and that I love her.

So many fucking regrets! Should have bolted to Canada. I am sure Rachel would rather have me alive in the Great White North rather than dead. She would have forgiven me, I know it.

As I pondered whether to go inside or cower outside, the North Star once again made its presence known to me. An almost blinding ray was at first cast upon me then onto the tent.

It never even occurred to me that my Dad might a be in the tent, fuck I bet Jake is in there too. I was excited and without hesitation I opened up the tent and walked inside. Thick blue smoke enveloped the whole interior. I could see the silhouette of a lone male inside. And once the smoke cleared enough, I quickly realized that the male exudes power and respect, more power than I have ever felt off anyone in my life.

He looked over at me with a serious scowl on his

face and ordered me to sit down. I knew exactly who he was. Crazyhorse, the most feared Sioux warrior of all time. I sat as ordered as he passed me the pipe. I inhaled out of respect for the elder warrior. The smoke burned my lungs and made me cough. This seemed to piss him off as he said *ENOUGH*.

He spoke to me in Lakota Sioux and for whatever reason I knew what he was saying and asking of me.

"Did you murder those two for revenge?"

"Yes, I did."

"Where they worth losing your own life for?"

"Yes."

"Why?"

"My Dad taught all his children there is a revenge, then there is a Strongbow revenge."

My answer made him smile.

"I followed you into many battles. You are a great warrior young Strongbow."

"Coming from the greatest Sioux warrior of all time, thank you. I have been taught well and my family bloodlines are also great warriors."

The smile Crazyhorse had now left his face.

"Only half of your bloodline is great warriors. The Hun are respectable, but not in the same class as us."

"My Grandpa Kohler was a career soldier. An officer, loved by his men and fearless in battle."

Crazyhorse smiled once again.

"Do you plan on putting the yellow man's poison through your body again?"

"Not at all."

"You have earned your right to hunt with your Dad, brother, and Red Cloud. But I have other plans for you young Strongbow."

"And what are these plans?"

"In time, your sister Rachel and daughter Katrina will help the Sioux people. They will help more than any male warrior ever could for our great Lakota nation. You must help them along the way. You must be their protectors. Keep them safe as others will try and harm them. Are you willing to do this for the Sioux people, or do you want to hunt with your family?"

"Can I talk to my Dad and brother?"

"No, next time you talk to them you will have fully crossed over to the hunting grounds."

"My Dad would want me to protect Rachel and his Granddaughter. When will this take place and who am I protecting them from?"

Crazyhorse picked up the pipe and smoked it; the whole tent was so thick in smoke I could no longer see him. I then felt a draft to my left and realized the flap for the tent was now open.

I heard the sound of the drum beat and I knew I was to follow where it was coming from. I stood up and as soon as both feet were outside the tent I blacked out.

10

DAY 155: I once again hear the sound of the drumbeats. I struggle to open my eyes as every inch of my body is in intense pain.

I see an intravenous drip inserted into my right hand. And the sound of the beating drums was actually the sound of a heart monitor hooked up to me. I really have to think hard and shake the cobwebs. Am I back in the Philippines in an army hospital; was the last couple years just a dream?

I look around the room and I see my left wrist is handcuffed to a bedrail. Things are coming back including the warm fuzzy blanket feeling from the morphine. Heroin's dirty little sister is flowing through my veins.

I try and call for a nurse, but my throat is parched and is killing me. I struggle to raise my right arm as my shoulder feels dislocated, but I muster enough strength and run it around my throat where I can feel a fresh scar where they did a tracheotomy just like they did in '72.

I see a button for a nurse; I struggle to grab it and once I do, I desperately keep pushing it until she comes in. She is not alone as a uniformed cop is right behind her.

"How do you feel Mr. Strongbow?"

I try and talk, but my throat is killing me, so I signal to her that I need some water. The nurse leaves the room and the cop stares expressionless over me.

As I am waiting for the nurse to come back, I keep trying to replay my crazy dream, can't fully remember it, just snippets, dark snippets to be honest. Fucking morphine must be clouding my memory and thought process. The nurse came back in with a cup full of ice water with a straw.

She holds the cup for me and tells me *just little sips please.* Eventually my parched throat is quenched. Hospital food may not be the best, but it certainly is better than prison food, so I asked the nurse if I could get something to eat.

She said that would be the doctor's call as I am on fluids only right now.

She explains that I have a catheter and a colostomy bag also hooked up. I closed my eyes and know from experience I have one hell of a journey of pain and misery ahead of me.

I asked the nurse what is going on with me. She told me the doctor will be in shortly and he will explain everything. As soon as she left the room, I thought *fuck waiting for the doctor*. So, once again, I struggle to move my arm and the first place I go to is where it hurts the most, my gut.

I feel a fresh raised scar with stitches coming from it. Pretty long scar at that.

In no time at all I drift off into another slumber, fuck, you would think being out cold for thirteen days I would want to stay awake. Not at all, I was hoping this was only a nightmare and once I wake up again all will be good in my life.

Not sure how long I passed out for, but I never did hear those drums beating away waking me up. I heard someone calling my name.

As I come to, I see three men in my room. The one calling my name I am pretty sure is a doctor, the other two standing behind him I know for sure are Detectives. That hair on the back of my neck is never wrong.

"Mr. Strongbow how are you feeling?" asks the Doc as he shines a bright light in my eyes and asks me to follow it with my eyes only, not my head.

"I would feel better if you put that light away, my head is pounding. Doc."

"Well, that is normal for what you have been through. Can you wiggle your fingers and toes for me?"

I did as instructed and then asked him who his two friends were standing behind him.

"They are not my friends; they are two San Francisco Detectives who want to ask you some questions. I just want to see how you are doing and want to make sure that you have the strength to answer their questions."

"How about you answer a couple of questions first, Doc. How am I doing and what all did you guys do?"

"You are doing surprisingly well. I was expecting some paralysis and brain damage. I don't see either. You came in here with a perforated liver from a knife would. You broke your collarbone, and it looks like it's not the first time. A couple broken ribs including one that punctured your lung. That impeded your breathing and that is what the tracheotomy scar is from. The nurse in the prison opened your trachea first and she saved your life. I also saw that you have had back surgery including a steel rod put in your lower thoracic region. It bent upon impact with the ground, so we put a new steel rod in. Your medical reports show it was implanted by an Army doctor; I wouldn't let one of them cut the fat off my steak."

"I had no choice at the time. They also pulled out a couple bullets."

"I think if you were a cat, Mr. Strongbow, you have almost used up all of your lives. These two policemen want to ask you some questions. I have already told them you have suffered tremendously and will be weak. I will be by later to check on you again."

I thanked the doc. The two detectives who sat and listened to everything the Doc said to me asked how I was feeling.

"You heard the Doc; I am still pretty fucked up. Who are you guys exactly?"

They both pulled out their badges, one was gold, and his name was Detective Hastings of the San Francisco homicide unit. The second was Detective Cullimore also of the homicide unit.

Hastings asked all the questions.

"Mitch, what do you remember about the night you were stabbed and fell four stories?"

"Everything is really fuzzy to be honest."

"Do you know who stabbed you?"

"I really don't feel comfortable talking without my lawyer present."

"I see you as the victim Mitch, if you have done nothing wrong as I believe, you won't need your lawyer present."

That line has to be the first thing they teach cops, always trying to trick you and trip you up.

"My head is still spinning from the accident and morphine flowing through me. Your partner is taking notes, I would hate for my current mental state to be used against me."

"Mitch, we are not here to charge you with anything, we just want to know exactly what transpired that night. Cruz was a multiple murderer. He was an evil person. You did the taxpayers of California a great justice."

Funny he didn't mention Mutt, nor will I.

"Like I said, have my lawyer here, let my brain try and clear and I will answer whatever you want."

Cops don't ever let things go and they always play to win.

He pulled out his notebook and said, "Your sister Rachel has been by several times to see you. Prison officials have told her you are not allowed any visitors. Now, we can always tell prison officials that it would be a positive step in your healing process if she were allowed in. She was very distraught, Mitch."

"My lawyer's name is David Levy. His office is in San Francisco. He works for the Hall Morrison law firm on James Street."

"Seeing your lawyer is more important than seeing your sister?"

"My sister is in her second year of law school. I am willing to bet you she has already approached the courts about seeing me."

Both detectives started to snicker which pissed me off. Then, there was a knock at the door and a uniformed cop walked in with a piece of paper in his hands and Rachel right behind him sporting an ear to ear grin.

Rachel was shocked to see me awake and raced over and gave me a kiss with a shit load of tears running down her face. The uniformed cop gave the detectives the paper which turned out to be a court injunction allowing Rachel to visit me seeing how she is my next of kin. Not knowing if I would come out of this coma, it would have been Rachel's choice if they pulled the plug on me.

Detective Hastings read the court documents and was pissed. The last thing I want is for Rachel to be on a cop's hit list. Fuck, one Strongbow has to be cop free, so I told Hastings that either he or Rachel can contact Levy. I reiterated I will tell everything that went down with Levy here.

Hastings said he would contact my lawyer and then I could tell my side of the story. I thanked him and then the two detectives left the room.

Rachel with a shaking voice asked me what happened. I told her the whole story; well…almost everything. I didn't tell her I was ready to accept death and wanted to take Cruz to hell with me. I also told her the two guys were all responsible for Jake's murder.

Rachel's face changed, it went red and her eyes were as angry as her tone of voice.

"You promised me that you have changed your ways. You were going to be a law-abiding citizen. Don't Katrina or I mean anything to you?"

Her voice was shaky.

"You two mean the world to me. They came after me. I didn't go looking for trouble. I will tell the cops exactly what happened, and I won't be charged; this was a clear case of self-defense. You're going through to be a lawyer you know the law, what do you think? Please believe me Rachel, I don't need you mad at me."

Rachel smiled, but tears still spilled down her cheeks.

"I would be prejudice and not charge you. Were there any witnesses?"

"I am not sure; I hope so…to exonerate me."

"Uncle Karl said he has disowned you, so who do you have as a lawyer now?"

"David Levy. He is good and Joseph O'Reilly highly recommended him. I think that says it all."

"Joseph has done a good job staying out of prison, he must be good. I do worry about you going back to San Quentin and another Thunder member seeking revenge. I think Levy should see about you going to another prison to serve out the rest of your sentence."

"Rachel, I believe every prison in the States will have a Thunder member. I will be fine. Realistically, I know the screws are keeping a closer eye on me now. Other cons will know this. Anyone attempting to kill me would be foolish. If it were me, I would wait till I was released from prison before getting even."

Part of what I said to Rachel was the truth, but I know deep down someone in the Thunder will earn their patch by taking my life. And I will do what I have done for the past six years; kill those who attempt to take it. I found myself starting to drift off to sleep again. Never did get a chance to say goodbye to Rachel or that I loved her.

*

I woke to the sound of men talking. Three men I recognized and one I didn't, Detectives Hastings and Cullimore and my lawyer David Levy, the fourth was assistant district attorney Sims. Before the cops and A.D.A question me, Levy asks for some private time with me first. He reminds them that it's an amendment right, so the three of them leave the room and Levy breaks out his pen and note pad. He asks me to tell him everything that went down and to leave nothing out.

And that is exactly what I did including the history between Jake and the Thunder and his death, or make that murder, at San Quentin.

Levy said that if I am not sure of the question not to give an answer for the sake of giving one. Be smart and stick to my story and never let emotions get in the way. I could tell him that I am happy both those bastards are dead, but don't admit that to the cops or A.D.A.

Levy, once he was satisfied with our conversation, asked the A.D.A and the two Detectives to come inside and that I would be willing to answer any questions. With the help of Levy, and sister morphine, I told the coppers everything that went down. I stuck to my story, and I guess the truth. I would give myself a 9.9 out of 10. Nothing is certain with coppers. They can twist things around. The A.D.A thanked me for telling my side of the story in depth. I can't see any murder charges coming my way.

I stayed in the hospital for another couple weeks. They wanted to make sure I could fully walk before sending me back to prison, and to make sure I didn't get any infections from the surgery.

I was slowly taken off the morphine. First off the I.V. drip, then the periodic needles. The recovering addict in me almost wanted to purposely fall out of bed and hurt myself just to stay high.

But that Strongbow warrior in me also knew I needed a clear and strong mind to head back to prison. I will have a huge target on me, and I fully expect this will not be the last time I see the inside of a hospital. I just hope it is not the morgue I visit next time. Fuck, I got lucky this time.

I was taken back to San Quentin by two uniformed cops and a prison official. I would not be heading back to my cell. I was to spend the next couple weeks in the prison infirmary continuing my rehab.

Just as when I first arrived here, the first-time people stopped what they were doing to look at me. A few nodded, a few looked away, and some

I could hear whispering that I was a dead man walking.

I was checked over by the prison doctor and then assigned a bed. The walking boss in charge of the infirmary was pretty stern with me, told me I am there till either my strength is back, and if I fuck up, he will kick me free after I spend thirty days in the hole.

I know I need my strength, speed, and flexibility back if I am to survive my final year in here. *Bigger picture, Mitch.*

One of the first people I saw in the infirmary was Billy Davidson; he looked like shit, frail, pale and could barely make eye contact with me.

Not even *thanks for saving my life*, sweet fuck all. I was more than a little pissed to be honest. I even tried to strike up a conversation and he said he was too tired to talk and just wanted to rest.

I really wanted to lose it on him, but the walking boss was always within ear shot. Fuck both of them.

That night, Herschel brought us dinner. He was

ecstatic to see me. He said I looked great, I said *really?* He said yes, as last time he saw me he thought I was dead. This made me laugh. I asked how he was and if everyone was leaving him alone. He said yes, but his eyes told a different story.

"Herschel don't lie to me. What is going on? Muslims giving you a hard time?"

"I think every single Muslims goal in life is to wipe out Israel and every Jew on the planet. I am used to that, and no, Albert has stepped up nicely, and yes for a modest fee which I am happy to pay."

"Then what is it, Herschel? Don't bullshit me. I want to know what is going on. It could save my life."

"Well… it's just that this guy from the Thunder arrived while you were in the hospital. Albert said he is the National President."

"So, what's the word on the street, he is coming for me, seeking revenge for Mutt and Cruz?"

"That's the strange thing Mitch. No one is saying anything. It is quiet, maybe too quiet."

"You got a name for this guy?"

"I think Herman, he is huge, Mitch. And you know at how these guys all want to be part of the Nazi's? Well, this guy is a Nazi general, even speaks with a German accent."

The walking boss told Herschel to quit chattering like a schoolgirl and head back to the kitchen. I thanked Herschel and told him to make sure Albert knows I am back.

"He already knows, Mitchell."

That made me snicker, what stopped it quick enough was a National President of the Thunder here at San Quentin. Yeah, he will command all kinds of respect from up and coming Thunder members or hang arounds. I am in no shape to fight anyone. I don't see anything that I can even use as a weapon in here.

*

After dinner, as much as it pained me, I started to do squats while hanging onto my bed post. I am going to speed up my healing and rehab process.

I would try my best and just tighten my stomach muscles for thirty seconds at a time. Every single exercise I could think of from the helicopter crash rehab I would do.

Needless to say, it also knocked the wind out my sails and I was tried and fatigued really quickly. I don't remember falling asleep and when I woke up, I was still in a dreamlike state. There was an angel dressed all in white standing over me. Not the typical Sioux vision I normally have.

"How are you doing Mitchell? I am so glad you are alive!"

My head was fuzzy, I was weak and parched. I tried to talk and focus but was having problems. The Angel passed me a drink of water and a pill.

By the time I swallowed the pill and finished off the drink I realized the Angel was a real human. It was Amy; she was the night shift nurse.

"I heard you saved my life."

"You saved my life once. It was the least I could do."

Perhaps it was the painkillers, the fatigue, and trauma I was going through, or just a case of stupidity, but what I said next shocked Amy.

"I was there when they killed Salvador. He will never hurt anyone again."

"I didn't hear that Mitch; I don't want to know anything, and I never wanted him killed."

"No one ever hurts anyone in my family or close to me and gets away with it."

And then I drifted off to sleep again.

*

The next morning, I woke up with cobwebs in my brain. I sort of remember being woken up by someone and my gut tells me I said or did something I shouldn't have; you know that gut gnaw feeling?

I looked over to the table beside my bed and saw an empty glass. Everything is now coming back, and the gnawing has now turned to fear.

Why the fuck did I tell Amy that? Fuck, would she go to prison authorities or the cops?

All day I was waiting for homicide detectives to pay me a visit. They didn't, thank fuck.

I fought to stay awake until I saw Amy start her shift. Once everyone was asleep, I hand singled her to come over. The screw on duty also saw me raise my hand and he came over first and asked what the problem was.

"I am really hurting and was wondering if I could get something for pain."

He said that he would have Amy come over.

Amy I could tell was still bothered by what I told her the night before.

"I am sorry if I upset you last night. Must have been the pain killers talking."

Amy really thought deeply before speaking.

"Mitch, was he killed because of what he tried to do to me?"

"No, he was just the filth of the earth scum who pissed off the wrong people."

"Honest, Mitchell?"

"I swear on Katrina's life. He crossed the wrong people and paid for it with his life. I had nothing to do with the killing itself. I was just along for the ride. Having said that, if he had succeeded in raping you, I would have killed him, and it would have been a slow, and painful death for him."

"But he didn't, and for that I am thankful. It would really bother me if you were in here for his murder. No way could I work here. I would have asked for a transfer."

"I am glad I didn't kill him as you wouldn't have been able to save my life."

This made Amy smile as she went and got something to help me sleep. I see so much of Tash in her when she smiles.

That morning I woke up with a gnaw in my gut even before I opened my eyes. I really expected to see my angel of a nurse Amy standing at the foot of my bed.

What I saw was the devil himself. I was like a frightened schoolboy knowing someone in the playground was waiting for him once the school bell rang, waiting to give him the beating of his life.

And that person was none other than Helmut Fritz, the President of the Reno chapter of the Thunder Motorcycle Club. Dressed in prison blues. I didn't see one fucking screw, not one nurse or doctor. Just me and Helmut all alone. I had no weapons and was way too weak to fight him.

He looked pissed and had a real surly on his face.

"Do I call you Mitch Walker, or Mitch Strongbow as I am pretty confused and beyond pissed."

"Mitch Strongbow."

"I hope you are man enough to answers my questions truthfully as your life is on the line, and right now, I am officially the Judge, the Jury and the Executioner."

I nodded my head yes.

"Why did you lie to me and tell me you were Mitch Walker? I assume your girlfriend's name wasn't Jen?"

"No, her name was Lucy Thom. Because if I said I was a Strongbow what would you have done?"

"First off what do you mean her name was Lucy Thom, secondly what was your whole purpose of partying with me and my old lady, to gather info on the Thunder?"

"Lucy died of a heroin overdose that's why I am in here. No, I am a civilian; I am not a member, or striker, or hang-around for the Hell Hounds. I really like you, fuck, you served with my Grandfather that was not a lie. And Lucy and I were on the run from certain people. I trusted no one, survival mode, you know?"

"As much as I respect you keeping a low profile while on the run, the biggest question I want answers to is why did you kill two members of the Thunder in here?"

"Either I killed them, or they killed me. They came at me, Mutt stabbed me, and Cruz tried to throw me over the railing. He said he wanted me to die the same way my brother died at his hands. I was handed a seventeen month sentence. The last thing I want is to get in trouble in here and lose my good time or get even more time added on to my sentence for a fight I am not involved with."

"I wished you would have been honest and upfront with me right from the beginning, Mitch."

"You would have let those guys beat me to death, or even helped them the first night I met you. I never ever meant you any harm or disrespect. You actually reminded me of my brother, Jake."

"In my life I have to make judgment calls on the spot. I have always been how you American's say on the wrong side of the tracks all my life. I believe you. But this is my dilemma; I am national president of the Thunder or at least until they replace mc with someone on the outside. With you taking the life of two members, the rest of the Thunder leadership will expect me to react…especially with us both in the same prison. Normally, I would kill you myself seeing at how I have been sentenced to over one hundred years in prison, what is another life that I take? But you also saved my life, and I will never forget that."

Helmut walked to window, looked out and then walked back.

"I will spare you your life for saving mine. But we are not friends in here. Do not say hi to me, do not name drop saying you know me."

"Thank you, what about the rest of the Thunder members in here and their associates, what am I to do if they come after me?"

"I will let my boys know to leave you alone; you are a civilian and also a heat score in here. But Mitch, I also expect for you to behave yourself around my boys. Don't flaunt yourself or agitate them. If there is more trouble between the Hounds and Thunder in here, I fully expect you will be standing on the sidelines. I see you jump in and I will personally end your life. Understood?"

"Absolutely."

I went to shake Helmut's hand and he just looked at my outreached hand, said no, and then he walked away.

My heart was pounding; my balls were shriveled

right up. Yeah, scared shitless. As I lay in bed, I replay the whole conversation and warning that Helmut gave me, I also go back to what Joseph implied to me before I arrived here.

Let the gangs fight each other; I am part of his crew. Yeah, I killed the two guys who murdered Jake and I got away with it. No more pushing the envelope, fucking Billy Davidson won't even speak to me and I helped save his life.

*

I spent another twelve days in the infirmary before being sent back to my cell and back to working in the kitchen.

Albert made sure to have some homemade hooch via prune wine waiting for me. I asked him how D'Angelo was. He said neutered for the most part with me taking care of Cruz. Albert then told me about the Thunder's national president now residing in San Quentin.

Even before Albert could tell me his name, I said Helmut Fritz. Albert was shocked, when I told about the history and conversation between Helmut and me Albert was floored, beyond shocked.

"Strongbow, your whole fucking life is like an episode from the Twilight Zone."

He was right, they say everything in life is based on six degrees of separation, for me I believe it is only three.

*

The next morning, I was kind of nervous going to the yard. I honestly believed what Helmut said, but what if Cruz or Mutt has family or lovers in here seeking revenge? I know the Muslims are pissed about me killing one of their own.

I stuck close to our crew and watched for any unusual movements or gatherings. I also told Albert I must get back on the "juice" as I am down ten pounds of muscle being laid up.

Albert was doing a set of curls followed my dips, once he did his set, he said I was up. Not sure if I had healed enough and was a bit hesitant.

Fuck it, let's do it, as soon as I felt my muscles burning and that adrenaline flowing, I felt alive and any anxiety I had about being in the yard went away. I was ready for the battle once again.

I also realized I was getting a lot of space and respect in the yard. I guess killing three people in a matter of weeks and that I was willing to kill myself to take another life, people realize just how fucking insane I am.

11

I've found peace for the past three weeks, as has the prison as a whole. The rest of the cons are leaving me alone or are giving me lots of space. My body is back to normal or at least as normal as a beaten and tattered body can be. I have put back on all the weight I have lost after the murders.

I look and certainly feel a lot stronger. Feels good lifting heavy and pounding the fuck out of the heavy bag in the yard. Flexibility is back.

When Rachel comes to visit, she is not teared up on first arrival or when she leaves. Fuck, Tash as promised, even sent me a photo of Katrina starting grade two.

Joseph and Donnie have visited me a couple times as have a couple other friends including Kerry with her baby Lisa, but not Fraser which I found kind of weird. She said he was out of town working. I have a countdown happening and have just under three hundred days left.

But prison life is like living in the Gulf of Mexico during hurricane season, a rain poncho does shit to protect you. Just when you think the day will be nice and sunny, you blink, and storm clouds come rolling in.

I was in the library deciding what book to read in my cell that night, quit laughing, I love history, when I was approached by Chris Downs and Nicky "All Thumbs" Balzamo.

Nicky is a made man for the Battaglia family out of Vegas, and Downs is a member of the Jokers Motorcycle Club which is just a puppet club for the Thunder. Downs also gave Herschel a shot in the head for being a Jew when he first entered the prison.

Nicky said he had to talk to me about something important. The hair on the back of my neck stood up. I never liked or trusted Downs and what Nicky was about to tell me tested my faith in everyone.

"I know you are good friends with Albert,

but word just came down from Mr. B in Vegas that he is a rat and is to be killed. I am giving you this warning as Mr. B really likes you. So, you either step aside and let us do our job or die along with him."

My gut flipped and heart skipped a beat. Fuck, Albert knows everything about the Capello murder I committed. He set the whole thing up. Was I just being played? Am I on his list of people he is about to rat out or has already ratted out?

"When is this going down?"

"You don't worry about when this is going down. You just stay the fuck out of our way."

Downs smiled at me after hearing Nicky's very direct answer. But something about Downs' smile didn't sit with me well.

They both left the library and I had to sit down and struggle with what to do next. I thought I was going to be sick to my stomach. My three-hundred-day countdown can soon become three hundred years.

A huge, and I mean fucking huge part of me didn't believe a word Nicky said. Albert is one of the most solid guys I have ever met. I put my life on the line for him.

If I go back and confront him then what? He goes into P.C. and Hastings and Cullimore or those two fucking FBI dicks Stone and Calder reappear with hard-ons for me? Let me tell you, there will be no lube, it will be a high and dry ass fucking.

Think Mitch, think! Time for a little deception, I think I will tell Albert I hear there is another rat in here about to take down some high-end mobsters and see how he reacts. Yeah, his eyes and facial reaction will tell me all I need to know.

Then I will distance myself from him and let Downs and Nicky do what must and should be done. Maybe because I have been trying to turn over a new leaf in here or perhaps the criminal Gods saw an injustice coming, fate stepped in.

On my way to confront Albert, I saw Helmut and a couple of his guys in the hallway. I remember very clearly what he told me about getting involved with any of his men but something about

Downs was clearly bugging me.

Deep breath in, "Excuse me Helmut, can I have a word in private?"

Helmut eyed me up and down and with no facial expression.

"What do you want Mitch?"

"I want to talk to you about one of your men, Chris Downs."

Helmut's whole face changed to a nasty and evil face I've seen before. He told his guys to wait up ahead for him.

"He is not one of my men. He has decided being muscle for D'Angelo is more important than loyalty to the Jokers."

Fuck, today is all about twists.

"I totally respect you and the conversation that took place in the infirmary. Would I be safe in assuming I wouldn't be breaking my promise to you if I were to inflict pain upon Downs?"

"Not at all."

"And D'Angelo?"

"He reminds me of Mussolini, and we know what he did to the Germans during the final months of the war. Just don't get me or my name involved, understood?"

"This conversation never took place."

Helmut clenched his jaw, patted me on the shoulder, then walked away. Glad to see that not only is the hair on the back of my neck never wrong, but also that gut instinct of mine was not affected by Mutt knifing me there.

I picked up my pace to track down Albert and let him know of everything that went down. He wasn't in his cell. Fuck, he has to be in the yard which is also the best place to kill someone.

So, I hauled ass, well as fast as I could, considering my body is still hurting. The yard was full so I headed to our designated area knowing that would be the most logical spot and once there, nothing. Frankie Knuckles was there, I asked where Albert was. He said he had a visitor come. Fuck, this was also how they got to John Derksen.

Frankie asked if everything was good. At this point I am not sure who to trust so I said yeah. Left the yard and hauled ass once again to the visitors lounge area.

My body may not be up to par, but my eyesight is still in fine form. I spotted Albert just leaving the visitor's lounge. I also saw in the reflection of a window Downs and Balzamo hiding in the washroom doorway. I know if I yell to Albert, I will be giving these two fucks another chance to kill him.

I have also learned how to get in and out of the general housing unit of the prison and there is a rear entrance to this washroom from the library. So, you go as fast as you can without drawing the suspicion of prison staff.

As I go through the library Miss Borden the librarian stares at me, am I that obvious? Fuck, if I can't fool her, I won't fool any screw.

I manage to get through to the washroom without being stopped. Back into a killing stealth mode. Silent death at its most evil. I have no weapons and there is nothing you can use in a bathroom;

everything is bolted down in a prison.

Everything but toilet paper. I soaked the hell out of one roll, yeah, I know not a weapon but a perfect distraction.

With a drenched roll, I snuck up and went inside the one stall. I stood up the toilet seat and threw it as hard as I could.

Maybe I should have been a QB instead of a linebacker as the roll nailed Downs right in the side of the head, the force of it made his head hit the wall. He cursed and Balzamo went to see who threw it.

I sat on the toilet seat with my legs up off the floor and ready for battle. As soon as he opened my stall door to have a peek inside, I kicked the door as hard as I could. He went flying backwards.

The momentum sent him flying into the wall. He dropped his knife at the point of impact, with one fell swoop I picked it up and drove it right into his neck. I repeatedly stabbed him and only stopped when Albert dragged the lifeless body of Downs into the bathroom.

He too had his throat sliced.

"Thanks Mitch, fuck they would have blindsided me. Fucking Balzamo, never thought he would switch sides and work for D'Angelo."

Albert now spat on Balzamo's lifeless body.

"We have to split not spit. See if any screws are around and let's slip into the laundry and get a change of clothes. Bloody clothes are always a giveaway."

Sometimes lady luck smiles upon you, even in a men's only prison. We were able to get a change of clothing from Tommy the Greek who automatically threw our bloody clothes in the wash.

My only concern was the librarian who saw me go into the washroom. Could be a problem but right now the yard is our safest spot and best alibi.

Albert and I were having a game of chess when we heard the riot alarm go off. Like the model prisoners we are, we hit the ground spread eagle.

One by one you are told to get up and form a line as several shotgun toting guards have their weapons trained on you.

All of us are lined up against the wall as the screws check all of us any signs that we were involved in the two murders.

After about an hour, Albert and I were both told to head back to our cells and once again the prison was to be locked down for the next seventy-two hours.

I didn't even attempt a fish line conversation. I believe I got away with another murder and saved a good friend's life.

*

The next morning, I was abruptly awoken by a screw saying to come with him. I knew not to ask where, as too many ways to give away your inner most fears without realizing it. I just nodded my head yes.

Fuck, here we go again. Fucking librarian must have ratted me out and said she saw me racing to the washroom.

I go with the screw, what the hell else can I do? Albert also watches me leave as I roll my eyes at him.

As we are walking, I am thinking of stories to help get me out of the murder charge. I know not to say anything without Levy present.

My guts are rolling, and I'm feeling uneasy. So easy to kill in the jungles of Asia, not here. I am a bit surprised as we walk right past the interview rooms. I also notice the body language of the screw is really relaxed. I also realize I am not handcuffed or put in shackles. What the fuck is going on?

I am taken to the library as the screw says Miss Borden wants to see me. My head is totally spinning, and brain doesn't have fucking clue what is about to happen next. Miss Borden thanks the screw and says she is fine.

Miss Borden is about mid-thirties. Full figured woman with her red hair up in a bun. Dresses very conservative, a black almost floor length skirt. A sweater and underneath it and a white blouse fully done up right to her neck. Wearing old lady eyes glasses, kind of sexy in a strait-laced kind of way, but she also reminds me of that one aunt who lives in a one bedroom apartment with thirty cats.

She doesn't smile at all.

She introduces herself as Miss Charlene Borden and says, "In prison, there is always stories floating around, some true, most false, some just down outright lies. But a little birdie to me that you are related to Red Cloud, is this true?"

That is not the question I was expecting, not at all.

"Yes, he is my great grandfather."

Her smile got huge as her face lit up, pretty sure I saw both her nipples come to life.

"Please follow me inmate Strongbow to my office."

I must say she has quite the wiggle in her walk. Once there she tells me to take a seat. A seat I might add that is facing the wall, not the door.

"I have read a lot on your great grandfather as I have nothing but total respect for the Sioux people, but Red Cloud was also my nickname in school." She then touches her hair.

She then looks over once again at the screw out in the hall, what the fuck is she up too?

She grabbed my hand and put my thumb right in her mouth, and then rolled her tongue around it. Took off her glasses, smiled at me with her big blues, undid my zipper, pulled out my cock and started to stroke me. What a dirty whore, love it.

As I was blowing my load, I kept thinking, if me batting her home will save me from the electric chair, my ass will be fried for premature ejaculation. I swear I was so nervous of being caught, and so unexpected, I came within twenty strokes. Felt like I was thirteen again.

I just sheepishly stared at her and shrugged my shoulders out of embarrassment. She whispered in my ear that next time she wants my cock deep in the back of her throat.

Not sure if Rachel would ever believe me when I say to her next time. I love spending time in the prison library, so rewarding.

On my way back to my cell I was still in disbelief as to what happened, my knees were kind of weak and I still had droplets of cum dripping down into my boxers, so I knew it was not just a jailhouse dream.

I told Herschel what happened, and he smiled in disbelief. He said he must make a movie out of this, a perfect porno script.

"Topper LaRue and the scarlet librarian."

We both burst out laughing. Over the next couple days, I was not summoned from my cell by any prison officials. Looks like Albert and I have gotten away with murder. Make that four murders for me. I also believe D'Angelo must be murdered as soon as the lockdown ends, as he will just go out and recruit more cons to either kill Albert, or myself.

Once we were all free what is the first thing I did? Was it to talk to Albert about the future killing of D'Angelo? Fuck no, it was straight to the library to see Charlene Borden. I totally see her in a different light now, portraying the typical shy librarian, who is kinkier than all fuck.

She was organizing books when I came up behind and said, "Wow."

Charlene turned around with a big smile on her face.

"Mitchell, how nice to see you, how is your Strongbow?" she said with a giggle.

If there wasn't a screw twenty feet away from us, I would have thrown her down on the ground and fucked her right then and there.

So, I put my head down towards my crotch, she looked at the massive bulge I had in my pants, and said, "Oh my, please follow me to my office."

She told Gates the screw, that I am helping her write a paper for her thesis on the Sioux culture.

Gates made his way over to us, eyed Charlene up and down, then eyed me up and down, no doubts saw my bulge and said, "Sorry Miss Borden, you and Strongbow can work on your project out here in the open. Prison is still kind of hot."

He then shot me the death stare, as if to challenge him so he could throw me in the hole. Jealousy, or him just being a controlling goof, not sure.

She apologized to me, but you could tell she was

pissed at him.

We played the game as Gates made sure he was within earshot of our conversation. She would ask questions about my family history, where our property was. I told her about the hunting longhouse. She said she would love to see it. I said maybe one day I will take her there. She stared at me like a thirteen year old girl with a celebrity crush. I really dug it.

I lasted about an hour, sure as fuck Gates hung by us. Guess I am going to have to plan my sexual visitations when he is not working. There must be history between them, my gut tells me so.

After I left, I headed straight to Albert, it was time to discuss D'Angelo. He is the only person causing us grief in the prison. Ninety eight percent of the population know to leave us alone. One percent are more fucked then us and the other one percent will kill for cash. I should know, as I too kill for cash. So many killers in here but few can get away with it.

In the bible there is some quote or fable about an eye for an eye. In prison it is usually a life for a life. Fuck, I took Mutt's eye, and his life. Does that make me a bible pusher?

On the fifth day of the lockdown being ended I was approached by Helmut in the yard. He asked me to play a game of chess with him.

At first, I was kind of shocked as I know he was pissed at me for duping him and taking several lives of his club members.

I was matching him move to move, there was no conversation at all which was even more puzzling. I was nervous even though Albert was standing behind me. I was expecting to be shived. Yeah, I thought for sure he was going to break his promise with me.

Then Helmut exposed his knight to be taken, I was puzzled by this move as I would be two moves away from checkmate.

I took his knight with my queen. As soon as I did this, Helmut took my queen and said *checkmate*. I was shocked, I walked right into his trap.

"You see, Mitch, sometimes you have to give up something to get something."

"And what do I have to give up, and what all do I need?"

"You have told me you are not a Hell Hound of any kind."

"I am telling the truth"

"I believe you, my spies in here say the same. But Billy Davidson is a Hell Hound. He is talking a lot of shit right now about coming after me with your help. Is this true?"

"I haven't talked to Billy since before the events of me protecting myself from your guys."

Helmut snickered, looked around and said, "I am willing to exchange you Davidson's life for D'Angelo's life. How does that sound, Mitch? You do know he wants you two dead."

Is this another trap just like him setting me up in chess? Fucking Davidson won't even look at me or talk to me. And I have no idea why.

I looked at Albert who now had this smirk on his face while nodding his head yes.

"Am I to take Davidson's life and you will

kill D'Angelo?"

"No, I want Davidson all to myself. D'Angelo will not shower unless a couple of my guys are standing guard for him. That is where I would kill him. I will make sure my guys go for a piss when he is showering."

Helmut with his ice-cold steel blue eyes stuck out his hand and asked if we had a deal. I looked at Albert who nodded yes. I shook Helmut's hand and said deal. Helmut said he would let me know when D'Angelo is set to take a shower. I asked does he need anything more from us. Just stay out his way was Helmut's response.

We also knew prison officials expected there are more deaths to come. They will be doing steady shakedowns looking for weapons. But, as I was taught in Special Ops, you improvise. Don't always need a sharpened weapon to take a life.

The next morning, just after nine, I was approached by one of Helmut's men. He said D'Angelo will be taking a shower in ten minutes.

Albert was working the early shift in the kitchen, so this was another killing I had to do myself.

On the way to the shower, my plan was to choke him with his own towel. Silent death and a weapon that will not leave fingerprints.

As I got to the entrance of the shower room, it was steamy as fuck, looked like merry old England. Helmut's two men looked at me, nodded, and then left. As I walked into the shower, I didn't hear any water running, I was confused. Fuck, was I set up? I looked around as best as I could and was ready to be attacked, fucking cock sucking double crosser!

Then, out of the corner of my eye, I saw a shadow coming towards me. I squared him in the nuts and then with speed and extreme power I swung behind him and snapped his neck.

His body hit the floor real hard. I squinted and waited for the next person to come at me, but nothing. As I looked at the ground, I was it was D'Angelo. I felt for a pulse and nothing. I left the shower area quickly and headed back to my cell.

Once back there I tried to dry my dampened hair and changed my clothes. I had no sooner changed when the prison riot alarm sounded.

I sat on my bunk and waited for the process to evolve while sitting pretty.

A couple hours later, I was starting my afternoon shift. I let Albert know that D'Angelo was dead. Albert smiled and said great job. Albert also drilled into me the importance of *no one*, including Joseph and Donnie, knowing that I killed an under boss in the Mob.

I assured Albert no one would ever know.

A couple hours after that, I was approached by two screws and asked to come with them. As much as I was hoping Miss Borden needed her weekly cock fix, I had this whole burning in my gut that it had to do with the murder of D'Angelo.

Yep, taken down to the interview room and shocked to find out they wanted to know if I knew anything about the murder of Billy Davidson.

Even though I knew it was coming it was still shocking to find out he was dead. They said he was castrated before he was killed. That part kind of bothered me, but that is the price of doing business.

I said I knew nothing and then they asked who would want him dead.

"Well, this wasn't the first attempt on his life was it?"

"Guys, believe it or not, I am not a Hell Hound. I was almost killed last time because people thought I was involved with Hell Hound business."

I then sheepishly asked, "Normally a castration is for rapists and child molesters. Was he ever known for that?"

Surprisingly neither one answered me. I was then asked if I knew anything about the D'Angelo murder.

"They stick to themselves. I know he is some big guy in the syndicate, but that's about it."

I don't know if they believe me or not, I guess to a certain degree they must have as I was told I could go back to work in the kitchen.

That night after work, in the showers was the first time I saw and had a chance to talk to Albert. He too was taken down for questioning. He had the perfect alibi. I reminded him who told him when he first came here that working in the kitchen was a good idea.

The prison would be once again locked down for another week. I did sense a lot of the tension was gone. At least for now.

Charlene would also have me drop by as she now decided she wanted to write a book on Lakota Sioux Chiefs, especially when Gates was working nights.

So, after I would tell her family history and stories that were passed down to me from my Dad and Grandfather, she would blow me till I came in her mouth. She was a kinky ginger, but no complaints here.

Helmut was still not the friendliest towards me but now he would at least nod at me in the yard. Speaking of not the friendliest, my cousin Jerry paid me a visit and wanted to know if I knew anything about Davidson's murder. I said I knew nothing, you hear stuff.

Jerry's back went up and asked me what stuff. I said he was castrated and asked if Billy liked to play with little kids. Jerry got pissed and assured me that if he ever suspected Billy of this, he would kill him himself

Before Jerry left, he told me to find out who was responsible for Billy's death. I assured him I would ask around. You know if I wanted someone killed, I would just have to drop his name to Jerry and say they killed Billy. But that's not who I am. Revenge is best with my own two hands.

In San Quentin, like any other prison in the States, there is always a high prisoner turnover rate. A lot of them come in pleading their innocence and mope around at first. Some come in angry at the world saying they were framed.

I trust the ones who come in and say I was stupid and got caught. Next time I know what not to do to keep my ass out of a federal prison.

A couple weeks after the D'Angelo murder, there was a new prisoner who was bunked a couple cells away from me.

His name was Jesus Gonsalves. Said he was from the Bay Area and was doing a deuce for assault.

Yeah, just the way he approached me in here raised my suspicions.

He also only seemed to know which guys in the Dirty Dozen that had criminal records, and nothing about the rest of the guys or girls.

It was like he was a Dirty Dozen member. He said we used to get high quite bit together while at Polk High.

I must have been high not to remember Jesus as the guy is pretty fucking big. He must be at least six foot six and weights in close to three hundred pounds. Jesus was also assigned to the kitchen with us and assigned to my shift.

Right from the beginning he would ask me questions about life in here and who I trusted so he could also trust them.

I pulled no punches and told him I trusted no one including him and if he wants to survive, keep his mouth shut.

One day on our way to yard, a guy bumped into me, I am sure it was an accident as most cons give me lots of space.

Jesus lost it on the guy and started to lay a beating on him. He told the battered and bloodied guy to apologize to me.

I am looking all around and waiting for the riot alarm to go off, but it didn't.

I told Jesus to fucking mellow out. I can handle myself in here. As soon as he said I am sure you have in past. Everyone knows about the murdering ways of Mitch the "Bitch" Strongbow, I had to walk away. Albert took me aside and said he was willing to take Miss Borden off my hands seeing at how Jesus is my new boyfriend.

I told Albert that isn't even funny. I then asked Albert what he thought of Jesus.

"He either has a man crush on you, or he is a rat for the cops, fuck maybe even a cop."

"That is what I am thinking. He ask you anything about me?"

"He asked if you were a full patch for the Hell Hounds. When I said no, he said he heard that to get in the club you have to kill, and did he think I would kill for the club."

"For fucks sake, Albert! Why didn't you tell me this before?"

"He just asked me this morning when you were in the shower. This is the first time I've seen you today, man."

"If he is a Cop, we can't kill him, fuck even if he is a rat we can't hack and whack him up into a million pieces as you know he will be watched even more carefully. Suggestions?"

"Keep it like it is for now. Tell him fuck all till we find out exactly who he is."

"I think I am going to talk to the south and north Mexican gangs and see if anyone knows anything about him. He has to be related to one of them."

So that is what I did. I talked to the Shock Collar from the north Mexican gang and told him I knew nothing of this guy and he knows all about me and did him or any of his members know Jesus.

I asked the exact same thing to the south Mexican Shock Collar. Both Shock Collars said they would let me know within twenty-four hours.

I thanked both and asked if they needed anything in return. Both thanked me and said they hoped I would do the same with my guys.

Absolutely was my response. I do have respect for career criminals who live by our own creed. As promised, both shock collars approached me in the yard, and no one knew shit about this guy.

Herschel also approached me later that day and told me that Jesus asked about me and Albert's relationship with D'Angelo. I said to Albert we have to act sooner than later. We both agreed that killing him was not the answer. Albert said since the D'Angelo murder we have had our cells searched a hell of a lot more often.

So tomorrow, while Jesus and I are working our early morning shift, Albert will put a shiv and a couple joints in Jesus' cell.

Jesus' cellmate Fred must be at least a hundred years old and a model prisoner who has less than one month to go in his ten-year sentence.

*

The next day came, and during shift change

Albert told me all was set for Jesus to take a fall.

Two days later while we were working, the screws did a surprise cell inspection. What was surprising was that Fred was charged for both the drugs and weapon. My blood was now boiling. That fucking pussy Jesus is a cop or rat.

I stared at him during our shift and said nothing to him. After our shift when we were in the yard is when I went after him. He was playing cards with a couple other guys from the kitchen. I eyed him the whole time.

Jesus caught on to me eyeing him with discontent and asked what my problem was.

"You're a fucking cheater."

Jesus smiled and asked me to repeat what I said.

"You're a fucking cheater. Every hand you won you cheated on and I despise a cheater."

He sarcastically told me I was fucked, no cheating going on. The other three guys threw their cards down and now started to trash talk Jesus who didn't have a clue what to do.

He might not have, but I did. He called me a fucking liar. Perfect. I jumped on top of the table and kicked him right in the face, and then jumped back down. The three guys from the kitchen now started a rain of flying fists on him.

Within thirty seconds the riot alarm went off. Neither me nor the three guys laying a beating on Jesus were the first to hit the floor. It was Jesus himself, who was now starting to have seizures.

I was of coursed charged with partaking in a fight. Sent to the hole for the next thirty days and had three months of my good time taken away.

And if I did my math correctly which was always a strong point in school, I had no good time left and will have to do all twenty two months.

At least here I know no fucking rats or cops will be setting me up. The downside is no weekly hook ups with Charlene Borden. Back to spanking the monkey thinking of her.

The other three guys also received the same as me, thirty days in the hole. Not sure if they had lost any good time or not.

As soon as I was released, I headed back to my cell. As I approached the fourth floor, I could hear someone shadow boxing. They certainly had their breathing down pat.

As I got closer, I could see shadows coming from inside my cell. Since when did Herschel learn to shadow box?

I was shocked; stunned as it was not Herschel. It was my old celly George Daniels. I had to shake my head; fuck was the last couple months just a fucking dream?

"Mitchell, you look like you have just seen a ghost."

"George, I thought you were moving to Florida with your sister?"

"I lasted two weeks, too many old fucks living there. It aged me, so I bought a ticket and always wanted to check out Hollywood."

"And what did you do in Hollywood to end up back here?"

"I always wanted to check out Grauman's Chinese Theater and specifically the Dukes footprints and signature. All was good when a group of teens told me if I wanted to stand in the same footprints of Duke, I had to pay them twenty bucks each. I told them to fuck off that they could now pay me fifty bucks each or I will smash their heads so hard their faces will be the newest exhibit."

"Did you hurt them bad?"

"I killed the big mouth, crippled another. They got some decent shots on me, broke a few of my ribs, I was in the hospital for a bit."

"Let me guess you were the only one charged seeing at how you are a violent ex-con?"

"You're not just a pretty face, Mitch. Yeah, I will end up dying in here. I was sentenced to life behind bars."

"And them?"

"Not a single charge. The kid who was crippled, his old man is a cop, surprised?"

"No, the cops look out for their own, call in favors. What happened to Herschel?"

"His lawyer appealed his conviction and they settled on cash and time served."

"Have you heard anything about the guy I dropped to get thrown in the hole for?"

"He disappeared like a phantom in the night. Albert believes more so that he was a cop not just a rat. I heard you had a run in with Cruz and Mutt. Glad you're alive and those two are dead. Never liked either one. Let's go to the yard and hit the heavy bag."

Not sure if being in the hole all alone for the past thirty days made me a little more tense or not but walking into the yard my back was up a bit. Cat on a hot tin roof. Especially with Albert and Frankie working in the kitchen right now and no one else from our crew around. George and I headed right to the heavy bags.

"Okay, Mitch. You go first, let's do some combos, I will yell them out, three-minute rounds. One –two-three-four to the body."

George didn't yell out the second set of combos, so I turned around and knew why.

All five Shock Collars and their second in command had now surrounded the boxing area. Helmut who was the Shock Collar for the Nazi Reich told George to play somewhere else.

George snarled at Helmut and said he ain't going nowhere.

"Mitch, tell Grandpa to go for a walk, we just want to talk to you in private. If we wanted to you dead, it would have happened as soon as you step foot in the yard"

I believed Helmut.

"I will be all right, George. Thanks."

"So, what's up?"

"Ever since the death of Billy Davidson your crew doesn't have a shock collar. None of us trust Maganini or Bisiganni. Made mobsters all have their own people to take orders from on the outside. You are very well respected in here, Mitch. And you have mine too. You're a smart guy who commands respect. All of us have come to an agreement that you would be the best choice. What do you say?"

"First off, thanks for the compliments. Quite an honor coming from all of you Shock Collars. And what if someone in my crew has a problem with me taking over Billy's position? Do I handle it or do you guys?"

"You handle it with our backing. The screws will give you more space in here. They know why help keep the peace and lately they are concerned with the amount of murders going on."

"Would I be insulting you guys if I talked to my guys first? I promise I will have an answer by the time lights go out tonight."

"That's fair, Mitch. Let us know one way or another."

"I will."

Then each one of the Shock Collars came up and shook my hand.

George came over after they left and asked what the fuck was going on. I told him and asked what he thought.

"I think you would be a great choice, Mitch. You made it to what Sergeant Major, correct?"

"Yeah. Not bad for no education, hey ma?" we both laughed at that comment.

"Then you know how to keep discipline among the troops. And you also know how important it is to have good leadership. I think you should accept it. All five Shock leaders approved. That is a good sign."

"And what if I pass on being a Shock Collar?"

"You will be treated like shit in here. Yeah, no one will stick their neck out for you including whoever replaces you. Mitch, you have what just over a year to go? Take the title, take the responsibility, and let others take the fall for you. Fuck, you have proved yourself ten times over in here already."

So, I decided to talk to Albert also before giving my decision. Albert wasn't so keen on me taking the Shock Collar position. He said with him being a made guy, he can't ever be seen taking orders from me. He said the Battaglia family wouldn't be impressed with either one of us.

"But Albert, think about it this way; I will

have a lot more power in here almost like your people have a politician or cop in their pocket. I would never center you out in front of others. I have too much respect for you and I do appreciate you are an officer in the Battaglia family."

Albert thought about what I said, his lips were pressed together, and his eyes went dark. Then he smiled and said I had a fucking point.

"Good, no more asking the Mexicans for favors, we can take care of business ourselves. Yeah, go for it Mitch, but remember, don't belittle me in the general population."

I shook Albert's hand and promised that would never happen. I then went and looked for Helmut to give him my response. I was of course stopped a couple cells before his and was told Helmut was expecting me.

Before I could proceed a couple of his guys patted me down for weapons. They said nothing personal, but I have been known to kill Thunder members.

A couple of those Thunder members still gave me the death stare, but Helmut kept them on a short leash. And now that I am a Shock Collar, fuck them even more. Must totally burn their asses.

Once a week, us Shock Collars would hold church and talk about any issues or conflicts within the prison walls. I knew to sit back and learn all the personalities first. Know who had the hottest temper, who would listen and think rather than just react.

Of all of them, Helmut was the calmest and coolest. Then again, the man was in a couple world wars. The Mexicans were the most emotional, with the Muslims having the hardest heads to get through.

All and all, it was a good first meeting. Prison officials knew these meetings took place and had no problems with them. In fact, we would settle differences in this room rather than with violence or death within the prison walls.

My first true test as a Shock Collar came when one of the new prisoners who I knew from the Airborne, started to work in the kitchen.

His name was Walt Gibson. He was a good soldier, good guy to have beside you in a firefight.

Like most Vietnam vets, including yours truly, he came home from Nam a little fucked up. Got heavy into the drinking. One night, on his way home from a bar, he killed a woman and her child.

Walt was sentenced to eight years in a federal prison. During our weekly church meeting, Marco Garcia asked how tight I was with Gibson. I explained we served together in Nam, why?

"Did he tell you why he is in prison?"

"Yeah said he got eight years for driving drunk and killing a chick and her kid."

"That's right, Mitch. That chick was my first cousin Theresa and her daughter Mary."

I thought of my Mom and Pam right off the bat.

"I assume you want revenge on him?"

"Yes, I do, is this going to be a problem between you and I?"

No way would I ever tell any of these guys what happened to Mom and sis, I never want them knowing any of my weaknesses.

"Not a problem at all. Do what you have to

do, Marco. I will not get in your way."

"That's good to hear, Bandeco."

Gibson's body was found stuffed into a duct. He was stabbed more than one hundred times.

Just before Christmas I had two very interesting visits. The first one was from Rachel. She said she and a bunch of girlfriends from school are spending Christmas in Germany, so she won't be seeing me over the holidays. She has always wanted to see where Mom was born and raised. She also wants to see if she can find Grandpa Kohler's grave. I said I needed a favor. I wanted her to buy Katrina something for Christmas from me.

"Mitch, she is Jewish."

"She is only half Jewish."

"Stan and Natasha are raising her Jewish. And secondly you are just a friend of her Mom and Uncle Glen's."

"Are you not getting her anything for Christmas, Auntie Rachel?"

At first Rachel didn't answer me. She just stared at me.

"Mitch, all you are going to do is to confuse her and put Natasha in a very uncomfortable spot. You get photos of Katrina as promised by Natasha. Just let it go, please."

"You still didn't answer my question. Did you buy her something for Christmas?"

"Yes, I did."

"And what did you buy her as I will go halves on whatever you spent. Down the road I never want her to think I never forgot about her on her birthday and Christmas."

"I see where you are coming from. I bought her some clothes. She loves the Partridge Family. For some reason, she thinks I know them personally. So, I bought her a lunch pail, posters, and some other stuff. But Mitch, you can't put your name on any of the gifts."

I didn't get mad, I thought about the bigger picture. I guess when it comes down to it the most important person in the world should know I care about Katrina. And that person is Rachel. The truth will come out one day.

Two days before Christmas my cousin Jerry came by to visit me. At first, I thought it was family being thoughtful, you know, Merry Christmas, peace on earth and goodwill to all men, bullshit.

Jerry told me that Szoke was just sentenced to thirty years for smuggling dope from Mexico to California. Richard Nixon's newest law enforcement group called the Drug Enforcement Agency and those sneaky bastards, tracked Szoke's plane all the way from Mexico to when he landed in Death Valley.

Szoke, so far according Jerry, has kept his mouth shut and Jerry wants to make sure it stays that way. He asked me to put Szoke under my wing; keep him calm and cool and make sure he stays solid.

I asked Jerry what happens if he doesn't remain cool, then what? Jerry smiled and slid his index finger from one side of his jaw to the other.

12

December 31, 1974: Another New Year's Eve spent locked up. So many people making resolutions for the upcoming year, I wonder how many of us in prison here promise to say quit smoking? Start a diet and exercise program? Be a better human being to others?

Quite frankly, none of us in here have any discipline to commit to these fucking stupid resolutions or we wouldn't be locked up behind bars in the first place.

So, my New Year resolution was simple and actually something I plan on keeping. In three hundred and sixty-five days from now I will be ushering in 1976 as a free man.

Albert broke out the prune wine that he had fermenting for us. It was a nice little buzz. I didn't bother to usher in the New Year, why be reminded.

*

A week or so later, Szoke appeared in our range. He looked like shit. He was sporting a black eye and lookcd like he hadn't slept in a month.

He almost stammered when he talked. His head was steady on a pivot looking around, the fucker was scared shitless.

"Szoke, good to see you man. You all right?"

"Fuck, Mitch I am not sure."

I looked at his black eye and asked who did it.

"A couple black guys."

Fucking guy couldn't even look at me while talking.

"No one will ever hurt you again in this prison now."

"I wish I would have just crashed my plane and fucking died, man."

"That's not cool to say. I know this is a shitty place to be, but do you know how many fucking guys I saw stuffed into body bags would switch spots with you?"

"I am sure if they went through what I went through they would have wanted to stay dead."

"What the fuck are you talking about? You got busted, you took a couple shots to the head. You're a solid citizen in the criminal underworld, you will be fine."

"Oh, I will be anything but fucking fine, man. Not even close to ever being fine, you don't fucking know, man."

"What don't I know?"

Szoke now had a tear roll down his face as his eyes watered.

"Never mind," said Szoke as he stormed away.

I let him vent and if he doesn't want to talk, fuck him. Three days went by and Szoke's cell mate came up to me and said Szoke hasn't showered yet since coming to our range and he is starting to smell like vegetable beef soup. I thanked him for not taking any action. I said I would deal with it.

Normally, when someone refuses to shower and starts to stink, guys will jump them and beat them with bars of soap placed into a sock, its actually called a blanket party. Or they will just grab them and throw them into the shower clothes and all. And of course, this is normally followed by a beating.

So, I grabbed Albert and said to Szoke that some of his fellow cons want to nickname him "Pig Pen" and he should grab a shower and get into clean clothes. He looked at us and said everyone in here should mind their own fucking business…that also included us.

You wanna take it personal but you can't. I understand the anger Szoke has in him right now. By the time he gets out of here he will be collecting his old age pension.

I just nodded and said to Albert let's go.

Later that afternoon, one of the guys in my crew had a visit and he was giving a couple vials of hash oil. He gave me one so once again I went down to see Szoke. The guy loves his smoke, and this buzz may help him relax a bit.

I swear I could smell the B.O. coming from him three cells away.

His celly just looked at me with disgust as I entered the cell. I told the celly to go for a walk as I looked at Szoke just lying there staring into space.

"Hey look what I stumbled across. You wanna catch a buzz?"

"Really? Dope is why I am in here, the only buzz I want is to be out of here. I want my freedom, man. I want to be like a bird and fly out of here. Maybe I should have taken that deal from District Attorney."

Right away my back went up and the fire that had been smoldering inside of me, ignited. I put the vile in my pocket and grabbed Szoke off his bunk and pinned him against the wall.

"You don't ever rat. There are people on the outside if they heard you talk like this would make sure people in here would take your life. Give your fucking head a shake!"

I drew back my fist, Szoke said to do it, kill him and take his meaningless life.

I realized right then and there he was not feeling sorry for himself. He did wish he were dead.

I stormed out of there and headed for the infirmary and to have a talk with Amy. The guy needs some valium or something.

Amy could tell something was up by my face which I am sure was red from my blood pressure being through the roof.

"I need some valium for a friend in here."

"You're a recovering addict. Mitch, you know better to ask me for drugs."

"Amy, I swear on Katrina's life they are not for me, they are for a friend from the outside who just arrived. He is having a really hard time adjusting and I am worried about him."

"Why don't you ask him to come and see me? I can help him. Who is it?"

"This guy won't leave his cell, not for a meal, not to shower. Fuck all. I can only protect him for so long. He smells Amy, he fucking reeks, and this guy is super clean usually."

"Tell me his name and I will have him evaluated."

"I can't, that would be like ratting."

"If you don't help me, I can't help your friend."

I thought deep about giving up his name. Not like I am ratting him out to the cops.

"Szoke. He is in cell 403."

As soon as I said his name Amy's whole face changed, something was up. She looked around to make sure the screw didn't hear what she was about to say.

"Your friend Szoke was raped on his first day in here. You are a good person and good friend, Mitchell. I am willing to help him, but he also has to want and accept the help. Talk to him and suggest he comes to see us here."

That smoldering fire was now a full inferno. I had this incredible rage inside me as I headed right to

Szoke's cell. On the way his celly said he can't take anymore of Pigpen and his ways.

He got a shot in the gut for that. As he hit the ground gasping for air, I picked him up by the hair and said to come with me. The guy was terrified, and he should be as right now I am in a killing mood.

I stormed into Szoke's cell and grabbed a hold of him and said let's go. Szoke now started to scream to let him to go. I threw him into the wall and put my right hand around his windpipe and started to squeeze it.

Szoke's eyes started to water. He couldn't breathe. After thirty seconds I let go of my grip and told his celly to get a shower going for Szoke. A couple screws saw what was going on and rushed right over before we made it to the showers.

"What the fuck are you doing?" they asked.

"Pigpen is getting a shower."

Normally the screws would assume you are going either beat or ass fuck someone in the showers.

But they too were disgusted by the body odor coming from him and I am sure they heard the same complaints that I did.

They told me to let go of him and they will make sure he gets a shower.

At dinner time I noticed Szoke was not present. So, I once again hauled ass to his cell. Just like earlier in the day he was just lying on his bunk staring into space.

"Let's get something to eat."

"I ate already." I looked around and saw a couple empty chip bags in his garbage.

"Chips? Are you fucking serious? The slop in the kitchen is healthier than this shit. Get up off your bunk now and come with me."

Szoke just looked at me as if to challenge me.

"You want a fucking repeat of this afternoon?"

Szoke mumbled something under his breath, not sure what, guarantee it was not good.

On the way to the kitchen we ran into Frankie

"Knuckles." He too was on his way down to eat.

We were a couple of minutes away when suddenly Szoke stopped cold in his tracks. He looked as if he had seen a ghost. He went white and started to tremble a bit. His eyes got big as he looked at a couple of cons across the hall in their cells.

I looked at the cons he made eye contact with, funny as they were staring back at Szoke. It wasn't until the one blew him a kiss when everything became clear. This had to be one of his rapists. I told Szoke to stay put and told Frankie to come with me.

I headed right for the cell of the kissing con, he looked at me and asked what my problem was. I kicked him right in the nuts and told Frankie to stand guard. The con was now cursing me as he doubled over in pain.

I grabbed him by the hair and smashed his face into the wall a couple times. He was now a bloody mess drifting in and out of consciousness. Once again, I grabbed him by the hair and made eye contact with him as I wanted him to clearly hear what I was about to tell him.

"You ever look at him, talk to him, or even come within breathing distance of him I will kill you myself you fucking rapist. You hear me?"

He didn't answer me, he just growled at me so I pulled on his right ear as hard as I could. He now rolled on the ground screaming, so I laid a couple kicks into his gut and then left.

This was the first time I saw any signs of happiness coming from Szoke since he first arrived. He nodded at me and smiled even if it was only for two seconds.

I hope he knows deep down I will protect him at least while I am in here. After that, I'm not sure. But in prison you live one day at a time and some days that does not feel like twenty-four hours, it feels like an eternity.

*

The next morning at breakfast, Marco Garcia sat at my table and said we need to talk. I asked here or in the yard, he said here was fine.

"Yesterday you laid quite a beating on Hugo

Lopez, why?"

"He needed to be held accountable for something."

"I would like to know if this was business or personal?"

"A bit of both, he raped a good friend in here. I was asked by some heavy hitters to keep him safe."

"I wished you would have come to me first."

"I didn't think I needed your permission as to who I punch out in here. He is not one of your crew."

"He is a repeat offender, he was always one of my crew, he just didn't make his way out of the bull pen into general pop yet."

"Well, I didn't know he was one of your guys. Now that I know make sure he stays out of my guy's way and we will have no problems."

"Well there is a problem as Lopez does expect some sort of retribution for the beating you put on him."

"Lopez is lucky I didn't fucking kill him. I let you have full access to Gibson without saying fuck. As far as Szoke goes, I am taking a stand. I am also a Shock Collar just like you."

"Strongbow, you are going to cause tension over this."

"If there is tension it is caused by you. Let it fucking go, man."

Garcia looked at me, smiled, and then left. I know that smile; a shit storm will be headed my way. I think I better tell Szoke for the next little bit to make sure he is within view of me.

I looked all over and couldn't find him. I ran into my celly George and asked if he saw Szoke, George said he was in the interrogation room.

He said a couple screws came down and took him away. I told George what Garcia said and asked what he thought. George laughed and said Lopez was Garcia's bitch his last bit in here. Now it makes sense, perfect fucking sense.

"Those anal bandits take care of their own. You better keep a close eye on Szoke, or will they care of him," said George.

I hung around Szoke's cell waiting for him to come back. Twenty minutes or so went by before I saw Szoke making his way towards me. I started heading towards him and Szoke stopped in his tracks as soon as he spotted me. His eyes went big, he looked scared.

"Szoke, what's going on man?"

"Nothing man, ah nothing at all why? Why are you here, did I do something wrong?"

"Relax man, just making sure you're all right. Who came to see you?"

"Oh um, the cops."

He was stammering and starting to sweat a bit. Fuck, you could almost hear his heart pounding right out of his chest. His actions were really starting to make me suspicious. Jerry said to make sure he stays solid or take him out.

"What kind of cops and what did they want?"

"Just cops, they wanted nothing Mitch, you

have to believe me!"

I didn't believe him, and I also didn't believe they were just cops.

So, I looked around and saw no one watching and I threw a punch right into his gut and pinned him against the wall.

"Do not fucking bullshit me, man. What kind of cops and what did they want?"

Szoke was struggling to catch his breath as I winded him with the shot.

"F.B.I. Mitch, I told them nothing."

"Look at me. I want to hear everything they asked you."

"Mitch, you have to believe me, I said nothing as I didn't know what they were talking about."

I looked Szoke in the eyes and told him, "You're fucking pissing me right off. What the fuck did they ask you?"

"They asked if I knew anything about the Texas Hell Hounds being decapitated."

I dropped my fist and now it was my turn to get nervous as my heart wanted to jump out of my chest.

"And do you know anything about this?"

"I don't know shit about this. I told them I am just a pilot. I am not a club member. All I know is what I have heard around the campfire. Those guys were robbed and had their heads cut off. Jerry thinks it was someone in either the Oakland or San Antonio club. And I am in prison because Jerry wanted all dope flown in and no more ground travel."

"I believe you. I know you are solid, or you would have rolled on everyone and be hiding in Butt Fuck Alaska. Sorry for hitting you."

"I am doing what everyone expects right, Mitch?"

"You are being a solid citizen. I am just tense these days. The guy who raped you, Lopez, is playing wife to Marco Garcia who is the Shock Collar for the south Mexican gang in here. So, make sure you keep in view of me."

Szoke slid down to the ground with his hands covering his face. He was crying as he sat there. I didn't know what to say or do. I put my hand on his shoulder and said all will be good. But it isn't going to be good, it's going to become *anything but* good as I heard a screw yelling at me to get away from Szoke.

I was shocked and said I ain't doing shit. Three screws now came running towards me. One of them had a pump action shotgun pointed right at my head. They yelled at me to get on the ground.

Truthfulness be damned. I hit the ground like they said. Two of them jumped on me while the guard with the shotgun made me clearly understand that if I fight back, he will blow my fucking head off.

I was handcuffed and whisked away to a cooling off cell. About thirty minutes later a walking boss headed straight to me and said he had witnesses sign a statement that I assaulted Szoke.

He came right out and asked me why. But I didn't assault him; I hit him but not to hurt him in a fit of rage, fuck.

"I never hurt him. Ask him."

The hesitation and answer sealed my fate.

"He says you didn't touch him. But that bruise on his stomach and the witnesses say otherwise. Stick out your wrists so we can cuff you. Strongbow, you are going to the hole for the next thirty days."

Fucking rats. At first, I didn't put my wrists through the slot to be cuffed until I was asked if I want to do ninety days instead of thirty.

I stuck out my wrists and begrudgingly let them cuff me. They then ordered me to kneel with my feet crossed and to put cuffed wrists behind my neck. I was shackled and once again on my way to the hole for another thirty-day stint.

This time they were wrong. I find out who ratted me out they will be in for a royal beating once I get out. Giving a rat a beating is worth thirty days in the hole.

It took a couple hours before the rage in me lifted long enough to realize that Szoke will be in trouble with me in the hole. I must get word to Albert somehow to babysit him until I am out.

*

Sadly, I never did get that chance to get word out as the screws that would bring me my food were not on the take, and on day seventeen of hole time the prison riot alarm went off.

I automatically thought of Szoke. Fuck, I really hope my intuition is off. I started to pace back and forth; I could feel an evil energy headed my way. Bad joo joo. It crept through the cement walls and floors down here in the hole, right through the clad iron door and into my lungs, and tormented brain, and soul. Nothing was stopping it from finding me; I knew exactly where it was headed. For the first time in a long time I felt everything closing in on me.

I had problems sleeping that night, my brain wouldn't shut down. I could really use a fix of heroin to kill the demons. Things just weren't right, and I knew it.

*

The next morning, I asked the screw delivering breakfast what happened.

I was told none of my business, same as the screw
bringing dinner. No one would say shit to me.
Fuck, these next twelve days can't go by fast
enough.

 So, every minute of every day I would push my
body through exercise to the point of exhaustion
and eventually pass out.

My thirty days in the hole ended on February 14th.
You would think this being a special day for
lovers, I would head straight to see Miss Borden.
Lord knows I am hornier than all hell.

But I have this knot in my gut ever since I heard
the riot alarm being sounded thirteen days ago.

I headed to Szoke's cell to make sure he was fine.
As I was walking up to the fourth floor my legs
were getting heavier with each step.

Once I finally got to the fourth floor I stopped,
took a breath, and headed to his cell. The closer I
got the emptier I felt inside until I heard music
coming from his cell. Led Zeppelin, Szoke's
favorite, thank fuck.

My pace picked up and as I was at the cell

before I yelled out, "Sounds like a John Bonham drum solo anytime now!" I jumped into the mouth of the cell and screamed out, "BONZO!"

But it wasn't Bonzo Szoke, it was some scrawny blonde-haired kid.

"Who the fuck are you, and where's Szoke"

"You mean the dead guy?"

I lunged and then grabbed the kid by the collar and held him against the wall with one hand and drew back my fist with the other hand.

"What the fuck do you mean the *dead* guy?"

"Hey man, I didn't kill him"

"You stupid little fuck, when did he die?"

"I don't know, they told me this is my new cell."

I threw the kid back down on his bunk and headed for my cell. George was in there having a coffee, he looked up at me and asked if I heard.

"I heard he is dead. How?"

"Lopez and Garcia went after him."

"I swear I'll kill those two cock sucking assholes!"

"Save your anger. Lopez is dead and Garcia is California's latest vegetable."

"Did Albert go after them?"

"No, Szoke got them both. We knew that they would go after him with you in the hole. So, we made sure Szoke had a nice razor sharp shiv. They tried to jump him on the way to the yard. He stabbed Lopez right in the chest, must have hit an artery. He then drove the shiv into Garcia's throat and kept stabbing him in the head repeatedly until a screw noticed what was going on. The screws told Szoke to drop the shiv and to get on the ground. I guess he was scared and tried to outrun them. Don't matter how fast you are an M-16 is always faster. They put a couple rounds in hum. He died on the spot, Mitch. Garcia is lying in a hospital bed brain dead. Machines are keeping him alive."

"I warned that fuck to stay away from Szoke. I hope they keep him on the machines forever, death is to easy a way out for him. I am glad Szoke went down swinging."

George could tell I was wound really tight and he suggested we go out to the yard and go a few rounds on the heavy bag.

Right now, I had to hit something either the heavy bag or a human, so I agreed. I eyed every single person in the yard on my way to the bags. Even guys in my own crew said they're happy to have me back, I just nodded.

I am sure the smart ones could see the rage in my eyes and the stupid ones would feel the wrath of my knuckles. George and I just finished off our seventh, three-minute round when Helmut and a couple other Shock Collars made their way over to us. I was ready for anyone; I needed a good scrap.

"Nice to see you out of the hole, we need to talk, Mitch," said a sincere Helmut.

So, I took my gloves off but kept my wraps on.

"What's up boys?"

"The south Mexicans are having an internal war deciding who takes over for Garcia. All they are doing is bringing heat onto the rest of us. Mitch, every day the screws are ripping apart every single nook and cranny looking for weapons. The northern Mexicans are seeing the turmoil and taking advantage of this and flexing their muscles and paying back beating debts."

"What do you guys want out of me and my crew?"

"We have all agreed to let them handle this shit between themselves. All of us have agreed to stay neutral, I hope you will go along with us."

"If everyone else agrees, then you have my word my boys will stay neutral. Anything else?"

"Stock up on food, this could be a long lock down from the screws if all hell breaks loose."

"I thought about quitting work in the kitchen, not now. Fuck, clean clothes and grub always must be cooked to feed the population. Now boys, what I could use is a nice buzz as I need to shut my brain down for a bit, you know? Can anyone hook me up with anything?"

"Chose your poison and method of travel

Mitch, through your nose, lungs, veins or gut?"
Helmut smiled devilishly.

I looked down at my veins which may not have
been hankering for a fix of heroin, but my soul
certainly needed it. I touched my nose; my nostrils
always liked the burn from a rail of coke, my
lungs could always use some blue smoke and a
good coughing attack and the Injun in me always
liked the firewater. So many choices and all so
right and all so wrong and all so right.

"Surprise me, Helmut."

Very good was his answer as he left.

I then headed for the showers as I was drenched
from the workout and showers in the hole only
come once a week.

On the way back to my cell you could tell the
whole prison was on edge. The screws and the
cons eyed me just as closely.

By the time I got back to my cell, it was ripped
apart my stuff was strewn all over the place.
George was in the middle of putting everything
back in the cell.

"Fucking screws are going after all the shock leaders and sending their own statement. Mitch, I know when this place is ready to explode. And this place is a powder keg with the wick already lit."

"And what then when a full-scale riot happens?"

"It's like the gates of hell open up and Satan himself casts a spell over the prison. No matter how meek someone is, they turn pure evil and those already fucked are out of control and everything they do, everything they have built up, is let loose. All debts are collected in the forms of lives taken and blood spilled. Trust no one. You get yourself into a corner kill whoever is coming at you. No prisoners Mitch, pardon the pun."

I have no grudges with anyone right now. I killed who had to be killed. But I do worry about Amy and Charlene. Would like to give them the heads up as to what is going on and when it is supposed to go down. But none of us really know. I guess the Mexicans will decide when and I better be ready as I know I have made a few enemies in here.

With the screws ripping apart my cell on a regular basis, not sure where I could hide any weapons…kitchen maybe.

After dinner I was chilling in my cell getting caught up on letters sent to me while I was in the hole. Frankie "Knuckles" gave me the heads up a couple of Helmut's guys were headed my way.

The one handed me a book and said page 218 was the best page in the book. I thanked him and headed right for page 218.

Every page after that had a hole cut out which contained a foil object. I opened the foil and the contents. There were dark little rocks, at first, I thought they were hash, but they were kind of slimy. Not heroin but judging by the smell I would say opium. Perfect choice I must say.

I didn't let anyone know what I was up to. I never want anyone in my crew to think I am weak mentally, but Szoke's death is really fucking my head up.

As soon as lock up happened, I asked George for one of his cigarettes and then took out the tobacco and rolled up a couple joints with the opium.

Like a good celly, George knew I was up to no good and asked if all was well. I said yeah just want to get mellow. I asked George if he wanted a hit or two and he said no. I lit up the first joint and laid on my cot and watched the blue clouds of smoke play out.

Within three tokes I felt a nice buzz creeping into my tortured brain. A brain that kept replaying Szoke telling me that the reason he got caught was because of someone robbing and killing the Hell Hounds in Texas.

I visualized myself robbing and then decapitating the two. Fucking brain, can't remember their names, but I can recall every single cut it took for me to have their heads off and the color of the gym bag I left their bloody skulls in.

Fuck, Szoke would be alive and a free man if it wasn't for me. Why did I punch him? I know I couldn't protect him being in the hole. *Fuck Mitch, you really blew this.*

I remember us flying back to Vegas and him rocking to Zeppelin. He was such an easy-going guy, great pilot. I guess him being locked up was not different than a bird in a cage.

I finished off both joints, and for the first time in a longtime, I felt totally at ease.

*

The next morning, I was awoken by a screw asking me if I planned on still working in the kitchen. At first, I said no then I remembered what Helmut said about what happens when a riot goes down and I said yeah.

I was still pretty fucking buzzed out when I reached the kitchen. It was good seeing everyone again. I was told by the boys that shit is coming down any day now and to be prepared.

I started thinking how I fucked up with Szoke and not being able to protect him. I won't let that happen to Amy and Charlene.

Right after my shift I am going to warn both, tell them to take some holidays or get the flu, anything until this volcano erupts and all is back to normal. A female will feel the wrath of a thousand horny bastards once this place is taken over and make no mistake about it, the screws will not be able to protect them. So, right after my shift I wanted to try and make amends for my past failures and I headed straight to the library first as Amy had the later shift.

*

Miss Charlene Borden's big beautiful blue eyes seemed brighter than ever before. I could tell she was happy to see me out of the hole. I think my throbbing cock was more than happy to see her.

Right off the bat I said we need to talk.

"Mitchell, you horny bastard," said Charlene with a laugh.

"Oh, I am horny, but I need to talk to you about this place."

We went into her office and I asked if she knew what was going on in the prison. She had no clue and was a little shocked and quite concerned.

She said she has a sister in Florida who just had a baby, and she has been putting off seeing the little guy. I strongly suggested she go and finally meet her nephew. She thanked me for thinking of her and said, for a con, I was a decent guy. I was happy to see her smile. She then put her hand on my crotch area, and before she could get my dick out of my pants, a screw named Maxwell walked in and asked if everything was good.

Of course, was her answer. Maxwell looked at her, looked at me and then told me to find something else to do. I sensed jealously coming from him and not just by the eye contact he made but by the way he stuck out his chest and then frowned at her.

"I am allowed to be in here, the library is for all cons, fucking mellow."

"Strongbow, why don't you go the yard and scrape your knuckles on the ground like the rest of the Neanderthals out there?"

Fuck you, was my response. He then asked if I want to do another thirty days in the hole. Warning Amy was more important. I will be damned if I lose another friend while I am in the hole and not able to protect them. I turned and left Charlene and the library after giving her a wink.

Fucking loser, were Maxwell's goodbye remarks

to me, fuck him.

As soon as you stepped in the yard you could feel the tension. This place was ready to go. I then headed to yard and right to the weights where Albert and Frankie were doing squats.

I joined in with the boys, and as soon as we started to discuss what our game plan should be if a riot occurs, a couple south Mexicans headed by Chico Sanchez were coming straight for us. Everyone stopped what they were doing in the weight area as we became the focus to all.

Now, I have previous history with Chico. He too was 101st Airborne. He was approaching the end of his tour as I was just beginning my first tour. I believe right after Tet was my first encounter with him.

We encountered some captured Viet Cong, both male and female. They didn't want to tell us shit, so Chico grabbed one male and one female and covered them both is gas and asked them who was helping them. The male told Chico to go fuck himself. He lit them both on fire.

So, was I surprised to hear he was serving a

hundred-year sentence in hear for firebombing a completive drugs dealers house to the ground after he nailed all the doors shut? Fuck no, he is pretty whacked.

"Strongbow, always in and out of the hole like the tough guy he is. You heard Garcia is dead right? After all, it was one of your men who killed him. I have to say he did me a favor as I planned on taking over the South Mexicans anyway. Garcia was fucking weak, a fucking pussy. You and me, we got good history. I also plan on settling some scores in here with some of Garcia's loyal followers and some North Mexicans. You have a problem with any of that mister Shock Collar?"

Time for me to bank a favor from Chico and to also go along with the wishes of my fellow Shock Collars.

"Chico, I have no problems with what is about to take place. I will not stand in your way or impede you in your quest; I do hope that in the future you will respect my needs if something were to come up."

Of course, was his answer and then Garcia smiled and then gave me the Airborne in country handshake.

After Chico and his guys left, Albert smiled and called me a whore. And that I am.

I grabbed a long hot shower after we worked out and then a cat nap, knowing by the time I woke up, that Amy would be working and I could warn her of the upcoming storm headed our way.

The shower was great, I lay down on my bunk physically and mentally exhausted, but I couldn't sleep. As soon as I started to drift off, I swore that I heard Szoke calling my name. And each time I would wake up more startled then the last time. I was also starting to sweat a ton.

Fuck, I could use another hit of Opium as last night was one of the best rests I have had since entering this hell hole. I looked at the clock and I had thirty minutes before dinner. I feel like shit, and Amy's shift has now started. I better go see her and warn her.

There is always this big fucking Black screw, Jones, who has major league attitude towards me.

Just getting into the infirmary on Amy's shift is a challenge, so I better think of a good reason to get in and be seen by her.

I will say my neck has totally stiffened on me and I feel a migraine coming on. Even better, I will say I think I have flu…that will keep Jones way from us.

As soon as I walked in, Jones came at me with attitude. He came a little closer and said I looked like shit. Flu, that is all I had to say. He backed away and went and got Amy.

As Amy came around the corner, I saw so much resemblance to Tash; same body structure, cat like eyes, and same blonde hair color. As much as I have a love hate relationship with Tash, I get butterflies seeing Amy in a fleeting moment thinking it is Tash.

"Mitchell, you don't look very good. You think it's the flu?" I just nodded my head as Jones was still within earshot of hearing me.

She put her hand on my forehead and said I felt warm. She said to stay put while she grabbed a thermometer,

As soon as Jones walked away, Amy put a thermometer in my mouth as she was taking my pulse.

I tried to talk, but Amy told me to keep the thermometer under my tongue or she wouldn't get an accurate reading. I squeezed her thigh and took out the thermometer and put my finger over my mouth and said *shh*.

"Mitchell Strongbow, if you don't keep that thermometer in your mouth, I will stick it up your ass."

"Your life is in danger, Amy."

Amy heard that fine as she went as white as her uniform.

"You're scaring me Mitchell, what do you mean?"

"There is going to be a prison riot sometime soon. Take holidays, go see your Mom or Abby. This place won't be safe for you."

"Mitchell, every day I come to work I put my life in danger. I see the way most of these guys look at me. I will be fine. Now if you don't keep the thermometer in your mouth your life will be in danger," said Amy who drew a fist at me.

I sat there like a good patient all the while thinking of different ways to convince her that all hell is about to break loose. The funny part is that I was starting to feel like I actually had the flu and when Amy pulled out the thermometer, she said it read 103.

"Mitchell, you have the flu. I am going to have you stay here in the infirmary until it has passed. Mainly because the prison doesn't need the virus running rampant. Officer Jones, prisoner Strongbow will be staying with us for the next twenty-four to forty-eight hours. Can you please accompany him to bed seventeen please?"

Fuck, this worked out well as I can keep a close eye on Amy's safety, except for the flu part. I wonder if smoking the opium had something to do with it? Makes me wonder if Grandpa put some Shaman Sioux curse on my body if I started to use heavy drugs that effected my soul that is still in the healing process.

Then again, opium is a natural drug much like

peyote, so why the curse Gramps?

Within ten minutes of getting into bed I felt like death warmed over. All of my joints were now starting to hurt. Everything from my eye lids to my toes ached.

Amy brought over a couple aspirin and told me to make sure I keep pounding back the fluids. I promised I would, and then before I knew it, I was fighting a battle between puking and staying awake. I closed my eyes and was startled by the sound of thunder, the problem was that it was a clear night, the thunder was coming from my guts having internal explosions.

The hairs on my arms now started to stand up and I felt my anus tightening up for the upcoming storm, not sure how long I could hold back as I raced to the washroom.

Jones the fucking goof grabbed a hold of me from behind and asked me where the fuck I was going.

"I am either going to spray the bowl or spray you full of shit."

I am sure either the paleness or sweat coming

from me confirmed my story.

My pants weren't even fully down when I started to spray. I felt like an embarrassed kid who knew the belt was coming his way. Contractions were now coming from my asshole, I couldn't stop shitting and the smell was rancid, so bad that I puked in the sink, then back to the toilet and back to the sink one more time.

By now Amy, and Jones were both in the bathroom. She was very sympathetic, and he was yelling at me what a fucking loser I was. Not sure what was burning more, my asshole or my temper. I looked at Jones and told him to fuck himself. Amy told Jones to back off that I am sick.

"Sick or not, he should be cleaning up that mess he made!"

Amy told me to have a shower and not to worry about the mess.

I got into the shower to clean myself up, I felt weak and feeble. The water couldn't get hot enough to warm me up. I was shaking from the time I left the shower to the time I dried off and jumped into bed. Amy gave me some anti-nausea meds as I laid there and shook as if I was coming off heroin again.

Within a matter of seconds, I passed out cold. Within minutes I was having a sickness nightmare. The problem is that they are so fucking real. Deadly realistic.

I was back in high school, Polk High. First day actually, a minor niner. Rhonda Ryan was yelling at me to come and help her as the Italians, including Luch, were coming back for revenge and this time it was her they came after. They also brought more Diego's with them. I went to leave my classroom, but the principal slammed a ruler on the desk and said I had detention. Rhonda was on her own.

Just like Dad taught us, I told the principal to go and fuck himself. I went to leave the room, but the door was solid steel. There was no window to break and as hard I tried, I couldn't pry it open.

I looked at the principal and told him if he didn't open this door right now, I would tell my Dad and he would surely beat him up.

"Unacceptable behavior, Mr. Strongbow!" screamed the principal as he pulled out the strap.

Once again, fuck you was my response. I grabbed the strap out of his hand. I went to whip him with it, but the Principal didn't show any fear. If anything, he mocked me by laughing at me. I was confused and getting more pissed when I realized the strap had turned into a cobra snake. The head on it was huge. Its eyes were pure evil. I wanted to look away, but I was spellbound. The snake pulled its head back, its menacing eyes went blood red as its razor-sharp fangs came towards me like a bullet from a sniper's rifle.

I was painfully bitten repeatedly time after time until I hit the floor and felt my life force diminishing from me. Paralyzed, I was losing all my senses except for sound and sight. I could still hear Rhonda calling for me, and this time, Amy was a Doctor saying there was nothing she could do to save me.

Beaten and battered I closed my eyes attempting to save enough strength to breathe when Amy said I was dead. Call the meat wagon and have him buried.

A loud growling engine could be heard approaching the school. Amy yelled out for it to turn on its siren as I was starting to decay, and little snakes were now coming out of my open wounds.

The siren was so loud my body jolted and then jolted again but this time it jolted me from my dream. I was drenched in sweat, as the siren from my dream was in fact the prison's riot alarm going off. I tried to jump up out of bed, but the flu reminded me that it wasn't such a great idea.

Jones came running towards me with his baton and told me if I get up, he will make sure I was the first casualty.

I yell at Amy to get out of here right now. Jones also says any talking from me will result in a broken jaw. I am too weak to lay a beating on this fucking loudmouth, but not so weak that I can't inflict a little damage.

By now, the other cons are starting to get out of their beds. Sick or not, violence, fear, and that adrenaline rush makes us all heal.

Within a matter of a minutes you hear the chaos

going on outside the infirmary, you hear weapons being discharged, you hear blood curdling screams.

The hair on my body was standing straight up. Like being under a full raging moon I am drawn into the madness of the riot and feel much stronger as do the other cons that now rush Jones and start to beat him.

A couple cons ask Amy for the keys to the drug cabinet, she tells them she can't give them up, she would be fired. They tell her she will be dead if she doesn't give them, being fired is the least of her worries. A frightened Amy now looks at me as I tell her to give them the keys.

I also tell them all if anyone harms a hair on her head, I will fucking kill them. Just like at Monterey, I am here for her.

Three of them all gather in a pack and say, "One against three, you ain't that tough, Strongbow."

Two members of the Thunder were also foolish enough to think the same, they are now buried, wanna join them, tough guys?"

The three walked towards me. I had zero weapons and felt like shit. I am running off pure adrenaline and battle-hardened rage right now. The three separate and are circling me.

I am eyeing which one of the three is the biggest threat. I know I will have to kill him quickly to take care of the other two. I am ready for battle when the door to the infirmary is kicked open.

Albert, Frankie, and a couple other guys from my crew are with them.

I look at the three and ask, "Who's the bitch now?"

And like that the fight was on. I went right after the ringleader. I am drilling him in the head as he is now saying it was just a joke. Fucking liar. I don't stop until he is a bloody mess and knocked out cold. Fuck, I feel alive! Fuck the flu.

Albert tells me the whole prison is in a full-scale riot. He also knows I have a thing going on with the librarian and informs me that a bunch of South Mexicans just took over the library.

"Charlene! Fuck, did she get out in time?"

I tell Frankie and a couple guys to stay with Amy.

"Frankie, I am holding you responsible for her safety. Take whatever drugs we can make cash off or can use as collateral in the riot."

Amy is shaking and asks for me not to leave. I assure her I will be back in twenty. As I leave the infirmary, I saw exactly what I heard, fucking madness has erupted it has the same feel as a psychiatric hospital. I see blood all over the halls and injured cons everywhere.

Little fires are burning, and it is like the whole prison has been flipped upside down and the mess that comes from it.

I also see Helmut and his boys looting the kitchen. This would be the perfect time if he still had a grudge with me to get even. He calls out my name as he and about a dozen of his men approach us.

The guy is pure evil, he of all people must get off on what is going on. Must remind him of being back in the S.S and going through the countries and cities in Europe.

"Strongbow, where are you going?" I swear

his German accent just got thicker.

"I am going to the library"

"Do you plan on reading during the riot?" laughed Helmut.

"A friend of mine might be in trouble."

"A certain red headed, big breasted friend? I hear you two are like love birds. I also hear Chico and his men have the library. You might need some weapons."

"Yes, you heard good about me and her, and yes I do need some weapons."

"A fool would go down there with no weapons; I also hear you and your men have taken over the infirmary. I will trade you kitchen knives, which are better than any homemade shiv, for some of the prison's finest narcotics, deal?"

"Deal, but the nurse up there is family. She is not to be attacked in any shape or form."

"We are not like the soulless pricks in here. I give you my word, no one will harm her."

Helmut stuck out his hand and we shook on it;

yeah, he is pure evil but he has honor if that makes any sense at all.

I told George to go with Helmut and his men and to let Frankie know we just did a deal, and all is good. Helmut gave me four carving knives and wished us luck. I thanked him and said we will be heading back to the infirmary as soon as I know what is up with Charlene.

You realized quickly that the inmates for the most part had taken control of the prison. It was utter chaos. The deeper you went into the prisons underbelly you saw total madness and if you couldn't see it for a minute or so you heard it or smelled it.

Screams of prisoners seeking revenge upon other prisoners. Unlucky screws caught in the middle of the spider's web of insanity were being tortured, only the lucky ones were killed right away.

The most blood curdling screams were coming from protective custody. It was home of the lowest form of human life in a prison, rapists, child molesters, and fucking rats.

I hope this part of San Quentin is cleansed of all

forms of the filth of humanity. Kill them all.

We get about twenty yards from the library and our presence has their one sentry running inside leaving six muscle headed Mexicans out front

"They know we are here, Albert."

"Your presence is always known, Mitch. Let's see if your lady friend got out ok."

By the time we walked another five paces the six guys in the front became twenty. All were armed with either shivs or chair legs. This was not good.

Pedro Lopez, who is Chico's second in command, asked what we wanted.

"Is Chico in there?"

"He is in there, but he is taking care of business. I don't think he wants to talk to you, Holmes."

"Well, me and my crew took over the infirmary. I think he will want to talk to me."

Pedro smiled and said I was right; Chico will want to talk to me.

I didn't hear any female voice or screams coming from inside the library. That was a good sign. Chico came out with a big smile on his face.

"Strongbow, you have control of the infirmary and all of its contents?"

"Absolutely."

"Then let's talk business. I want to buy all the painkillers in that place, what do you say?"

"I think we can do business. Is the red headed librarian in there?"

"Yeah, she is, why you want your turn?" laughed Chico and several of his men.

Time to spread the bullshit in the Mexican fields.

"Her dad is a good friend of mine who also is a full patch in the Oakland Hell Hounds. I will trade you all the vials of morphine for her."

Chico looked at me as he scratched his chin and pondered my deal.

"I worry she will rat us out to the cops, some of the boys had their way with her, I think she would be better dead."

Four of us against twenty armed, murdering Mexicans. I don't like the odds.

"If I don't get her out of here alive, I will be killed. I promised him she would never be harmed. I will give you my word she will not say shit to the cops. I will tell her dad this is a deal I made with you. You can always use muscle on the outside."

"I have enough men on the outside loyal to me."

"You can never have enough people in your debt. I promised you earlier I would support you as a Shock Collar to accept you as the new South Mexican Shock Collar. Helmut is in the infirmary right now waiting for me. He knows I am down here. You will have both our blessings."

Chico talked to Pedro and then said, "I want all the morphine vials and valium. I also want your word that if she rats, your life will be forfeited for hers. And finally, that screw Maxwell...I want you to kill him"

"Deal, but I want no witnesses to me killing Maxwell."

"I have to see you take his life myself, well that is unless he is someone's son you plan on saving," laughed Chico.

"Let's go inside, just you and I."

I told Albert I would be back in five.

The library like the rest of the prison was busted up. The sign that read *Shh* was ripped of the wall and had blood stains on it. And there was noise coming from inside, loud screaming. Two of Chico's men yelling at a beaten and bloody Maxwell.

They were screaming at Maxwell to eat the cum out of Charlene's ass. It sickened me to see her hurt laying on the ground naked. Her whole lower body was bruised, she was whimpering on the ground face down.

I flashed right back to Jansen's raping of Lucy. I gripped my knife really tight and told Chico to get his men out of here or I will slice and dice them right now. Chico ordered them out. They looked at me when walking by and smiled. Those two will die in time.

I took off my shirt and told Charlene to put it on. I told her it was going to be ok.

She was crying and blood was flowing from her nose, her one eye was starting to swell shut already. As she came in to hug me, Chico reminded me of our deal that included Maxwell.

I then said to Charlene to go in the bathroom and get cleaned up. She didn't want to. She was terrified and still trembling in fear. I promised her I will not leave her, and that she will be leaving the prison as soon as she gets cleaned up.

She was like a ghost. I walked her to the bathroom, and she went inside. I walked over to Maxwell; he was being a total goof to me and spat on my shoe. All the rage I had brewing inside me came out as I pulled him up by his hair and sliced his throat from one ear to the other.

As he lay there now gurgling and taking his final breaths, I looked at Chico and said, "Good?"

He smiled back and said, "Good."

He also said I better have a talk with *Red* as he calls her, and that is what I did.

I walked into the washroom and saw Charlene sitting on the ground crying, her head was in her knees.

I gently lifted her head up and said, "If you want to live, come with me. You will not be safe if you stay here."

I had to help her up off the ground and when I did, I said, "I have promised my life for yours; you have to say you don't know who did this. If you tell the cops or prison officials, they will come and kill me. I will get even with those who did this to you. Do you understand me, hon?"

She nodded yes, but I also know she is in a state of shock. Right now, I just want her out alive. I have a feeling I will be dealing with Chico sooner than later and not in a good way.

As Charlene left the washroom with my arm around her, Chico stopped us and asked if she knew what would happen if she told the cops who did this to her.

"You will kill Mitch. I won't say anything. I will say I was jumped from behind and didn't see who did it."

"Very good, stick to that story or he will die a very painful death," said Chico as he smiled at me. I told Chico I would meet him at the infirmary in twenty.

I kept my arm around Charlene the entire time. She stopped cold and put her hand up to her mouth once we were outside the library. She saw all the South Mexicans watching us. I told her we must keep walking towards the bullpen. That is where Prison staff and the Cops were gathering.

The five of us walked together and if anyone had any other thoughts of raping her, we would have killed them at the first sight of a hard-on. The five of us were certainly attracting a lot of attention and not in a good way.

We are moving way too slow with Charlene being so beat up physically and mentally, so I grabbed her and threw her over my shoulder and did a fireman carry to about twenty yards from the bull pen. All you could see were cops and prison staff in riot gear that were armed to the teeth.

I yelled, "I am bringing a prison employee out!"

I was instructed via megaphone to put her down right there.

I also recognized the sound of an M-16 hammer going back. So, I did as instructed and put Charlene down. I looked at her and told her she was now safe.

"Please don't say who did this to you. I will get revenge on them. I promise just like I promised to take you to safety."

Charlene teared up and nodded her head yes. I kissed her on her forehead and then started to walk backwards towards my crew.

I watched a team of cops rush towards Charlene with their weapons pointed at me the whole time. Once she was in the custody of them, I turned around and thanked my guys for being there for me. Albert said I will have to kill Chico.

"I know I do, more than likely Pedro as well."

"You kill one Mexican you might as well kill another. Any idea how? They out number us almost ten to one in this place."

"Yeah, I do, I will slice his throat and you know the North Mexicans will get blamed for it. As far as Pedro goes, let's see how he acts with his boss dead. He might be excited to take over and be the big taco in this place."

By the time we got back to the infirmary there was a fair amount of tension between my crew, Helmut and his crew, and Chico and his crew. If Amy wasn't inside, I would start brawling with them all. But I know if I go down so will she.

I told Chico and Helmut to meet me in the Doc's office.

"Boys, there are enough drugs in here for all of us to get high and make some cash off. Let's not be greedy pigs at the trough as there are close to two hundred cops and the National Guard outside the prison walls ready to fry our bacon, pardon the pun. I made promises to you and I will live up to those promises. Let's divvy up the drugs right now."

"Chico, how about your guys take Jones out of here. I want no witnesses."

"What do you want done with him and what

about this nurse?"

"The nurse is family; she lives and if anyone goes near her, I will kill them. As for Jones, I really don't give a fuck, just another douchebag to me."

"You mean another dead douchebag, Strongbow. Too bad she is family... are you fucking her too?" Chico said.

"Not fucking her. And no one else will either"

"Relax man. I am good, give me my drugs and then we will get rid of the rest of those low life North Mexicans."

I did as Chico requested. I gave Helmut his drugs also and then told Amy she must leave now. I will escort her out just like I did with Charlene.

Amy looked at me as if I had a third eye and said, "I am not leaving, Mitchell. There are a lot of badly injured people in here. They will need my help."

"Amy, there is about to be a royal fucking rumble between the South and North Mexicans.

Once they go at each other again I fully expect all hell to break loose. The Muslims will come looking to rape you and then they will kill you. No, you have to leave."

"Mitchell Strongbow, I will not leave." Amy's face went beet red in defiance and anger.

"I am pretty sure Jones is dead, who is going to protect you?"

"You will, just like at Monterey. I know deep down you are a good man with a good heart. I see in you what Natasha first saw. I know you have gone down a bad path, a path of crime, but I believe if your Mom and sister weren't killed by that cop you and my cousin would be married and you would be a great father to Katrina."

I squinted my eyes and said to Amy, "Last chance to leave, hon."

She folded her arms and shook her head no.

"Albert let's set up this place as our fortress as we will be staying here until the riot is over."

Albert smiled at me and said this might be a safer place to secure then out in West Block.

We tried to fortify the place as well as we could. My biggest fear was other gangs coming for the drugs and, of course, Amy. We told her that if all hell breaks loose, she is to head to the doctor's office in the rear of the infirmary.

After a few hours a couple things went down that made me scratch my head. Number one, Amy didn't ask about her co-worker Jones at all.

That raised a huge red flag for me, and cons started to come in looking for medical aid. They heard that Amy stayed on. We decided to only let the wounded cons in. Their buddies would wait outside.

Watching Amy in action reminded me of my Australian nurse girlfriend back in Nam. I am still bothered I never got to say goodbye to her. I wonder if her marriage ever got back on track.

Shortly before midnight, we heard a lot of commotion heading towards the infirmary. It was Pedro and a whack of the South Mexicans. They were all hyped up and it wasn't until they approached the front doors, did I realize they were carrying a bloody Chico.

Pedro was actually showing concern about his Shock Collar.

He was livid saying Amy must help them. I told Pedro he can come in with Chico, but the rest of the guys have to stay out if they want help. I didn't trust those fucks at all. Pedro agreed and so Chico was brought in. He had bubbles coming from his blood-soaked chest.

I knew exactly what it was right off the bat, a sucking chest wound. Amy asked how I knew this; Nam was my only response.

She asked if I could help her with Chico. Of course, was my answer, I would now get my chance to finish him off. Pedro stood by us the whole time. Amy told Pedro to hold plastic wrap over the gash in Chico's chest while she was busy trying to find a vein to start an I.V. She asked me to draw up 10CC of morphine and to put it into his I.V.

I just smiled and thought perfect, it will be 10CCs but not morphine. I went back and drew 40CCs of San Quentin's finest cleaning solution.

I brought it back and stuck it right into Chico's

intravenous bag. Within two minutes, Chico was dead.

Pedro was devastated and starting to swear in Spanish, some of it I picked up on, death to the North Mexicans. He then stormed out and I said to Amy that it was going to be a long night and it was.

Amy must have looked after twenty seriously wounded cons. She worked until she passed out from exhaustion. Amy finally laid down on a cot to rest; I covered her up and kissed her forehead. She was truly an angel.

I too was bagged between the energy of the riot and the flu that I had been fighting. I laid on the cot beside Amy. Within a millisecond I had passed out cold even with the riot going on throughout the prison.

It seemed like I just fell asleep when I was woken by a sound I haven't heard in several hours. The sounds of weapons being discharged. I jumped up to see what was going on. Amy, god bless her pure soul, was still out cold.

Albert and Frankie were already awake.

Frankie said the gun fire and megaphone screaming were getting closer. I told all the guys when the cops and National Guard come in don't resist or you will be shot.

I told George he'd better warn Amy when a couple tear gas containers were shot through the front door of the infirmary.

Vietnam was my first taste of tear gas. Tet in '68 to be specific. We used it in a lot of the smaller buildings that were too dangerous to storm. Fuck Charlie, we shot it in and then went to where he would try and escape and then opened fire on them.

I yelled at my guys in the infirmary to get on the ground and once again reiterated, *don't give them an excuse to shoot you.*

Sure as fuck, the National Guard came charging in with their M-16s pointed at us asking who they should shoot first.

The guys did as instructed, but that didn't stop the Nazi Storm troopers from laying the boots to us as we were lying on the ground.

Wounded cons laying in hospital beds had rifles pointed at their heads while the bed sheets were pulled back.

Amy was choking and a guard knocked her to the ground with the butt end of his rifle. I rolled over and sliced his Achilles tendon with a knife. He hit the ground screaming; too bad his gas mask made his screams incoherent.

Then while lying down, I ripped the mask off the fallen guard and started to give him punches in the head. In my rage I got on my knees to add more force to my blows.

I didn't hear the other guards come at me, the only sense I had was about a millisecond before the butt end of a rifle landed full force on the back of my neck. I was knocked cold.

The riot started with me in a hospital bed and ended with me in a hospital bed, only this time it was the infirmary in the Oakland Jail.

I had no clue where I was. My head was pounding. Pounding so hard I started to throw up within a minute of being awake.

My right arm and left leg were handcuffed to the bed. I called for the nurse as I was starting to puke on myself. Of course, it was a male nurse with no sense of humor who just stood back and watched me barf. I was yelling at him in between hurls.

"Are you going to fucking help me you cocksucker?"

He smirked and then threw me a towel.

"Can you at least un-cuff me so I can take a shower and get some clean clothes? And how about something for my head? My fucking eyes are still burning from the tear gas!"

"My instructions are you are to be handcuffed and shackled at all times. And you have a concussion, so no meds for you."

"So, what the fuck do I do, lay here in my own vomit?"

"For now you do. I will let one of the officers know what is going on. Apparently, you are a really dangerous person, and you make staff here nervous."

I wiped myself as well as I could, threw the puke

filled towel clear across the room, closed my burning eyes, and tried to sleep.

I must have finally drifted off as I was startled by four screws who said they were taking me to the showers.

At first, I had to promise no violence towards jail officials, or this would be the last shower I would ever take here, and I might be staying for a while. I promised I would be good. They then shackled both legs, undid my handcuffs and off to the showers I waddled.

It was essential to get the smell of both the tear gas and puke off me. I stayed in there until they told me it was time to get out. The hot water felt so good. I was given Oakland Jail clothes to wear. Once dressed, I was not taken back to my hospital bed, but I was walked down to an interview room. A couple detectives from San Francisco who interviewed me in the past and an in-house detective from San Quentin, were there to interview me.

That was the reason I was allowed to get cleaned up; god forbid I get puke or get riot blood on their fancy suits.

"Mr. Strongbow, once again you came out of another recipe for disaster unscathed for the most part. I will reintroduce myself; I am Detective Hastings, and this is my partner Detective Cullimore from San Francisco homicide and I am sure you know Detective Trower from San Quentin."

"I sort of remember you two; I took a pretty nasty blow when the National Guard came storm trooping their way into the infirmary, and yes I know Trower all too well."

"Seeing as how we all know each other, I would like to ask a few simple questions about the riot."

"I think I should stop you right now. Two things. Number one, any questions, I want my lawyer present, and secondly I have a concussion, anything I say won't hold up in court."

Hastings looked at Cullimore and his demeanor changed as he pulled out his little black notebook.

"Funny thing Strongbow, last time we went

to ask you questions you also had a concussion. You seem to be pulling this shit all the time."

Trower got up and put his hand up to Hastings.

"Detective, he has a medically documented concussion. He has every right to ask for his attorney and seeing at how he is still under the umbrella of the California Penitentiary system, and specifically under my care, if he doesn't want to answer any questions that is his constitutional right."

Trower looked at me and nodded.

"And I also sent a message from the warden and the rest of the staff at San Quentin, we all thank you for your courageous actions that kept two female staff safe from further harm or impending death. Charlene Borden will survive, and her injuries will heal in time. She credits you with saving her life. I also have a statement from Amy Rosenstein; she credits you for sticking by her and keeping her safe from harm while she attended to wounded prisoners. Mitch, the warden wants to offer you all your good time that you have lost in the past and he also has the

Governor's approval to let you do the rest of your sentenced time on parole. Mitch as soon as the doctor here clears you, you will be a free man."

Now my head was really spinning. Fuck, am I having one of those dreams other cons have told me about, the one where you are finally set free and as soon as you walk out the front gate you wake up back in your four by six-foot cell.

For the first time in a year I was actually happy, smiling, fucking butterflies even, and then I saw it. My smack in the face from reality that woke me up. Just the way Trower looked at Hastings and Cullimore.

"My first day in San Quentin I learned something really quickly. I learned that if someone offers you a comb and you think they are being nice you are wrong, dead fucking wrong. That comb will cost you something as little as a pack of T.Ms. or he wants you to suck his cock. Nothing in here comes either easy or free. Now what else does the warden want so I can stroll out of here and enjoy the spring weather headed our way?"

"You're right Mitch, nothing comes easy or free in here. This riot took the life of several correctional officers including Maxwell and Jones. Two officers who were supposed to ensure the safety of Borden and Rosenstein. They paid the ultimate price with their lives. We want to know if you witnessed who took their lives and who was taking part in raping Borden?"

"My lawyer would bust my balls for talking without him present, but I have fuck all to hide. I was down for the count with flu when the riot alarms first went off. By the time I became fully coherent, Jones was dead. I saw fuck all with Borden. By the time I got there, Maxwell's body was lifeless. There were several Mexicans with their pants down around Borden. I saw no one in the act with her, but why else would they have their pants down."

"I would like some names not just Mexicans," said Peterson.

"That's all you are getting from me."

"The warden won't let you walk free over this little information. Come on Mitch, we know you are a decent guy. You saved two lives; you got fucked by the D.A. for your girlfriend's death, you're a distinguished war vet, you shouldn't even be in here." said Hastings. Fuck, he should win an Oscar for his performance.

"You see, you are not taking away anything I didn't have. And some of the lifers in here have told me that always looking over your shoulder, wondering if a vindictive cop or pissed off parole officer will throw you back in here and get you more time for fucking up your parole, that is when something is taken away from me. I will do my final seven months knowing I am a solid citizen in here, knowing I saved two females from the savages in here, it's who I am."

Hastings and Cullimore stood up, eyed me up and down, and then Cullimore mockingly called me a hero. I just smiled and nodded my head, not in agreement with him but knowing if I get the chance, I will show him what a fucking superhero I am and knock him out cold.

As soon as they left, Trower looked at me, shook his head, and said, "Fucking cops."

I was kind of shocked at him cursing at the two dicks.

"You were never a cop?"

"No. I cut my teeth like you in the military. I was an M.P. for ten years. My last three years were spent at Leavenworth. Can't say I liked it seeing young kids rather serve time in that hell hole, then go back and fight in Nam. The number of guys who go AWOL is astounding. And for the record, I was being serious about you being a decent guy. I am not into this good cop-bad cop shit."

"Thanks, I try. So, what happens next?"

"We'll try and find out what caused this riot and who was behind it. We know it was a pissing match between the South and North Mexicans, but we need to find out if it was over drugs, territory, or just bottled up anger for the past bit. Do you want to come back to San Quentin?"

"Yeah I would like to finish off my final seven months there. I ain't telling secrets as you know I am a Shock Collar. I get a lot of room in there and less people pissing me off."

"I will give the rubber stamp to you coming back. It might be two to three weeks though. Lots of interviews and normally when we ship out the main troublemakers to other prisons throughout the country, problem is that we get other troublemakers coming back."

He almost left the room, turned around, came back and said, "I am curious about one thing. I know you are a Shock Collar, and you wield a lot of power inside and that lots of people gave you room after the Mutt and Cruz deaths. Did Charlene and Amy mean anything more to you? You really risked pissing off a lot of these prisoners who haven't been laid in years and for some decades."

"Off the record and no repercussions to either girl?"

"I give you my word."

"I had a daughter with Amy's cousin. I first met her when she was fifteen at the Monterey Pop Festival. And as far as Charlene goes, she is writing a book on the Sioux, she respects my culture, my beliefs. She has a lot of respect for the Sioux."

Trower looked at me closely, shook his head yes, and said ok. I didn't lie to him, just didn't tell him that Charlene is my prison girlfriend.

"Keep out of trouble in here and I will see you in a couple weeks or so. You need anything?" "Just make sure I get my mail sent over and if family asks where I am, tell them here. My sister has been through enough with losing one brother in San Quentin."

Trower promised me that he would take care of everything. I was able to milk two more days in the infirmary before being taken to a pod. Before I was taken to this pod it was a visit and chat with the Warden.

He reminded me of Sydney Poitier's character in the movie *In the heat of the Night.* A real serious dude.

"Strongbow, I don't like what I am reading in this report that was sent over from San Quentin. I don't like the look of you either. As fast as I am able, you will be shipped back to San Quentin where you belong."

I looked at him and smiled; this seemed to have pissed him off.

"What are you smiling at, you think this is funny?"

"I think it's funny that Trower and the Warden in San Quentin thanked me for saving two female prison officials lives, and yet you are my busting balls for what? Trust me, I want back in San Quentin as quick as I can where I am treated with respect."

"Respect because you are a Shock Collar, a gang leader in there? Respect because you killed two inmates? Your life will be nothing but a revolving door in the penal system, Strongbow. You will never have my respect."

This time I laughed. I swear I could see his face turn beet red as he yelled at the guard in the room to throw me in the hole for five days. No sense in even arguing with this bastard; I looked at the guard who was standing beside me and asked if the Warden's breath was always this bad.

He closed his eyes like fuck, did you just say that? Yeah, I did, and it cost me another five days. Ten days to get back into fighting shape. Two hundred and forty hours later, I was released from the hole.

I felt good, strong, fast and ready to see who wants to get stupid in here with me.

I was taken to a pod where the cons were already sentenced and waiting to get sent out to pens across the states. I could tell as soon as I entered the pod, everything that I learned in San Quentin, I brought with me.

I eyed every person; I knew who was the king of the pod which was a huge black dude and who his soldiers were. I could tell who was solid and who was going to have a really hard time in prison.

So, knowing I don't have a crew in here, and I am on borrowed time, I decided to stay nice and mellow.

Plus, you are only allowed one hour of yard time a day and locked up the majority of the time, I have fuck all to prove in here.

That is the plan, but you know me staying out of

trouble and keeping a low profile never works out that way. The first day was pretty uneventful. Maybe I was wrong.

The next morning as I was washing myself in the wash basin, I noticed a couple of blacks staring at my SS Wolf tattoo.

Now you are only granted one hour of yard time, so I did what I normally do in the hole. Tons of pushups, burpees, lots of abs, and shadow boxing.

I was breaking a good sweat when four of the Blacks including the one that was the size of a house head my way. I had no crew and no shiv. This was not good.

"You the same Strongbow in San Quentin, right?"

"Yep, I know who the fuck I am. Who are you and why do you want to know?"

"My name is Aadil and I am from the Muslim brotherhood."

I didn't even give Aadil a chance to finish what he was about to say. I know he wants revenge for me killing the Muslim in the yard.

I kicked him right in the nuts with my left leg and then threw and overhand right. He was out cold.

I managed to get a quick elbow into one other guy as I know I had to get at the monster right away. He was my biggest threat.

The monster was faster than I thought as he came charging at me. I didn't have time to land a punch, kick, knee, or elbow.

I was like a tackling dummy as he sent me flying. I hit the ground hard, and by the time I refocused, he landed on top of me. He was starting to throw bombs, fuck he had to weigh over three hundred pounds, and we are talking a sold three hundred pounds of muscle.

The only thing I could do was to try and get him in close so he couldn't land any more punches as I felt myself getting weaker.

Desperate times call for desperate measures; I bit into his left ear as hard as I could. He screamed in agony as his went from punching me to grabbing his ear which was pouring blood.

I stood up quickly and spit out a piece of his ear

before squaring him as hard as I could, right in his nuts.

He was done; but his two buddies weren't. They yelled they were going to kill me. I said bring it and wiped the blood from my right eyebrow.

They decided to separate and come at me from both sides; the one on the left came first or at least tried to, I kicked him right in the knee, and he hit the ground, but not before I kicked him in the head.

Knowing the other one was coming fast, I spun around and caught nothing but air. I saw a twelve-gauge shot gun pointed at my head and a very angry screw telling me to hit the ground.

I smiled and did as told. And then, I was jumped on by a whole lot of angry screws throwing punches into me. Fuck, I wasn't resisting. I was handcuffed and leg shackled before being taken to the hole.

My face was a bloody mess, and I don't know who did the most damage. I asked to go to the infirmary, but no one came to hear my requests.

I was cut pretty good above my right eyebrow; I had another gash right in the middle of my head at the hairline. My nose was sore, not broken just tender, as were my ribs, but the biggest pain in the ass was I had my lip split open as it was rammed through my teeth.

A couple hours had passed before I heard someone outside my cell. They opened a slot and told me to stick my hands in between.

I did and was quickly handcuffed. I was then told to kneel and face the opposite corner. I was told any sudden movement and I would be shot in the back. Once again, I did as instructed and had my ankles shackled.

I was taken to an interrogation room when a Jail Detective and Jail official wanted to hear my side of the story.

"Pretty simple, four guys come at me I have to do what I can do defend myself."

"And did you know any of the four before the attack?" asked the Detective.

"I didn't know them at all."

"So, this was just a random attack, you did nothing to taunt them in any way?"

"I am half white and half red. I think they came at me because of that reason. You think I am going to start something being a cherry in this pod and no back up?"

The Detective agreed with what I said. The jail official had my files from San Quentin on him.

"Well Strongbow, I have two inmates in the hospital, hopefully one of them will not lose his hearing and they will be able to sew his ear back on. You are what I call an alpha male. And this show of force just cost you sixty days in the hole. I hope your ass is back in San Quentin by the time the sixty days are up."

He then told the two screws to take me to the hole. I smiled at him and asked if the nurse can look at my wounds.He assured me they would heal within sixty days, *what a goof.*

Off to the hole I went, recovery, meditation, and training time. If anything positive ever came out of my time in the army, it was learning and loving to be alone.

It just took me a cleansing with my Grandfather to realize that being alone with myself wasn't such a bad thing after all, forgot how happy it made me.

It appears that the jail official and will be happy. After eighteen days in the hole, the door opened and the screw said I would be taken back to San Quentin that morning.

This time I journey home was by paddy wagon. And guess who was heading to San Quentin with me? The Muslim with the big mouth Aadil, and this time he didn't have any muscle with him.

There would be just the two of us and I was the last one put into the wagon and as soon as he looked at me, the black man went white.

"You are coming to my turf now where I'm a Shock Collar. Do you know what that is?"

He didn't say a word, the fear in his eyes said it all.

"Basically Aadil, I am the king of the castle and I have all these white knights under me. Knights that will do whatever I ask. And what do think I am going to ask them to do for me? Come on Aadil! You're the strong silent type suddenly? Well, I will tell you what they are going to do for me. I am going to tell them to make sure you meet Allah. But I want it slowly, and just like your buddy, it will be one body part at a time, and can you guess which body part I will cut off first?"

I was having fun with mentally tormenting him as I should, fuck him.

"Fuck, Aadil. If those hundred virgins are waiting for you, guess what? They will still be virgins as the boys are going to cut your dick off."

Aadil looked away but not before I saw his eyes well up. The drive didn't take long for me, but for Aadil it must have felt it went on forever.

Normally I hate bullies, but right now I have no problems being a bully or being a villain. The whole time I stared at him and yet he wouldn't look over at all. Before we knew it, the paddy wagon had stopped.

The back door opened, and the screw said, "Welcome to San Quentin, ladies."

Fuck me, the smell and sounds told me I was

home and as idiotic as this sounds, I am glad to be back here rather than stuck in the hole in the Oakland jail.

Aadil and I were taken to the bull pen for processing. It was nice with so many cons welcoming me back.

Even a couple of the screws who are normally dicks to me nodded at me. I am sure I gained their respect for saving Charlene and making sure no harm came to Amy. If only they knew I sliced Maxwell's throat I wonder how I would be greeted back; I am sure a beating and sixty days in the hole to start with, and then a date with either the electric chair or gas chamber.

I was processed in no time at all. The booking screw said my cell stays the same.

Before I left, I looked at Aadil and said, "See you on the range unless you end up in the morgue first."

Once again, he made no eye contact, fuck him!

All through the prison I was welcomed home. As soon as I hit the fourth floor, I was greeted as some kind of war time hero. Everyone was giving me hugs including Albert and Sammy.

We headed to my cell where George called me a sexy bastard.

I asked, "Weren't you neutered already?" That comment made us all laugh.

George then handed me all my mail and there was a lot. But before I decided to go through it, I asked Albert what all has gone down since the riot.

He said the South Mexicans have a new leader named Tito as Pedro ratted out on his brothers rather than face murder charges. They were going after him for Maxwell's death. I am glad I kicked everyone out before ending his life, and the only witness has been buried for a couple weeks now. Funny at how all it took was one Mexican who started to rat and the snowball effect started. I was happy to hear that as I never trusted that bastard.

Albert also said for now the tension pre-riot has left the prison. The South and North Mexicans have called a truce and have agreed to terms with boundaries regarding dealing and other illegal activities.

The only thing sort of festering is between Helmut's crew and the Muslim Brotherhood and it has to do with some of the soldiers not liking each other from the street.

I told Albert about my run in with Aadil and several of his Muslim crew while in the Oakland jail.

Albert asked what we should do, "Once he gets into the main range, he could become a problem."

I agreed, "We should kill him before he leaves West block."

That was the easy part, the hard part is that neither one of us have a reason to be in West Block. So, we would need someone solid to do our dastardly deed. A lifer would be perfect as he has nothing to lose.

Albert was going to contact his one screw and get a list of the cons currently in West Block for us to go over.

As much as I would like to get Helmut and his crew involved, I want this as quiet as can be.

It was time to go through all my mail. Three weeks' worth. The one that caught my eye was from Queens New York.

I recognized the handwriting. It was from Natasha Hotz; fuck, that last name still irritates me.

She thanked me for the birthday gift for Katrina and for keeping Amy safe. She went on to say that it shows that good people are put into bad spots, and bad situations for a reason.

Two things come to mind after reading this. Thank God for Rachel as I had no clue that March 17th had come and gone, and I also must find out what Rachel got her before I respond. And secondly, I am currently plotting and planning on killing someone so that still makes me a bad person in a bad situation, but I am working on it.

I always check the return addresses on my letters as a way to keep my brain sharp. I received a letter with no return address. This intrigued me to say the least.

It started off saying, *My mighty Sioux Warrior, I know your mail is censored, but I wanted to thank you personally for saving my life.*

I knew it was from Charlene even thought it was never officially signed. I could also see tear stains on the paper.

She promised in time she would be in more contact, but right now she couldn't think about this place or what happened. She ended it by saying that my Grandfather and my Grandfather Red Cloud would be proud of me. Not sure if my Grandfather would be proud of me, Crazy Horse certainly would be.

At lunch I was shown a lot of respect from my fellow cons including Helmut who came over and shook my hand as he welcomed me back.

Helmut asked where I got shipped to and I said Oakland jail. He asked if the fresh scar above my eye was the result of a dance in Oakland.

I said yes and told him the whole story. For the most part he laughed. I picked up on Black Paul, who was a couple of tables away, was also listening to me telling my story. I didn't pay any more attention to it until we were in the yard. I was working on the heavy bag when Black Paul came over and asked if he could have a word with me, sure was my answer.

"Mitch, I overheard your story about what happened in Oakland and I need a huge favor from you, man."

"Can't guarantee shit, but I will listen, go ahead."

"That cat you had a run in with, Aadil well his real name is Andre Dawes."

"Same last name as you, cousin?"

"He is my brother. Look Mitch, he is all fucked up, these Muslim bastards have brain washed him. I also know that people who piss you off in here end up on the wrong side of pain. He is my only family."

"Paul, he came at me with three other guys. He is lucky he was in Oakland lock up and not here as I would have killed him with members of his crew."

"That is what I am nervous of, that he is now here, not in Oakland lockup."

"And you should be nervous. I wasn't

looking for any trouble in Oakland and he came at me. Paul, I am a Shock Collar. My crew and Helmut's crew will be watching for retaliation. If I don't go after your brother, I will be seen as weak."

"Come on, Strongbow! No one will ever see you as weak in here. You are a legend. I helped you get out of town when the cops were after you and I mean you were a major league heat score. I didn't shy away, I helped you out like a brother."

"You were paid well, man."

"You're right, I was. Let me pay you to keep my brother safe, how much?"

"What is your brother's life worth to you?"

"I don't have the kind of money that I know you will want, but I have all kinds of cars on the outside. You're out in a less than a year, Strongbow. I will give you a set of wheels in exchange for my brother's life."

"You definitely have my attention. What kind of wheels? I don't want something hot that will have my ass thrown back in here the first time Jon Q Law pulls me over."

"Fair enough, I have an El Dorado that you would look sharp in."

"I want something fast and small. San Francisco streets are challenging enough for a V.W. never mind an El Dorado."

"I got you on that one, Strongbow; you get a chance to see the movie Bullet since you have been home?"

Paul could tell by my smile that I had seen the movie.

"I will give you a '68 GT Mustang, stick and all. It hauls ass, but you have to give me your word that no harm will come to my brother by you or any of your crew."

"I will give you my word that no harm will come to your brother from me or my crew. But he can't be flexing his muscles or yapping off to me or anyone else, or you will be held responsible, understood?"

Paul stuck out his hand and said deal. I shook his

hand. We agreed that Donnie Terek would pick up the Mustang from Paul's girlfriend. She would sign the ownership over to Donnie and when I get out, Donnie would just sign ownership over to me.

Albert came over and asked what deal I just made with Paul, I told him, and he asked if I changed my name to Strongbowlini. Then he asked if I was working for the Battaglia family as I just made an excellent extortion deal. I thought so myself, at least now I can tell Rachel she can keep my other car.

Before dinner, I went up to the infirmary to see Amy. As I walked in, she didn't notice me, I watched as she did her stuff. She stopped, turned around, smiled from ear to ear before coming over and hugging me.

She hugged me really tight while whispering *thank you* over and over. The screw didn't step in which surprised me. When Amy broke away, her eyes were filled with tears and she apologized for being so emotional.

I reminded her that she once saved my life, and at

one point I thought we were going to be family.

This made her laugh as she was now wiping away the tears.

"That would have been one way of putting my Aunt in a box. You are a good man Mitchell Strongbow. Don't ever forget that."

"You're a good person as well Amy, I knew that from the first time I met you."

Amy blushed, thanked me, and said she should get back to work. As she turned around the side view of her face was identical to Natasha, same eye shape, cheek bones, and lips.

I think I will be going in for early lock up and tossing one off. Fuck, I never thought I would see little Amy this way!

*

Over the next couple days things were back to normal for me. Rachel visited me as well as Joseph and Donnie who picked up my new car. Rachel bought Katrina a bicycle from me for her birthday. I asked if she also sent a pack of baseball cards to put in the spokes so it could sound like her Daddy's Harley.

For the first time in a longtime I was content. I had served over half of my sentence and really just wanted to keep a low profile and stay away from all the prison drama. I know I shouldn't say it, but I can picture myself walking out the front gates of this place soon.

But sometimes drama finds you even if you aren't looking for it.

One night after dinner, George and I were playing chess. I was enjoying a tea even if the old bastard was beating me. I felt like I pulled a muscle in my back. I had a decent workout that afternoon but felt nothing out of the ordinary.

I found the back pain was getting worse and the pain had also spread into my balls. I couldn't get comfortable, so I tried to stretch out, but nothing.

I started to sweat and before I knew it, I was throwing up. George went and found a screw to tell him something wasn't right with me.

The screw looked at me and said I looked rough. He told me to stay there and he would call the infirmary.

Trust me, I was going nowhere. It felt like my balls were going to explode. I noticed my breathing was becoming very shallow. As the pain was getting worse all I could think of was that someone poisoned me and that I was dying.

Amy and a couple orderlies showed up as a crowd of fellow cons showed concern. Amy asked where I was sore. I explained everything as best as I could. Fuck, I have been shot and stabbed before and this pain was right up there.

Amy told the one screw to call an ambulance as she drove a syringe of morphine into my thigh. Right away I felt the rush of the painkiller taking effect. I smiled at Amy and said I was with the wrong Jew all along.

I sort of remember her blushing before closing my eyes. They managed to get me on a stretcher as Amy hooked up an I.V.

The rest was a dream like sequence, the only thing that kept it real was that I felt every single bump in the back of the ambulance on the way to the hospital.

Once there I had to repeat to the E.R. doctor my symptoms. Me being buzzed out said they must have poisoned me.

The doctor asked, "Who?" Charlie of course, was my answer.

He just stared at me in disbelief and asked, "Charlie who?"

"The Vietcong, Charlie has been trying to kill me for years."

Doc said he had no time for this and sent me off to get X-rays done.

And with being a guest of the state of California, there was no waiting time, or line for me. Pics were taken right away, then I was taken to a room, handcuffed to the bed with a cop stationed outside my door. I drifted off into a state of semi-consciousness almost like at the Inipi.

I drifted back to the Monterey Pop Festival but with a twist. I was jerking off in the tent again and the zipper came undone, it was not Muriel who poked her head in but Amy; a topless Amy who came inside and pushed me onto my back and continued to jerk me off until I shot all over her exposed breasts. She then snuggled up beside me and told me to go to sleep and everything would be good. I did as I was told and then was awoken when the Doctor came in the room with a butt ugly nurse.

"Mr. Strongbow, you have a monster kidney stone, four it total but the big one I would say is over two centimeters. It is preventing the rest of the stones from passing."

"So, what does that mean?"

"You will need surgery. We are going to keep you over night and hopefully you will have surgery in the morning."

The nurse then put a fresh I.V. bag on and said that I was not allowed to eat. Trust me, the last thing I wanted was food. I only wanted more painkillers flowing through my body.

As soon as the Doctor and Nurse left, I passed out and continued my lucid dreaming. All of them were sexual. Right back to the first time Kerry Dubrowski let me play with her breasts to the first time I lost my cherry to Lucy Thom, the Vigoda sisters, and of course, Natasha and I doing anal the first time.

But each time Amy would be somehow incorporated into the sexual session. And each time she would have this amazing glow to her.

The most realistic session was I was back working on the Straddleport cranes. Amy was in the cab with me. I was overlooking the Bay as she was giving me the best blowjob I have ever received in my life and I have had at least a hundred chicks suck my cock. She was able to deep throat me and stroke my cock without missing a beat; her timing was that of a rock drummer.

It didn't take very long before I felt myself ready to explode and Amy didn't disappoint me as she swallowed every ounce of cum.

She kissed me on top of the head before leaving the cab. The cab door slammed as if the wind grabbed a hold of it, so loud it woke me from my delusional, erotic dream and when I did, I saw a shadow leave the bathroom and then leave the room.

I struggled to stay awake and make sense of what

just happened.

Was it real? I was way too weak to even call for the nurse. I remember touching around the head of my cock and it was gooey, then I passed out again.

*

I woke up the next morning delirious not knowing where the hell I was, fuck, I have been in so many hospitals over my lifetime I had to figure out why I was in, and even what city, state or country.

Yeah, the morphine was still doing a number on my brain. I pushed the call button and within a couple minutes a nurse came in. By then I remembered why I was there and asked if I am still going in for surgery.

She said yes in about an hours' time a porter will be taking me to the operating room. I thanked her and asked if I had any visitors last night. The nurse looked confused and told me that only hospital staff were allowed in my room.

It had to have been a wet dream then, the morphine does funky stuff to the brain, totally lucid.

Eventually a male Asian porter came up to take me to surgery. He kind of fucked me up as I still don't trust any males that are Asian, especially while on such a hard-core drug.

Not sure how many surgeries I have had in such short yet troubled lifetime. But the operating room always feels cold, morgue cold.

The anesthesiologist asked me if I have ever had surgery before. I smile and say about a dozen times. I feel my vein with the I.V. in it getting cold. I look up and see the anesthesiologist injecting something into my tube it hits me hard as I feel myself go under.

I glance to the corner of the room and see Katrina looking at me and smiling. Makes me feel good. Really good as the anesthesiologist then puts that black balloon thing over my mouth.

I can taste onions and the balloon mask the rubber smell coming from it is nauseating.

Then you are out cold and at the mercy of those in the operating room, whether you like it or not.

I eventually wake up and as per normal when having surgeries, throw up and yes, I was still handcuffed to the bed.

The nurse came over and gave me a syringe of Gravol right into my thigh.

I asked her how the surgery went. She grabbed the chart and said looks good and that I have a stent up me for the next ten days.

I know I stuttered when I asked what a stent is and up where exactly. Once she told me it's up my urethra and the doctor will take it out while I am awake, I had a head rush of fear. I asked for another shot of Gravol in the other thigh.

I was taken to a private room for the night and then would be shipped back to San Quentin in the morning.

The nurse said I had to pound back the water as I still had little stone fragments inside my kidneys, which is really dangerous as my kidneys are under duress and I have to get out all the fragments. The Doc also wanted to make sure I don't have any excessive bleeding.

So, like a good patient I start to pound back the fluids and my first piss felt like I had razor blades coming out of my pee hole. Fuck it hurt and yes there was a fair amount of blood.

You know you want to stop drinking as each piss killed, but I want my kidneys working normal and my poor cock has been through enough grief today. Fuck, maybe my ESP knew how much pain would be coming and granted me that wet dream last night. Fuck, it was so real.

Several times I would wake up in the middle of night to piss. Of course, I still hand the one arm handcuffed to the bed. You know how hard it is to piss into a jug with only one arm? The second time I knocked the jug all over myself after pissing into it. Then I did something I haven't done in a long time. I lay back in bed and closed my eyes. I was choked up and I am not sure why. I have been more beaten up then this. I keep thinking everyone was proud of me for my actions in the riot and the piss jug becomes my failure.

I pushed the button for the nurse to come in once I half-ass composed myself.

This chick was a royal fucking cunt, right off the bat she said, "What Strongbow?"

"The jug spilled, and I am covered in piss and blood."

"And what would you like me to do about it?"

"I would like to shower and get clean clothes and clean sheets."

She went into the washroom and came out and threw me a washcloth.

"You're a Strongbow; you know how to clean up bloody messes."

Then it hit me like a lightning bolt, I know exactly where her attitude was coming from.

"I am not Jake and I really liked Liz O'Malley, a lot."

"Funny as we are all convinced Jake killed Liz. I heard you are in prison for killing your girlfriend. No, you're not Jake but you are another Strongbow with another dead girlfriend. Great family trait!"

Handcuffed or not I will kill this bitch. I pulled at my handcuff and all it did was rip the shit out of my wrist.

The nurse called me a fucking loser and then left the room laughing as I sat there in piss and blood. If anything, her face and actions are now burned into my brain. *She will pay for this!*

That rage stayed with me for the rest of the night and after every piss I poured the jug all over the floor. I never slept; the vengeance factor fueled me.

*

The next morning the surgeon and a nurse came into my room. They asked what happened and I said I spilled the jug by accident; I also said the nurse on nights was amazing and I would really like to get her name or even address as I would like to send her some flowers because was so helpful to me.

He half smiled and said, "The gesture is nice Mr. Strongbow, but she gets paid very well. And you have been able to pee I see. So, I am going to recommend you be released back to the federal prison system. Continue drinking water the more the merrier. What prison are you at?"

"San Quentin."

"I have full confidence in the medical staff at San Quentin in also taking your stent out. Any complications and they can call us. Good luck."

"Thanks Doc, you think I can at least get showered up and put on clean clothes before I leave?"

"I will see what I can do. I will also give u a report of the surgery for the doctor at San Quentin for you to take with you."

Twenty minutes later, two cops came in and said I could have a shower, but I would be handcuffed in the front and have my ankles shackled.

I said that was cool. Even though I was cuffed and shackled it was still nice to have a shower all to myself. I was still horny, but no way would I jerk off with this stent up me, kind of freaked me out to be honest.

I was giving a clean set of hospital clothes, a decent breakfast and then the two cop's next assignment was to take me back to San Quentin. They were decent with me, so I did everything they asked without back talk or giving them grief.

As soon as I was brought inside San Quentin I had to go and see the doctor. I never liked the doctor here, he reminded me of the kind of doctor they would have at a German POW camp.

Our nickname for him was Doctor Sausage Fingers, I also believe he liked nothing better than to check out prisoners prostrates, fuck, he creeps me out.

I handed him the surgeon's report, he went over it and of course talked out loud and then looked at my crotch region and asked how it felt.

"It's kind of sore, can I get something for pain?"

"Hmm, maybe you should drop your scrubs so I can have a look?"

"Actually, not that sore"

"Hmm, I see. Well, if it gets worse come and see us. I see the surgeon would like the stent taken out in ten days."

He actually hand counted what the date would be in ten days from now, fuck, makes me wonder how many pain killers he has taken today.

"Come back on April 1st and I will take the stent out for you."

Fuck, April Fool's Day, how goddamn ironic is that?

I couldn't get out of there fast enough. I was hurting but I know someone in my crew would have just as good if not better painkillers then Doctor Sausage Fingers and I could get them without being sexually harassed.

The first thing I did when I got back to my cell was trade hospital scrubs for my jeans and t-shirt. Then I tracked down Albert who was able to get some codeine for me.

After a couple days of being buzzed, the pain went away with each piss. Before I knew it, nine days had passed since the surgery, but no way did I want Dr Sausage Fingers going near my dick. So, after dinner I went to the infirmary and asked if Amy would take my stent out. She laughed after I told her why.

She smiled and said ok but it must be on record that part of the stent was poking out of my pee hole. I agreed even if the thought totally grossed me out.

Amy gave me a valium to relax me, then ten minutes later she told me to jump up on the table and to take my pants down and cover myself with a towel.

As soon as I lay down, the dream I had in the hospital came back to me. I was horny but terrified as she pulled out a device to grab the eye of the stent.

"Amy, is there not like a magnet or anything that will pull the stent out?"

"You ever go fishing as a boy with your Dad?"

"Absolutely, why do you ask?"

"Because I am going fishing for the stent eye. You just sit back and relax."

Amy then removed the towel and saw my very terrified cock.

"Wow you used this, or should I say disappointed Tasha with this?" laughed Amy

I could feel myself going beet red.

"No, I have never had any complaints, I am just scared."

"I am just joking, relax, you guys and your manhood. I've seen you hard before, very impressive, Mitchell."

My head was now spinning between what Amy said and digging for the stent.

As soon as I was going to ask when she saw me hard, she said found it.

"Mitchell, I need you take some deep breaths, don't fight it, just try and relax."

I remember during one firefight I had a piece of shrapnel go into my thigh. The medic had to take it out and it didn't hurt one tenth of what this currently feels like.

I felt every single millimeter of this stent being pulled out my pee hole.

No more erotic thoughts, no more of even

wondering how and when Amy saw me hard. I started to growl and looked at a spot on the ceiling to focus on.

Amy said, "Mitch, we are almost there. I need you to take a deep breath and slowly release your breath."

I didn't answer her, I just nodded my head yes and did as instructed. The ceiling didn't help me focus, but looking at Amy's eyes did, I was drawn to them, they seduced and hypnotized me. They lit right up and when she said it was fully out, I didn't even feel the final pull. I smiled at her, enough to make her blush and ask what I was looking at.

"You're fucking beautiful, Amy."

Amy squinted her eyes and said she must have given me too much valium.

As I went to talk again the screw came over and asked if everything was all right. She said all was good as she told me to get dressed and to start drinking water; as soon as I pee, I can go back to my cell and take it easy.

I sipped the water and stared at Amy. Yes, the valium gave me a nice buzz, but I feel really close to her.

I eventually peed. It fucking killed and there was blood. I personally think I should spend the night in the infirmary, but Amy told me I need to go to my cell and just relax.

"I will head back once you tell me about you seeing me hard."

Amy bit her lip and asked the screw to make sure I get safely back to my cell. As curious as I was, I knew not to push the envelope, she has piqued more than my curiosity.

I took some codeine that night to help with the pain. If there is one thing that is bad about prison is that you are always battling demons. Mostly because you have so much free time on your hands.

I am not sure if it is the buzz from the painkillers or not, but I find myself falling for Amy.

I know she is married; I know Natasha is her first cousin, but I see the way she looks at me and I have to believe fate has done its part to bring us close, even in this hell hole.

She was cock teasing me tonight. You don't tell a guy in prison you've seen him hard, that itself is another mind trip. When?

*

The next morning, I had a spring in my step even if I was moving slower than normal. All I could think about was Amy. If my cock wasn't so sore last night, I would have jerked off ten times over. I have decided I want to spend more time with her.

I want to tell her I want us to be lovers in here, and when I am finally released. I am sure she too has desires with her husband away at the Naval Academy.

I will leave my job in the kitchen and work in the infirmary. I have more medical knowledge then the current cons working in there, and I will make sure one of them decides he no longer wants to work there.

I didn't let anyone in my crew know my

intentions. If Amy were to totally freak out, the last thing, I want is to lose respect with my men.

So, after dinner I decided I was hurting a little too much since the stent was removed and I should get it checked out. I walked there with butterflies in my gut and a bulge in my pants. Felt like a teen all over again.

I stood outside the infirmary door before going in and said last chance to back away and not lose face, Mitch. Fuck that, when was the last time a Strongbow backed down from anything in life? That's right, never.

I turned the door handle and an obese Asian nurse, who looked like Godzilla, was inside. I was stunned, maybe today was Amy's day off.

"Amy off today?" I asked her.

"Amy no longer works here," she said with no emotion at all.

"What do you mean? Where did she go?"

"Damned if I know. You need something?"

My heart sank into my gut. That dreadful feeling,

I know all too well is back with a vengeance. Abandonment at its finest. I turned and walked away. I reached the stairwell and wasn't sure where to go or what to do next. My head was spinning, I thought I was going to hurl.

One screw walked up and asked if I was all right or if I needed a nurse. Yeah, I did. I needed a nurse named Amy.

Albert will know where she went. I will get him to ask his screw on the take. Albert said he would ask and let me know what was up with Amy.

That night it took three codeine pills for me to pass out, it wasn't from the pain in my cock, but the pain in my heart.

At the breakfast table Albert told me he heard back from his screw on the take. It stopped me from eating and I lost my appetite right away.

Amy's husband graduated from the Naval Academy as a pilot, and now Amy has also joined the Navy Academy to serve as a nurse once she has graduated officer's college.

No Amy, no Charlene, looks like I will be

building up my arms by weights, steroids, and lots of jerking off.

My cock healed completely. I hope I never have to go through that pain again. I never received anything from Amy, which was kind of disappointing, but a couple weeks later I had a visitor.

It was Charlene Borden, she had on a pair of tight jeans that really should off her curves, a black sweater that showed those beautiful breasts of hers poking through, and wearing make up to accentuate her gorgeous flowing red hair.

She looked like a Goddess to say the least. I popped a hard-on right away. The screws weren't impressed that she, an employee of the California Corrections Department, was there to see me, a convict.

She said she wanted to thank me in person for saving her from those animals, and for also risking my life as she knows firsthand how ruthless San Quentin prisoners can be to each other.

I explained as best as I could why I did what I did.

"I really like you and not just because you were the only female in here who would give me hand-jobs. I see the good in you. I am a Strongbow, and my Dad raised all of us with values even if we walked on the dark side of life. You are right, they were animals and if I had a rifle, I would have shot every single one of them. I would do to them what I did to a fucking Texan that I walked in on raping my girlfriend; I would castrate every single one of them and then watch them bleed out. I have more respect for someone who kills for hire then a rapist."

Charlene teared up and asked if it was my girlfriend that died of the overdose.

"Yes, it was, she was never really the same after that and it has eaten at me ever since the rape took place. Lots of guilt. But I mean it, I feel like I have known you a longtime now."

"Mitch please don't let it eat at you. I know you never would have let it happen in the first place with her and you stopped those animals. I believe they would have killed me just like they did with officer Maxwell. And I kept my promise and didn't say I know who attacked me to keep you alive in here. Have you ever heard the Tale of the Kinsman?"

I shook my head no.

She explained that everyone has soul mates; people we have known in life over and over.

"We can have multiple soul mates; people you feel an instant connection with and like you've known them before. Soul mates get a good rap ...everyone wants to find their soul mate but there is something more powerful than that. Kinsman is the most amazing tale! When we were created, we were whole and fulfilled and happy, but we were a very selfish being. We were only out for ourselves and we didn't know the real power of love. So, the Gods decided to do something about it because they knew we needed to appreciate love as much as they did. They decided to split us in two, sending us off into our next life only *half* of a whole. The punishment for our selfishness was to search the world for our other half; alone and roaming life after life searching for the other part of ourselves that would make us whole again. We never feel complete until we find that our half of our soul.

And sadly, many people never find it. Doomed to live life after life as only a half shell of themselves. That is why so many people are unhappy. They have never found their Kinsman. But when you *do* find your Kinsman your life instantly changes. You know your soul a mile away. You are drawn to it, you hunt it, it calls to you and yours calls to it. And when you meet you are never the same. Your heart no longer hurts, you no longer feel lost, or sad, or unfulfilled. You are suddenly whole with that person and you both know you have found home. And after that you travel each life as one, as a whole."

I smiled at her and said, "I believe this, yeah, it makes sense."

I asked how long she's had a fascination with the Sioux for.

"All my life, Mitchell. My family went to Mount Rushmore when I was a child. Then we went to see where the Battle of Little Bighorn had taken place. I felt I knew the land. I had been here before. There was such a strong vibe, Mitch. Please don't think I am crazy."

"I don't think you are crazy at all. The Sioux are one of the most spiritual people to walk the earth. The first time I saw you, I felt like I've met you before, but not sure where. I know you are three years older than me. I know it is not from my family or the club. Where did you grow up?"

"I grew up in Denver, Colorado. Moved here for this job two years ago after a shitty marriage ended."

"I don't recall ever being in Denver."

We continued talking and Charlene would flirt with me by looking down at my cock and smiling or biting a nail.

Perhaps the screws had seen enough of her smiling, laughing, and cock teasing me as they told Charlene her time was up for her visit with me. Before she left, she asked if she could visit me on a regular basis. I said I would really like that, but what about her job here; pretty sure the warden wouldn't like that.

"I won't be coming back here to work, not after what I have been through. I am going to take some time off before deciding my future work plans."

And then I said something out of character, perhaps it was a sign of weakness on my part being locked up and feeling alone especially with no female in my life.

"Don't move back to Denver, I want you here. I am out in eight months' time."

Charlene blushed and sported an ear to ear smile and said she wouldn't move away on me.

*

Once a week Charlene would drop by, tease the fuck out of me, and send me photos with her wearing scantily clad clothing, no face showing, and always a spicy story. She promised when I get released, we will reenact every single one.

All in all, life was getting better in San Quentin. No one would fuck with me. I certainly earned the respect of every Shock Collar and the cons either under them, or not even in gangs, knew I killed Mutt and Cruz and basically got away with a violent double murder. They didn't want to tempt fate and see if I could also get away with murdering them.

The prison, for the most part, was running smoothly, there was enough dope to keep everyone happy and to make each gang in their money. We all knew not to get greedy and cause another riot.

Was up to two hundred and sixty-five pounds. Been juicing and steadily pumping iron with Albert and Frankie. My size and muscle would be put to the test, really soon.

I was paid a visit by my cousin Jerry, and Donnie Terek later in the week. They said there is a full patch from the Bakersfield chapter of the Hell Hounds was just sentenced to a life term at San Quentin and could I look out for him and let him in my crew.

I told them both I would, but he also must realize that this is my crew, and not his. The way both guys looked at each other I knew there was going to be trouble with this guy.

"Mitch, he is a bravado type of guy. He is loud, but he will back up whatever he says, he is solid. He took a murder rap for an executive."

I thought to myself what the fuck does *bravado* mean to them? To me it means a loudmouth dickhead whose ass I will have to back every time he shoots his mouth off.

"What is his name and how old?"

"His name is Carlos Khan, twenty-two years old, calls himself King Khan."

"Great a yappy fucking punk, and he gives himself his own nickname, who the fuck does that? Has he done time before? San Quentin is a man's world, not a boy's club where we sit around the campfire and sing songs. Khan, ain't that some Muslim kind of fucking name?"

"Just juvie time, and fuck Mitch, you are only twenty-five and this is your first time in a federal penitentiary. He is adopted, just give him a chance. Trust me, you will want him in your corner when shit goes south."

"Four years in the army taught me how to survive. That included creeping and crawling in the jungle, Charlie never saw me coming. Chaos Carlos will want all to hear him coming, fuck he would let out a Tarzan call, beat his chest, and then wonder why he got shot, or nabbed by the screws in here."

"Then teach him how to survive, Mitch. Think of him as one of your cherries in Nam," said a pissed off Jerry.

"You know in Nam those who didn't listen to me came home in a flag draped casket. But I will try my best, Jerry; I promise you that. As long as he listens, because if he doesn't, I will smack him back in line. I better not have repercussions come back at me from the club."

"Do what you have to do, just keep him safe and show him the ropes. He has earned the respect of Von Kruder. I personally told Von Kruder that I would talk to you and ask for your help. Don't let me down, Mitch."

As soon as they left, I headed straight for Albert and told him what I was asked to do. Albert smiled and shook his head, he strongly suggested that I talk to Helmut and let him know what was going on. This way I am also showing Helmut respect and I will tell him that I will try and best to keep Khan in line.

He went with me seeing as how he was my second in command.

We found Helmut playing chess with one of his guys. I told Helmut to come for a walk. Albert agreed to finish the game for him. Helmut said I looked serious and wanted to know what's up.

I told him what I was asked to do. Helmut looked at me and asked what happens if this guy gets out of line and goes after one of his men. I said come and get me and I will tune Khan.

"Mitch, I am telling you right now, if he starts with me, I will not hesitate to end his life. Things are good between us, I wanna keep them that way but I have my limits and if some mouthy or bragging Hell Hound flexes his muscles or gets out of line, I will handle it the Thunder way."

"You have every right to defend yourself, that goes without saying. I am not a patch, you know that. Personally, if this fuck starts to throw his weight around the only thing I ask, is that if you kill him, have it go back to the Muslims or Mexicans."

Helmut nodded his head and exhaled out his

nostrils. Why couldn't the fucking asshole come here after December fifth when I will be a free man, and not involved with prison politics or babysitting?

Albert talked to his one screw on the take who said Khan will be coming straight from the hole to here after he has served fifteen days. Yep, he was thrown in the hole for fighting. Albert also said the guy is young; he may look up to me and straighten out. I certainly hope for his sake he does; I am not going to war over a loudmouth.

13

July 4: Normally, families would gather around and watch a firework display after a day spent picnicking with the family.

There were no picnics in San Quentin, but fireworks were coming to our block via King Khan. Fresh from the hole.

We just finished breakfast and me and my crew were playing backgammon. A stranger was headed our way with two screws.

I went inside my cell to make a tea when I heard an unknown voice say, "Hey old man, where is Strongbow at?"

"Who are you calling an old man, punk?" mouthed back George.

"I am calling you an old man because you are fucking ancient. Now tell me where Strongbow is already, before you get any older and die on me."

"Come here you fucking punk and I will show you who is going to die."

I came racing out of my cell, looked at the new con, and said,

"I am Mitch Strongbow. Who the fuck are you to be mouthing off my celly?"

I got right in his face ready to drop him.

"Fucking relax, Strongbow. I am Carlos Khan from the Bakersfield Hell Hounds. I was told that you would be expecting me."

Time to nip this in the bud right off the bat. I grabbed him by the throat and threw him into the wall and cocked my other fist back.

"I know exactly who you are and now you will know who I am and what my rules are for survival in here. I will only say this once, so you better listen closely. This is a federal penitentiary where no one likes anyone loud. You are loud, and you are a heat score. Other cons will turn on you. Last week, they pulled this one kid who looked and acted just like you out of a ventilation chute, he was stabbed more than two hundred times, and no one batted an eye. Secondly, I am a Shock Collar, I am like your chapter president in here, you do as I say, full patch or not. That old man has killed ten times more people then you will kill your whole lifetime. He has taught me the ways to survive in here. You treat him with respect. Third, times are peaceful, lots of money to be made, and yes, there are Thunder members in here that I do business with and I respect. Not asking you to suck their cock, but I am telling you not to stick your nose in their business."

By now Albert, Frankie and the rest of my crew made a circle behind us.

"Each and every guy standing behind me is solid, they have proven themselves to me, you wanna be part of my crew, you earn mine and their respect. If you chose not to and want to go on your own, no hard feelings, but I am willing to bet the Muslims in here will be skull and ass fucking you within a week. They will come to me and ask what you mean to me. I will say fuck all. Now, what's it going to be Khan, you going to abide by my rules?"

He had a stupid smirk, and like a three-year-old said *fine*.

"Fine what? I want my crew to hear your response."

"I heard your rules man, I ain't fucking stupid."

I drove my fist right into his gut. I felt the wind leave his lungs as he hit the ground in pain.

"I think you are fucking stupid the way you just talked back to me. Again, what are my rules?"

Khan looked at all my men, all who were solid to me and would kill the stupid fuck without blinking an eye.

"You are the boss, what you say goes, keep a low profile and be respectful to those in our group."

"And what else?"

"Don't start anything with anyone else in here."

"And who am I thinking of specifically?"

"Guys in the Thunder."

I smiled at him and stuck out my hand to help him up off the ground.

"I will knock you down, but I will also help you back up. That is just who I am."

I then asked what cell he was assigned to; he said 430, *perfect* I thought. His celly would be a member of my crew named Pete Baldwin.

Pete is serving a life sentence for killing a politician's jerk off kid who would brag that he would never be drafted. Pete's younger brother came home from Nam in a body bag. Pete has always opposed the war and since he fought in world war two, he had a valid point. He said the Nazi's and Japanese deserve to die; he or his younger brother had no qualms with the foreigners.

Pete is early fifties, but solid as they come. He takes no shit from anyone and knows the way to survive in here.

I asked Pete to keep an eye on him and to try and teach him the ways to make sure he doesn't piss everyone off in here.

Pete said that was not a problem. He also asked what happens if he gets mouthy with him, being a full patch and all.

"Fucking drop him and then come see me," was my answer. "Just don't kill him."

We all ate lunch together. I made sure that Khan ate at my table. As soon as he saw Helmut, he gave him the stare down which did not go over well at all. Helmut headed to our table with a couple of his guys. Not once did he look at me, he was totally fixated with Khan.

"You got a problem, bitch?" asked Helmut.

Khan went to stand up, but I knew no good would become of this, so I grabbed him by the collar of his shirt and told him to sit the fuck back down.

Helmut looked at Khan, laughed at him, and then blew him a kiss which seemed to infuriate him even more. Khan broke free of my grip and lunged at Helmut. Let the free for all begin. Fists were flying and the riot alarm went off.

And with my history with the Thunder, I take no

chances and throw punches to hurt and maim.

I didn't stop throwing them until I heard a shot gun blast go off. All of us stopped except Khan. That was until a screw whacked him full force on the side of his face and he dropped to the ground unconscious.

We were all taken to the hole except Khan, who was taken to the infirmary.

*

After about an hour or so, Detective Trower came in and asked me what the hell happened.

"I don't know what happened, fists started flying and I just tried to protect myself."

"Strongbow, you are such a bullshitter. Fuck man, I thought you were a solid guy. Why are you insulting both of our intelligence? You're a Shock Collar as is Helmut; no one attacks unless the orders come from you guys. I am going to ask you again, what happened?"

"I don't know what happened."

"Fine. I am done wasting my time. You will

be spending the next thirty days in here trying to recall what happened. If you finally figure it out, let me know. Then again, I don't expect you to tell me. Too bad as by the time you get out of here, I am sure Carlos Khan will be running your crew with him being a full patch and all."

I may have smiled at Trower, but my mood was anything but cheerful. I wanna kill Khan myself now. Fuck Jerry and Von Kruder, this Hell Hound versus Thunder war should in no terms affect me. I am a civilian and yet I find myself doing thirty days in the hole for it.

And I know it won't end once I get out. I think I am going to put the next thirty days to good use and plot and plan how to murder Chaos Carlos Khan, so it doesn't come back to bite me in the ass.

After several days of intense exercise and thinking of the perfect scenario for the end of Khan's life, I had several thoughts, devious each and every one.

I will buy some of the purest heroin in the place and he will die of a drug overdose. The heroin will be a peace gesture between him and me.

I will watch him struggle to take his last few breaths and then I will make sure I am seen by not only my fellow cons but more importantly prison staff.

Second idea is if he doesn't do heroin or coke, I'll just hire one of the Mexicans to take him out. It sucks that I will have to pay cash for it, but it will be well worth it.

Thirdly, I slice his forearms wide open and let him bleed out; make it look like a suicide attempt that succeeded. They will think the poor bastard couldn't handle doing a life sentence.

*

Day twenty-two and I hear the riot alarm going off. My gut tells me I am somehow involved with this.

A couple hours later Detective Trower pays me a visit. His turn to smile.

"I am pretty sure you can hear the riot alarm down here right, Mitch?"

"Yeah."

"Any idea why it was going off earlier?"

"No, but I am sure it involves me somehow… seeing that you're here."

"Yes, you are correct. Carlos Khan was murdered by Helmut Fritz."

Now my back was up.

"Why were those two out of the hole before me?"

My question shocked Trower.

"You're not concerned about one of your guys being killed?"

"Khan was never one of my guys. I keep telling you I have nothing to do with the club or their ways. I have family in the club, and I thought I would teach the kid the ropes on how to survive. But you know what, he was an idiot. A total fucking idiot who got what he deserved. Now can we go back to why they were let out of the hole before me?"

"You are a repeat violent offender, each incident now you will do thirty days minimum.

Helmut was never in the hole and Khan once before. They actually both got out this morning. It didn't take long for both to find each other."

"It's a prison, pretty easy to find whoever you are looking for."

"It is a safe bet this was gang related. What concerns me is was this Hell Hound versus Thunder crap or your crew versus Helmut's crew."

I took a deep breath and didn't want to sound like a rat, but I also don't want any unwanted heat to come down on me or my crew. Khan ain't worth anymore grief and seeing at how the fucker is dead I told Trower what he wanted to hear. He has always been more than decent with me.

"I believe it is Hell Hound, Thunder shit. I have no problems with Helmut or his crew. And I promise you no one from my crew will seek retribution against Helmut or anybody in his crew."

"Helmut died, and this really worries me."

My stomach dropped upon hearing this.

"I worry this is just the tip of the iceberg and more violence will be the result of his death."

"Fuck, I am sorry to hear this, I liked him. He served with my Grandpa Kohler in the Second World War.

"I knew no man or amount of men could kill Helmut; he was hardcore solid. How did he kill Khan?"

"I was actually in tower one interviewing officer Mongrain about an earlier incident. Was more interested in making sure the witness statement was one hundred percent accurate. Mongrain was talking to me when suddenly, he says shit is about to get real. I asked what he meant. He pointed to the yard. It was like Moses parting the seas. All the prisoners made a path for Helmut and Khan to meet. Now, these two guys just got released from the hole five minutes earlier. Khan is all smiles as he is strutting like peacock towards Helmut, who is very stoic, stands his ground, tells Khan to bring it. Khan goes racing in wildly. The wily fighter Helmut now smiles, spits in Khan's face. For a millisecond Khan tries to wipe the snot off his face while still

running full force. It blinds him just enough that
he doesn't sees Helmut's foot coming towards the
kid's abdomen. It knocks the wind right out of
Khan, a wind he will never get back. Helmut
wraps his massive arms around Khan in a bear
hug. Helmut let out a growl, then with the strength
of a hundred boa constrictors, he stars to squeeze
the life out of Khan. Mitch, I am at least fifty feet
away at least thirty feet up in the air. The whole
yard is in awe, deadly silent. You could hear
Helmut snapping Khan's vertebras in his back.
The man was breaking his ribs like it was nothing.
Helmut only stopped because the broken ribs
punctured Khan's lungs, and Helmut's face was
full of blood. He dropped his prey to the ground,
cleaned his eyes and then like he did when he was
a wrestling superstar, the legendary champion
picked up a limp Khan over his head for all to see
in the yard. But he wasn't done with him. Time
for his trademark match ending Stuka maneuver.
He had Khan's head face the ground, his legs
around his shoulders. He yelled out, "Es Lebe Das
Dritte Reich!" And with all his might drove
Khan's head into the ground full force. At first
you heard the thud of Khan's skull being driving

into the cement. And if you were within twenty feet of the mayhem, you were sprayed with pieces of Khan's skull and brain. Helmut looked at the lifeless body of his foe. Then he raised both arms high in the air. He let everyone know he was the champion of San Quentin. He bellowed out at the top of his lungs an animalistic growl. Then without warning his legs started to shake, he broke out in perfuse sweat and hit the ground face first. None of us saw any wounds on him. Doc figures he died of a massive heart attack. Autopsy will tell us for sure. I will want a sit down with you and whoever takes over for Fritz. I am curious Mitch, who do you think it will be?"

"I honestly have no idea, that was their politics not mine. I hope someone reasonable. I have just over four months left on my sentence and I want to keep the same release date as when I came in. If it means avoiding a war, I will sit down with whoever takes over the Arian leadership."

"I am glad to hear this. Come with me as I have all the other Shock Collars in the Warden's office right now and two from Fritz's gang. We have a new warden who wants a sit down with all of you."

"Am I going back to the hole as soon as we are done?"

"As long as the meeting doesn't turn violent the remaining nine days on your sentence here will be shaved off."

"I am curious about one thing before we head to our meeting."

Trower nodded his head said go ahead.

"Why didn't you guys step in and stop Helmut and Khan before he left two dead cons?"

"That's a fair question. Well, unofficially Khan was telling anyone who would listen that he was going to kill Helmut first, then everyone else associated with the Thunder. Hot heads make our job extremely difficult. Stresses the hell right out of us to be honest. Prisoners, prison staff were all on edge. Sometimes the cons handle a situation that ties our hands. Khan would be a nightmare for all prisoners, not just us staff. When you were a kid Mitch, and you knew there was going to be a fight in the school yard, and you knew the school bully would take a beating. You ever notice no one would jump in, not even the teachers?"

Holy fuck, yeah, he was right. Never thought the term *jailhouse justice* also referred to screws.

As we were walking to warden's office, I still couldn't believe that Helmut was dead. I thought that old Nazi was the perfect model for the fourth Reich and their thousand year run.

Sure, as fuck every Shock Collar and their underboss in the prison was inside the Warden's office. The Chinese, Italians, Russians, North and South Mexicans, Blacks, and Muslims. My underboss, Albert, greeted me with a sincere smile.

Berry and Nicholson from the Arian group shot daggers at me, but the coldest stare in the room was from the new warden. I am normally good at guessing a person's ethnicity, but I couldn't figure out his.

He was very stoic looking, around mid-forties I would say. Decent shape and not from lifting, but I would say soldier shape.

His eyes had a thousand yard stare.

"Strongbow, how special of you to join us. Take a seat. For those of you that don't know who I am, I am Warden Goldstone."

A fucking Jew, just what I need.

"Yes, I am Jewish, but I am not your stereotypical Jew who can be pushed over through force or intimidation. Much like most of you in this room, I too have taken several lives. I was a soldier and prison warden in Israel before moving to this country and eventually becoming an American citizen. And the reason I am the new warden is that your past warden was weak and played games. I don't play games, nor am I weak or stupid. I know each one of you in this room has power over his men and the drugs, violence, gambling, and extortion that take place here. The only one of these vices that bothers me is the violence. You keep your people in line and I will turn a blind eye to the other vices. But heed my one and only warning. If the violence and murders continue to rise in here, I will come down on whatever Shock Collar and underboss who can't control their men. You will never see the light of day, and if you are a lifer with no hope of parole, you will spend the rest of your life in the hole. And yes, I do have the power to do that. Do I make myself perfectly clear?"

None of us answered him, only the weak and kiss asses would do that. Goldstone then said all of us could leave except me. I told Albert I would see him back at my house.

Trower and a couple screws stuck around. At first, I thought he wanted to interview me more about Helmut's murder.

That theory was shot down when he ordered all out of his office. Trower said, *really?* and Goldstone said *leave*, in a sharp voice.

Fuck, I now have a bad feeling, Goldstone specifically wanted no witnesses.

"Strongbow, you have been in this prison for just over a year and yet you have gotten away with killing the two cons from the Thunder. You got away with killing in the yard and with killing a rat."

"That's your opinion. Your staff cleared me

of everything as did the cops."

"There is also one other murder on the outside that you got away with, at least for now."

I snickered, smiled, and asked, "What murder, Lucy's?"

"No one ever loses sleep over a dead junkie. I will try and refresh your heroin induced, and if I might add, damaged brain. In 1967 I was first introduced to the name Strongbow. I despised it right from the first time I heard it. But for my cousin Barry Getz, he loved that name. Busting you and your brother should have been one hell of a feather in his cap but he was weak and stupid, booze was always his downfall. Wouldn't you agree?"

"He is nothing more than a murderer with a badge; he should be rotting in here."

"I strongly agree with you, but no one is able to find the man. He has turned into Houdini. It appears he vanished off the face of planet. I would have thought your brother Jake would have someone in the Hell Hounds go after him. Instant club membership with Barry's death. But with

Jake having died already, I thought Barry might be spared. Then you come home from Vietnam and suddenly Barry goes missing. Has anyone ever questioned you about his disappearance?"

My back was up, really fucking up.

"I don't know fuck all about him; I was trying to forget anything about the asshole."

"But I can give you all kinds of freedom that most prisoners don't get including solo time with the pudgy former librarian, Miss Borden, for every visit. You can fuck her all you want. I have read the filth she sends you. I will personally write a letter to the parole board telling them what a model citizen you have been in here and you will be released within a matter of days. I will tell them how you stopped Borden from a gang rape and made sure that Amy Rosenstein was protected from all prisoners during the riot. All I want is for my family to have proper closure, is he alive or dead?"

"You bloody fool. Are you accusing me of something? Because if you are, I want my lawyer present."

His whole demeanor instantly changed

"You will soon find out I am anything but a fool, Strongbow. You are now my top priority in this prison. I will fuck you up and all your vagabond crew of misfits and fuckups. They will regret having you as their Shock Collar. You will not win against me. I will let every Shock Collar in here know you are a rat. Now, tell me if he is alive or dead?"

Furious, I jumped up out of my chair and called him a fucking idiot. Goldman begged me to take a swing at him; fuck that, I don't want to serve any more time in this hell hole then what I have to, and more importantly, he ain't worth the charge.

I blew him a kiss and walked towards the office door. He was screaming at me to come back, even ordering me to get back. His loud and angry voice had Trower and several other screws come racing into his office.

I hit the ground face down and spread eagle as they came in with their clubs ready to beat me.

"Throw him in the hole right now!" yelled Goldman to Trower.

"For what?" was my plea.

"For disobeying a direct order and being a defiant bastard."

Trower just looked at me in disbelief as I was shaking my head. He told two screws to cuff me and take me to the hole.

But we didn't go to the hole. Trower took me to his office and asked what the fuck happened. I told him the whole story as I had nothing to hide or fear, well, maybe some fear with him threatening to let all hear that I was a rat. I don't care how tough you are, the only good rat in here is a dead rat.

"I want to see my lawyer; that fucking guy is a head case. He is a section eight. He is asking about his cousin and I have no clue what he is talking about. Fuck, just him wanting revenge on me for something I didn't do is beyond fucked."

"Mitch, I will contact your lawyer but for the time being I think you might be safer in the hole then general population."

I reluctantly agreed and gave Trower my lawyers

name and off to the hole I went, again. I was angry, right fucking angry, I should kill him seeing at how he is seeking revenge for his drunk, killing cousin. Fuck, I lost my Mom and sister Pam who were innocent and murdered in cold blood! My Mom was an educator, Pam was a college student who believed in making love not war. Getz was an out of control, power drunk, cop and I enjoyed beating him to within an ounce of his life, and then watching a train slice him into a million pieces.

Within a couple hours, Trower came and got me and said my lawyer was waiting for me. I told Levy the whole story. I also didn't want to sound like a whiny bitch, but I made it clear that I am now fearful for my life.

Levy was shocked and said two things can happen; he can approach the parole board and see if I can get my hearing sped up, or he would see about getting me transferred out of San Quentin and placed into another prison for the remainder of my sentence.

He also said he wants a meeting with Goldman before he leaves the prison today to let him know about my concerns.

So, back to the hole I go. Angrier, and I have to say, a little confused. Did Goldstone purposely come to work in San Quentin to get answers about Getz's disappearance?

I could really use a fix of heroin to help me sleep. My brain won't shut down, my muscles are filled with blood ready for the battle. A battle I never saw coming.

How many more relatives does Getz have out there? Do I have to kill them all?

So, for the next eight days I worked out till exhaustion. The only time I spent on a positive thought was fantasizing and then masturbating about Charlene Borden. I thought about us fucking our brains out. Her lips and tits are driving me crazy. She will be my first fuck upon my release.

13

Day nine came and I was released from the hole, and not by a screw, but from Trower.

He said we need to talk.

I thought *fuck, Goldman must really have it in for me now and Trower is also going to suggest what Levy did, for me to transfer out of here.*

"Mitch, three days ago Warden Goldman was found shot to death in his car. There was a note that read he was paying for his sins against the people of Lebanon, it was signed, PLO."

Trower said nothing more, he only stared at me and waited for my response. I smiled and reminded him that I have been in the hole the whole time.

"I have nothing to do with his death. I am up for early parole in a couple months. Why risk losing it? And to be honest with you, and I mean perfectly honest, I would rather have the pleasure in seeing that cocksucker take his last breath. I would want to inflect pain upon him myself. With his dickhead personality I am sure he made all kinds of enemies. In fact, I am willing to bet other cons have assaulted him in the past and he loved it as he would fuck up any chance of them getting early parole."

Trower nodded his head yes.

"That is who I would be going after, guys already released and with an axe to grind with him."

"I am sure the police have a long line of suspects. Anyways, you are free and if you want early parole, I suggest you keep a low profile between now and then."

I always try was my answer. I then left and headed for breakfast, which was being served. For me, hearing of Goldman's death was the perfect meal. It was good seeing everyone. It's amazing as you really don't leave the prison and yet it seems you are gone off the face of the planet.

Albert said some guy I served with came looking

for me while I was in the hole. I asked who, but all Albert could remember was he didn't have a common last name. So, I asked what he looked like. *Frank Zappa on steroids*. No one came to mind. I asked where his house is.

Albert said he wasn't sure as right now the guy is in the hole for punching out two Russians. One he sent to the San Francisco hospital the other was in the infirmary here for a couple days.

Now I was totally intrigued, "Well, he knows where to find me."

By lunch time I had visitor who I knew very well.

Charlene Borden came in to see me. She was wearing a short black mini skirt. A blue leather jacket and a see-through sweater, oh and of course no undies, or bra.

It took everything in me not to jump through the glass to fuck her. She made sure to show me her full, red-haired bush around her pussy. Her nipples were like my cock, erect the whole time.

She promised that she would not have another cock in her pussy, mouth, or ass until I am out.

For whatever reason I told her don't wait that long, if you have a chance to get laid go for it, just tell me the details.

I was a total voyeur when it came to her. Her sexuality reminded me of Lucy and when she said no cock will enter her, just her dildo or this one chick who keeps flirting with her, I felt contractions in my cock. I thought I was going to blow my load right then and there.

After she left, I found the first washroom and jerked off. This girl has not only my head spinning but my cock spinning out of control.

A couple days later I had two other visitors, Rachel and Jerry. Rachel, being ever so humble, thanked me for the car and said she would put some money in my jail account. I told her I have more than enough money.

"Just keep up your grades."

Jerry informed me that Fraser Dalton was no longer a club member. He was kicked out of the Hell Hounds. I asked why.

"Because he likes to stick heroin into his

veins. Club rule which I must abide by, plus I don't trust a junkie, nothing personal. Mitch, I know you two are close and wanted to tell you this myself."

"I appreciate you telling me, that's too bad. What about Kerry?"

"She is turning tricks so they can both get high. If he wasn't Caleb's brother, he would have… well you know."

I nodded my head yes. Normally when you are kicked out of the club you give up your bike and take a wicked beating. Those are the lucky ones. Most disappear and are never heard from again.

Rachel said one hundred and seven days till my early parole, "Do you think you're going to get it?"

"I doubt it, I had to do what I had to do to survive. I will more than likely do the whole sentence. Sorry sis."

I don't want early parole, too many eyes on me and I don't want more charges and getting another deuce of time added for fucking up my parole. I want zero rules or restrictions. I can't tell Rachel that I am going to work for Joseph.

*

A couple days later, the whole, *guy looking for me*, was gnawing at my gut. If he has a running feud with the Russians, I want to know who he is as I am not being shived for anyone who thinks we are connected.

I asked Albert to talk to his screw on the take and ask who beat the Russians up. Albert said the guy's name was Ocean Al Zaim.

"Oscar Zulu, no shit. I served in Special Ops and Sog with him. He is Syrian. His family fled Syria in 1949 as his cousin was the President until a coup ousted him. Albert, this guy is a fucking genius. He knows at least a dozen languages. We were once on a hot LZ and the pilot was killed. Oscar jumped in the pilot's chair and was able to get us out of there and back to base safely, even if we had a hard landing. I asked when he learned to fly. He said watching the pilots when we were on a Huey. I wonder what he got pinched for and what is his beef with the Russians, he is also known for having a ten-inch dick, I kid you not. The man was a legend. Momma San wanted no part of him or his weapon."

A couple weeks later we had a newbie come join us in the kitchen. He was none other than Oscar Zulu. I had no doubt in my mind that he was juicing for sure, as he wasn't this buff last time I saw him.

"Strongbow, you crazy son of a bitch!"

"Oscar, you crazy son of a bitch!"

We hugged each other and I said, "Fuck man, look at you all muscle bound and looking like a hippie. You actually look like Frank Zappa on steroids."

"I am on steroids, you need some?"

"Maybe. What's up with the Russians and you?"

"I was working for this Russian Vlad Fedorov, you know him?"

"I have heard of him. Bad ass right?"

"Yes, a bad ass. His wife Dominika had an

even badder ass. Vlad caught me *inside* her ass. He wants me dead now."

"You always were a horny bastard; fuck, you were always juggling nurses two or three at a time. And what brings you to this fine establishment?"

"Vlad set me up. He said he wanted to meet with me to clear the air. I agreed to meet him at a restaurant on the outskirts of Sacramento. Vlad knew that I would be packing a weapon. When I got there, no sign of Vlad just six cops waiting for me inside."

"You are sure it was him that set you up?"

"As soon as I walked in, they had their weapons out and waiting for me. No one knew I was going to meet him. You know I like to work alone."

"How much time did they give you?"

"A deuce less. I am out in July. When are you out?"

"Early parole is December fifth. I won't get it. So, in May I will be free to walk."

"I have a deal for you, Strongbow."

"I am listening."

"I know you are a Shock Collar and are feared by most in here. You command a lot of respect. I am sitting on a lot of dope on the outside. You help me stay alive until I am out of here, and I will make it worth your while."

"What are you offering?"

"Five gallons of uncut hash oil."

"I will keep you alive till I am out of here."

"I pay cash or dope whoever takes over for you."

I then called Albert over and told him the offer from Oscar.

"I will keep you alive once Mitch is gone for a gallon of hash oil."

Oscar said, "Not to insult you, but I don't know you".

"You're right, but I don't also know you from shit. I am a captain with the Battaglia family," said Albert with a proud but evil smile.

Oscar looked at me for reassurance to Albert's claim and I nodded my head yes.

"Deal," said Oscar and the three of us took turns shaking hands.

I asked Oscar what he is going to do once he is released from prison as Vlad will still want him dead.

"I will take care of that Commie cocksucker as soon as I get out."

"No, Oscar. You take care of us first; you give me Albert's oil for safe keeping."

"Strongbow, after all we have been through and you don't trust me?"

"We have been through a lot together, this is true. But you also trusted a Russian to meet with you and look where you are now."

Oscar smiled and said smart man. The number of Russian mobsters in here is small. Maybe a dozen or so. What concerns me more is Vlad learning I am now protecting Oscar and hiring one of the

Mexican gangs to kill him.

I think I better have a sit down with the other Shock Collars and let them know Oscar is under mine and Albert's protection. The Battaglia's have a lot of muscle in California.

*

The next afternoon after lunch all the Shock Collars agreed to meet with me in the yard.

I let them know Oscar is under mine and Albert's protection and if anyone has a beef with him let's talk right now.

After the meeting, Julio Ortega from the north Mexicans, took me aside and said he has been approached by certain people in here to kill Oscar. I said to Julio that I would appreciate him not accepting the contract.

"Mitch, I need money to help my family on the outside. I hope you understand."

"I do understand and respect where you and your family are coming from. How much are they offering?"

"$ 2,500. Oscar must have really pissed off the Russians, large."

"I don't know what he did, I don't have that kind of money, is there anything else I can do for you not to accept this deal?"

Julio looked at Albert and said yes there is.

"My wife has been threatened with deportation. You know the people to stop it?"

"Let me see what I can do, what is her name?" Albert asked.

Julio passed along the information to Albert. I thank Julio for his honesty and for not taking the contract right away. After Julio left, I asked Albert if he believed him.

He said, "Yeah. Keeping his wife is more important. He knows if we find out he is bullshitting us that she takes the risk of being deported; he showed us his weakness."

I also took Oscar aside and said, "I hope you have a lot of cash. That will keep you alive."

I assured him we made a deal, but rats in here will

want cash on any harm coming his way.

Oscar said that was not a problem.

We spent the next couple days getting caught up on our lives since we left Vietnam. Like me, Oscar has been an outlaw. He couldn't fit into mainstream America and all the bullshit that came with it.

*

About a week or so later, Julio thanked Albert for making sure his wife got a green card to stay in the States. All the threats towards Oscar seemed to die off quickly.

Over the next couple weeks Charlene came every Friday to totally tease me. She said she would write me hard core letters that would make Hefner blush. I said I never got him. I said the screws would read it, confiscate it, and then beat off as they would never have sex like what Charlene would offer me once I got out.

Levy came and saw me a couple weeks before my early parole hearing. I said again that I don't want early parole. I want out of here totally free, no strings attached to me.

I know Kurt Wilson will be waiting for me to fuck up my parole, just having a coffee with Donnie, who is an ex-con, would fuck my parole.

Trower heard word that I didn't want a shot at early parole, and he came to visit me.

"Mitch, people don't ask for early parole for two reasons; number one is guilt, I know you felt bad for your girlfriend's death, but you seemed to bounce back just fine. The second reason is you plan on making yourself a career criminal. If this means anything, I think all in all you are a pretty decent guy who had a lot of kicks to the balls. Did you not have a job you loved before getting into crime?"

"Trower, for a cop screw, I think you are decent, you treat us like humans not like the filth of the planet. Yeah, you know what I loved to do? I loved the Army, I loved the rush, the challenge, the discipline. If my body wasn't so beat up, I would have made a career out of it. They cut me lose I didn't quit."

"Can the V.A. help you find work?"

"I have a friend who owns a motorcycle repair shop. I plan on working for him. I like to tinker around. We have worked well together in the past."

"Is he a Hell Hound?"

"Yes, he is. I have zero interest in joining the club. Remember my brother Jake was betrayed by a fellow Hell Hound. If I learned in Nam, it was to only rely on yourself. Thanks for your concern. I will be fine."

I believed what I was saying, pretty sure Trower didn't.

*

December fifth came and went. Rachel dropped by and said I was making a huge mistake. I told her about what Kurt Wilson said, Rachel said I should contact the police and talk to his supervisor.

I just shook my head and smiled.

"Rachel, cops are as crooked as criminals. Fuck, I've seen stuff with my own two eyes. In May, I will be a one hundred percent free man.

No string attached. Kurt acts up and I will have my lawyer go after him. Right now, all he is going to do is deny what he said to me. Then he'll put word out on the street that I am a rat. That will get back to here, then I won't see the light of day and you will be burying another brother from San Quentin. I have a solid crew that looks out for me in here."

I don't think she fully understands how crooked cops can be. All she knows is what it says in her legal books and what she is taught in law school. I probably understand the law better than her with all the stories I have heard in here.

Just before Christmas, I had a visitor that kind of choked me up.

It was my Grandfather with Rachel; he came to spend Christmas with Rachel seeing at how she came home from school. Plus, he said it was a bitter cold winter so far in South Dakota.

He said I looked much healthier and stronger. He asked how the demons were. I was honest with him, I said from time to time I want to stick a needle into veins. He said I will be fighting demons all my natural life, and then maybe even after.

I thanked him for all his help, I then asked him if he thought Rachel would still be in school in the afterlife? A one finger salute from Rachel. She seemed to be a little more stressed then normal.

I asked what was wrong. Her eyes glared at me.

"Rachel, please tell me what is wrong. I don't want you going away angry, especially so close to Christmas. Santa may put coal in your stocking."

Her eyes squinted and several times she went to speak and stopped.

"Please just tell me."

"You are the only sibling I have left and yet we haven't spent a Christmas together since 1966, it's been years, Mitchell. And yet you chose not to be out this Christmas rather than not blowing your parole. Well shit, that tells me you will be getting back into trouble."

I closed my eyes and did the math. I opened them and said, "I am sorry, four years I was in the

Army. Rach, I promise you that next year I will spend it with you. Just promise me that you won't cook."

The look she gave me was more brutal then a one finger salute.

"As I have said before, I wouldn't even be able to have a drink of rum and eggnog with Donnie and Jeanie and they are good people. You like them. Wilson will make sure I fail and will have a huge hard-on for me."

Grandpa reminded us both we are family, all we have is each other. I then promised my grandfather that next year we will all have Christmas together, or may Crazy Horse himself, come and scalp me. I told them I loved them, and May will be here sooner than later.

I asked Rachel if she sent gifts to Katrina for Christmas, she said yes. I took a breath and asked how she signed it.

She smiled and said, "Aunt Rachel and Uncle Mitchell."

I looked at my Grandfather who nodded at me.

I thanked Rachel, no sense in blowing up. If anything, Katrina knows my name and knows I am family; one day she will know the truth.

If that was the most emotional visit; Charlene Borden coming in all but made up for it. Under her topcoat she was wearing a Rockette outfit; she also proceeded to suck a candy cane like a cock, totally teasing the fuck right out of me.

She said next Xmas she has plans for me, including me fucking her under a Christmas tree.

Yeah, I jerked off three times that night, I was going for number four when George said in a pissed off voice, "It will fall off, leave it alone!"

*

One good thing about working in the kitchen is the smell of turkey cooking. Took me back to being a kid. Mom would get up before dawn and start to stuff the turkey and get all the veggies ready. Us kids would race downstairs and see what Santa would bring us.

There was Mom already awake and on her third coffee. I felt a sadness come over me when I thought about how many Christmases Katrina has had without me in her life.

The walls felt really closed in that day. Fuck, even the screws that had to work were miserable, I guess they too wanted to be with their families. Well, fuck them.

*

For a prison cooked Christmas dinner, it was pretty good and us in the kitchen ate as much as we wanted. I was surprised Oscar celebrated Christmas, he said there are a lot of Syrian Christians.

George could feel my sadness and said he hasn't had a Christmas dinner with his family in over forty plus years. He said that I have a chance to make sure this will be my last Christmas behind bars and not to fuck up again.

He confirmed to me what I had always thought. There is nothing wrong with being a career criminal, it can be a very successful and rewarding life. The key, he said, is to surround myself with solid people who would rather do the time then rat me out. Amen to that.

New Years was the same. Albert was able to get a bottle of Wild Turkey for us. I never ask, I know better. He said next New Year's he, Sammy, Oscar, and me would all be free men. We toasted to freedom in 1975.

The more I got to know Oscar the more I realized he was a pretty hard-core drug smuggler. And we are not talking stuffing a key of blow up his ass and sneaking across the border. We are talking flying in hundreds of kilos of dope at a time.

And not just from Mexico to the States; we're talking from Syria to North America. He still has all kinds of connections and family over there. Opium and hash are what he mostly deals with. And of course, just like we did in Special Ops, he would exchange dope for guns and vice versa.

Albert was very skeptical as was I to a certain degree. He assured us he has his own plane, several boats, and knows who to bribe to get dope moved from all over the world.

I thought with Szoke dead, Oscar could fill a void. Pretty sure you can't put an ad out for pilots willing to fly under the radar, pardon the pun.

He said there is no reason the four of us can't do business or work together once we are all out. He said his only concern is his Russian enemies which he said he will take care of once he is released.

I thought of what George had preached to me. Albert, I know is solid. I have seen that firsthand, Frankie is a made man in the mob. He must be solid, or he would have been killed by now.

I think before I get in too deep with Oscar, he will have to prove to me how solid he is.

*

Albert took me aside the next day and his thoughts were the exact same as mine. Albert also said Oscar talks a big game, big enough game like an undercover would do. I said to Albert in Nam he was a scrounger, whatever we needed, Oscar would get for us. But I also agreed for the time being will keep him in our circle and keep a really close eye on him.

I know Joseph wouldn't trust him at all, same as Donnie. But if he is legit, he has all the connections and vehicles for us to make large cash and that's what it's all about.

Within the first week of the new year, Oscar was able to get his hands full of some Russian steroids for us. Same as some hash and hash oil.

Albert came right out and asked him where he got it from, the question caused tension as Oscar told Albert it was none of his business.

Oscar looked at Albert and said, "I don't ask you about your business in here, so don't ask me."

Albert was now pissed and started to curse at Oscar and call him a clown. Oscar then threw a punch at Albert and all hell broke loose.

Frankie jumped in to help his capo, Albert. I jumped in and I felt like I was in the middle of two friends fighting. Plus, Oscar promised me five gallons of hash oil for keeping him alive.

Several other guys in our crew also jumped in and we were able to break things up before the riot alarm went off.

Quite a few screws made their way over and when they asked what was going on, both guys said nothing, and all was good.

Oscar was not impressed and went back to his cell cursing and swearing in Syrian and yes, I knew exactly what he was saying as I have heard him curse quite a bit in Nam. I also knew to give him space and to calm down Albert before he has Oscar killed.

As soon as I came near Albert, he pointed at me and said, "Don't start."

"I am not starting anything Albert. Just making sure we are cool."

"Mitch, I don't trust the guy. He talks too big a story; you know the saying, if it is too good to be true it usually is?"

"I respect where you are coming from. The guy was solid in Nam. If we needed anything the army or CIA wouldn't give us, fuck, he would get it for us. Why don't you get your contacts on the outside to find out what they can about him? I am also curious as to whether the Russians want him dead because he was banging the one mob boss's wife."

Albert wiped the blood off his split lip and said, "If he is a hustler, cop, or federal agent I will personally drain every single drop of blood from his body."

"I will help you if he is not what he says."

Albert looked at me intensely and didn't answer. I have the feeling that I may also take a fall if Oscar is not solid or is now working for the coppers.

I headed to Oscar's cell; I knew not to warn him that Albert was going to do a criminal background check on him. That also includes from mobsters, crooked cops, and maybe someone in the D.A.'s office.

Oscar was pinching his bloody nose when I walked in. His face turned beet red as he started to curse Albert.

"Oscar, I don't want to hear it. You just started a fight with a Capo from the Battaglia family. They have more pull in here then the Russians my friend. What the fuck were you thinking?"

"I don't sell out the people I do business with. If I did, they would no longer do business with me. You notice I don't ask where you or the

Italian gets your dope from in here? You know why? Because what I don't know won't come back to bite me in the balls."

I thought about what Oscar said and it was the truth. He never asks any questions.

"Just keep your distance from Albert. Let me talk to him."

Funny, Oscar shot me the same dirty look Albert just shot me. I was kind of torn as Albert and I have never really had any tension between us. Oscar and I ate dirt and killed Charlie together.

So, I told George my dilemma because he'd seen this many times over in prison.

"Mitch, you and Albert could pass for blood brothers the way you two have been looking out for each other's safety and best interests in here. I don't know much about this Oscar character, but from what I have seen and sensed, he would sell his grandmother for cash. And with Albert he must be loyal to his people, he moved up the ranks being loyal. Oscar is a one-man crew. He is not used to being loyal to anyone but himself. You're a smart kid, Mitch. You know deep down who to trust."

I did know all along who to trust. Was kind of hoping it wouldn't come to choosing sides though. Fuck, nothing comes easy!

Oscar kept his distance from Albert which I was glad he listened to me.

*

A couple days passed, and Albert said let's go for a walk in the yard.

"So, I heard back from my people about Oscar, not a cop or federal agent, you know at how he said the Russians want him dead for banging that guys wife?" I said yes.

"He was not only banging the wife, but he was also banging the fifteen year old daughter. You better not shower with that fuck or he will be banging you."

"That's not even funny. So, what are the dynamics going to be with you two now?"

"I don't trust the fuck, but I want that gallon of oil he promised me. So, I will keep him at arm's length, but when he gets out and doesn't deliver with the gallon of oil, I will pay you to kill him or have someone else kill him."

"I fully respect where you are coming from. He doesn't deliver I will kill him as he will be breaking a promise to you that insults and strains my friendship with you."

Albert smiled and gave me little slaps on my cheeks and said I was as solid as they come.

So, Albert let up around Oscar, there was no love but no more fighting. Oscar on the other hand, seemed to be branching out to other gangsters of all races and creeds. Part of it was through dealing and some of it was through his own boasting of past adventures either in Nam or in the criminal underworld.

At one point I thought he would be able to take over for Szoke being our illegal pilot, not now. The guy talks to much. Joseph would put a bullet in him first and then me.

*

Over the next couple weeks, Oscar grew further

away from our crew. Part of it was the Russians and most of the general population knew we were protecting him. And for the bigger picture, it was because he would underprice us on dope and tailor-made cigarettes.

Albert was pissed, he said I should be pissed as you don't do that to someone in your own crew. I had to agree with Albert. It was a bullshit move on his part. I decided to have a sit down with him.

"Are you still a part of my crew?"

"Of course I am, Mitch. Why do you ask such things?"

"Word on the street is that you are undercutting us."

"I thought this was part of being an American, free enterprise."

"You are right. I guess if the Russians offer me six gallons of hash oil, I should take the deal and let them get even with you?"

Oscar stuck out his pointer finger and wagged it at me and said, "Mitchell, why do you have to be like this?"

I grabbed a hold of his finger and broke it.

"You fucking scream and I will slice your throat. You stop undercutting us as of right now. You will also apologize to me and Albert in front of the crew or whatever deal we had is off the table. I am a fucking Shock Collar and you are disrespecting me in front of my crew. You understand?"

Oscar was pissed and nodded his head yes.

"I can't fucking hear you, Oscar."

"Yes Mitch, I am sorry for insulting you and I will make amends in front of your men."

Now it was time for me to nod my head.

"Good. Now go and get your finger reset."

Oscar looked at me and reset his finger himself.

*

That afternoon while in yard, Oscar apologized to Albert and me. He said he never meant to cause any grief and offered us a dime bag of weed as a way to keep the peace. Albert said nothing at all. Truly no love for Oscar. I often wondered if

Albert would kill him or have him killed as soon as I'm out.

And then about a week later while in the yard, this guy went after Albert as he was doing chin ups. He was running on the track and then bolted towards Albert.

He has a shiv in his hand. Oscar's Nam senses must still be working just fine as Oscar dove and took the guy down within mere feet of a helpless and vulnerable Albert.

The attacker fell on his shiv. It went right into his jugular. There were so many witnesses including several guards. Trower didn't charge Oscar.

None of us knew the dead man. He was Puerto Rican and no known gang or mob affiliations which was strange. The only thing we knew for sure was that the guy was in for armed robbery and was from Davis, California.

The incident made some peace between Oscar and Albert, but it also made Albert kind of paranoid not knowing anything about the guy or why he wanted him dead.

Over the next month, Charlene would write me every day; she would always send photos, some made it to me, others I was sure some screw was jerking off to as it became part of his private perv collection.

Jeanie Terek popped by for a visit a week before Valentine's Day. I asked her to send a dozen long stem roses to Charlene's apartment.

Jeanie reminded me this wasn't the first time she's helped me out romantically. Yeah, I remember for Tash's sweet sixteen it was at a restaurant that she was working at. She gave Tash flowers from me in the back. Jeanie asked me how serious things were between us.

I said for now it is just a jail house romance, but I really, really like her. Jeanie smiled and said that it wouldn't be a problem.

I am not sure why I couldn't tell her I was really fallen for Charlene hard core. Was it because if I said more, she would think it is just a jailhouse thing? What dynamics would we have once I am out of this hell hole?

I told Charlene that I know she has needs while I

am in prison, and that I would never stop her from getting laid. Fuck, she tells me how much she likes cock. The only thing I ever demanded from her was to not get serious with anyone else while I was in here.

She thanked me and said she only wants me and will wait for me. I am skeptical and try not to think about her getting fucked on the outside even though it does kind of turn me on.

She reminds me of Lucy in that aspect.

14

March 17, 1975: My little girl turns seven today. Kind of an emotional day for me. I have a burr up my ass and anyone pissing me off today will take a beating of epic proportions.

I was quiet during breakfast and my crew picked up on it. Albert and George knew why and said this will be the last birthday in Katrina's life that I won't be in it. Albert once again offered to send someone to Queens to put a bullet in Stan's head.

I thanked him, but said I am fighter and I will win Katrina on my own. Funny, as now I don't even think of getting back with Natasha at all. Of all creatures and humans on the planet, I despise her most of all.

I can picture Katrina opening her gifts and asking them both to tell her about the day she was born.

Stan should have no problems telling her a bullshit lie. After all, he has been telling her the biggest lie of his life saying he is her Dad. Fucking prick.

I had two visitors that afternoon. The first one was Rachel. She of all people knew how rough of a day it was for me. She smiled at me for a bit and asked how I was doing today.

"You know how I am doing, Rachel. Not in a good mood at all."

"You are out in just over sixty days, Mitchell. Please don't do anything to stay in here longer."

"Unless they put Stan or Tash in here, I have no other plans to murder anyone else."

"I don't like to hear you talk like this, Mitch. That is something I would expect from Jake. You promised me that you have turned over a new leaf regarding them. Do you think Katrina would ever want to hear you talk like that?"

"She would never hear me as those two fucks won't let me near her, remember?"

"Neither do I. I will come back when you are not so miserable."

Rachel was pissed. She stood up to leave and then sat back down and let me have it.

"Did you know that I missed school today, drove two hours knowing how hard a day this is for you. Quit feeling sorry for yourself. You are in prison because of something you and Lucy did. Natasha and Katrina had nothing to do with it. You will always be her blood father, Mitchell. No one will ever take that away from you."

I took a deep breath and thought about what she said while staring at her.

"You're right sis. I just want to be on a level playing field in her life. A chance to know her. She keeps me going day after day when I want to relapse and start shooting heroin all over again."

"I am glad she keeps you grounded. I need you also in my life. We only have each other left. Mitchell."

"You're right. I think of the promises I made to you and Grandpa. No more junk. Now I feel like such a heel, but did you send her something for her birthday from Uncle Mitch and Aunt Rachel?"

"Of course, I got her something from us. You might find it kind of amusing if Tasha doesn't."

I snickered and asked what.

"A couple Barbie dolls and Big Josh doll. I thought about a G.I. Joe but pretty sure that wouldn't go over very well."

"Rachel, I would have given you a million dollars if you bought her a G.I. Joe doll. You think Tash will be pissed at you for the Big Josh doll?"

"Not sure, it's not her, it would be Stan, as let's face it he is not very manly. Can't see him hunting or fishing on Sioux land."

"I am more than willing to take him hunting, the only problem is that only one of us would be coming back."

We both laughed over that. I thanked Rachel and apologized for being a moody dick.

She said she understood today would be hard on me and that's why she came, family sticks together.

Fucking right it does. My second visitor was also sort of family. It was Joseph O'Reilly. Fuck, the Leprechaun himself showing up on this holiest day of all for the Celts.

I could tell he was not here to spread his Irish cheer.

"Mitchell, I understand you have a certain Syrian named... fuck, I can't remember or pronounce his name."

"Yes, I do. His name is Ocean Al Zaim, and we call him Oscar Zulu, why?"

"I have been contacted by certain people I have done business with in the past about him."

"Let me guess, Russians correct?"

Joseph smiled and said yes.

"I am also willing to bet they asked for me to step aside and leave him open so these Russians can put a grin under his chin."

Once again Joseph smiled and nodded his head yes. I know I have five gallons of hash oil on the line to keep Oscar alive, but I believe we can use his skills of being a pilot and his connections for our use once he is released.

"Joseph, did they tell you that he is a pilot with his own plane? Did they also mention he has several boats and connections all over the world? Szoke is dead and we need a solid pilot, one that is not scared of shit. I served with him in Special Ops and SOG. I think we should offer him a job once he gets out in July. What do you think?"

The wheels were now turning in Joseph's brain.

"And you trust him totally? I want no surprises from him. I like my guys solid. Is he a druggie?"

"Not a druggie. Just likes his pussy and that is why the Russians want him dead, he banged the one boss's wife and I also just heard he was banging the fifteen-year-old daughter. I have been in some tight hot spots with him and he never showed fear. I think we should, or you should talk to him once he is released and see what you think, sound fair?"

"Mitchell, I don't want to have a fucking pedophile working for me."

"I will talk to him and tell him to make sure all pussy is of legal age."

"Talk to him today and tell him I will be by to see him by the end of the week. If I don't like the vibe or if he gives me attitude you will stand aside and let the Russians seek revenge, understood?"

"No, I don't. I am kind of confused actually. You are going to interview him for a job here during a visit?"

"That's correct, lad."

Talk about fucking balls, made me laugh.

"I will let him know and yes I will step aside if you don't like the vibe from him. Thanks for giving him a chance and what about the Russians if we take him in?"

"Fuck the Russians, never did like or trust a commie."

Joseph never ceases to astound me with the size of his balls. I went back and told Oscar the situation. He agreed to talk to Joseph and even work for us. But he also said he will work as freelance only.

He hates having a boss and likes his freedom. I respect what he said I just hope Joseph does or he will make life interesting in here. The end of the week came, Joseph and Oscar met and talked.

Oscar told me that the conversation went well, and that Joseph agreed to keep him as a freelance. One thing that I saw in Vietnam that I never experienced was being a short timer.

These are guys who are close to the end of their tour in Nam or almost have enough points to go home. They have earned it on both occasions. I would watch some of the most battle-hardened soldiers get really nervous and downright scared.

We have all saw guys within a couple weeks of going home killed in action. I was planning on being a full-time soldier, so I never lost my edge.

But I am now down to just under two weeks left in my sentence and I am a little spooked. I gave up my Shock Collar position. I am trying not to get into any situations that I would put my life in jeopardy.

Yeah, I can see that light at the end of the tunnel, I must make sure no one shuts it off on me.

One of the hardest things is when Rachel comes to visit, she is so excited that I will be getting out soon. Jake never got that chance and I know she never knew if I would be carried out in a casket like him.

Charlene was also pumped for me and would totally cock tease me. She told me I won't be able to walk for a week; I will only be able to crawl from the bed for beer and food.

Joseph was all set for my release as my new employer. But I have to think there are still pockets of guys in here that would like nothing better than to take my life with me being so close to leaving.

Their last hurrah. I have killed two Thunder members in here. They were in my opinion, the biggest threat of all.

And of course, talking about biggest threats, the

legal authority in here if someone ratted that I killed that screw to save Charlene's life.

So, you make sure you are never alone and that those with you are solid, most notably, Albert.

Fuck, even as far as Oscar goes if a gang of Russians or any other mercs go after him, and it means I too will die if I intervene, it'll be nice knowing you Oscar.

You go in for early lockup. Shower time is when I would go with the rest of my crew. Jeannie came and saw me and said Joseph is having a welcome home party and asked who I would like there.

I said Rachel and gave her Charlene's phone number. I plan on spending a lot of time with her getting caught up on lost sex time. Before I knew it, my final night was here. Albert had a party for me that included some homemade hooch.

I drank just enough to catch a good buzz, but not enough to let my guard down. There is a saying, a good friend will help you kill someone, but a great friend will help you hide the body.

Albert will be like a brother to me from this point

on, not only a great friend. That night before I closed my eyes, I had one thought, or should I say final fear.

I wake up and find out I have only begun to serve day one of my sentence, and everything so far is just one fucked up, trippy dream.

*

The next morning, I still had that fear until George told me not to sleep in and miss my chance to walk out of this place a free man. As soon as my feet hit the floor the walking boss came over and told me to gather up my gear as they were waiting for me downstairs.

I asked about breakfast, not so much to eat, but to say goodbye to everyone.

"Strongbow, you leave now, or you will be stuck here for the weekend."

Packing my stuff now boss, was my answer.

I looked at George and realized I will never see him again. I will be an ex-convict and won't be allowed to come and visit him.

He will run out of life before he is eligible for parole again. Kind of sad, but it's the only life he knows. I gave him a hug and said he was the perfect celly. He told me I was a solid standup guy which meant a lot.

I had one last look at my cell and told myself what I am sure every con has said, never again.

The walk from my range and down the stairs made my legs feel really light, almost as if that ball and chain were free.

I was re-photographed, re-fingerprinted. The fucking amount of paperwork you go through was testing my nerves.

But I was not alone. There were four other cons as lucky as me getting their freedom today.

All four of us were different on the outside.

I looked at each one and wondered who will end up back in here. I am sure they all looked at me and thought the same.

A screw then said to come with him. He gave me an envelope with my personal properties I came in with, and also, the suit I wore at my sentencing twenty-two months. I sort of snickered as only the pants fit. My dress shirt and jacket were several sizes too small. I will say, all that muscle I put on while hitting the weights in here kept me alive.

I am also sure this extra muscle will be needed for my new job, in working for Joseph "The Leprechaun" O'Reilly.

Pandamonium Publishing House is a full-service publisher in Hamilton, Ontario, Canada.

For additional titles visit our website
www.pandamoniumpublishing.com/shop

www.ingramcontent.com/pod-product-compliance
Lightning Source LLC
Chambersburg PA
CBHW051521050726
47503CB00014B/350